WINNER OF THE
BRAM STOKER AWARD
AND THE *LOCUS* AWARD FOR
BEST FIRST NOVEL FOR
THE CIPHER

BAD BRAINS

"[Bad Brains] has more in common with Franz Kafka and Albert Camus than with Stephen King. . . . Koja hot-wires her characters' descent directly to readers' perceptions with her punk-poet writing. . . . [She] flashes from literary fiction to genre horror to artistic speculation so fast the reader has barely recovered from one attack before the next begins."
—San Francisco Chronicle

"THE MOST PROVOCATIVE VOICE IN CONTEMPORARY HORROR SINCE CLIVE BARKER. Her style is passionate, powerful, and unpredictable. In Bad Brains she [weaves] nightmares as lovely and soulful as they are grotesque and terrifying." —Fangoria

THE CIPHER

"This powerful first novel is as thought-provoking as it is powerful." —Publishers Weekly

"A TOUR DE FORCE of style, horror, strong emotion, fear and obsession." —Writer's Digest

"DISTURBING, UNIQUE AND UNFORGETTABLE. . . . [The Cipher] takes you into the lives of the dark dreamers that crawl on the underbelly of art and culture. Seldom has language been so visceral and so right, the phrases sometimes pinpricks looking for a witch's mark and sometimes knife thrusts to the heart."
—Scott Winnett, Locus

Also by Kathe Koja:

THE CIPHER
BAD BRAINS
SKIN

STRANGE ANGELS

KATHE KOJA

A DELL BOOK

Published by
Dell Publishing
a division of
Bantam Doubleday Dell Publishing Group, Inc.
1540 Broadway
New York, New York 10036

ISBN: 0-440-21498-X

Reprinted by arrangement with Delacorte Press

Printed in the United States of America

Published simultaneously in Canada

March 1995

10 9 8 7 6 5 4 3 2 1

RAD

I would like to thank Sandy Beadle, Lou Jacobs, and all those who answered my questions with patience and grace, especially Melody Asplund-Faith, who shared generously her time and expertise.

I am very grateful to Barry N. Malzberg for his invaluable critique.

And to Rick Lieder, as always, my love and thanks.

For Bud

PART ONE
GRANT

*Nobody speaks the truth when there's
something they must have.*

ELIZABETH BOWEN

HER HAIR ON THE PILLOW; AN EMPTY WHITE cup beside the bed.

Grant, familiar waking headache and he turned over, turned to touch her, long stern curveless body like an ax handle, like a mannequin made of steel; old museum bronze, she was beautiful that way. The cup atop a notepad like a rock to hold it down; STERNE-HUSEY in black caps and below it her handwriting, bad chickenscratch he could not entirely read from this angle: something about meeting someone at four. A client? A doctor? Beside him she frowned in her sleep; was she sleeping? Probably not. He was conscious of his erection, implement beneath the blankets, a tool the use of which he had not decided.

"What time is it?" and right again, she had not been asleep, her voice too sharp for recent waking and in it her day already planned, meeting by meeting, step by step; up on her elbows, "Grant. What *time* is—"

Forget the hard-on. "Twenty to."

Leaning over and past him to answer her own

question, "Eight forty-one," as if any information
he offered could not be expected to be accurate or
even true, sheet marks across her breasts and off to
the bathroom; first the radio, then the water. Eight
forty-two. He had nowhere to go today, no reason
to be up but her cool smile, she would pause on her
way out to gaze at him—supine, cocooned—and
say "See you tonight" as if he might not move at all
between now and then. And then she would leave
and he would be up, angry, washing and dressing to
sit at the half table in the kitchen, one knee pressed
too hard against the wall and what now? The rest of
the coffee she had made; what now?

They were calling it a sabbatical, to their
friends, his friends who knew better, her friends
who did not care, would not care if he were working, either: to them he was merely another of the
great gray race of laypeople; whatever else he did,
or did not do, or was, he was not one of Us.

Johnna was one of Us; Them. An art therapist.
Grant had once met a literary agent who told him,
"I make half a million dollars a year and my father
still can't understand what it is I do." Johnna's job
was like that, a walking title, clinician's coat with no
body inside, no form. She had disliked the story
about the agent; at the time he had not expected
her to, was surprised by her chilly frown.

"My father understands perfectly well what I
do." One hand on a glass of wine, expensive wine,
more than he could afford but he was still trying to

impress her, then. "As a matter of fact it was my father who—"

"That's not the point," smiling a little, a little more than necessary, trying to get her to see. "It's just that some kinds of jobs, see, are very, uh, non-concrete, they're very—"

The glass back on the table, lipstick on the rim, dark lipstick the color of wood, mahogany. "Taking pictures of fruit is concrete?" Thin lips, she had smiled then, or almost. Vulva-lips, one of his friends had called her; all she needs is a beard. At the time it had pissed him off. Now he said it out loud to himself, "Vulva-lips," coffee cold and falsely sweet before him on the table, her magazines and journals piled up where the salt and sugar used to be; she used neither; she needed room for all her things, books, *Phenomenology of Schizophrenia Expressed in Art, Prevalence of Recurrent Motifs in Psychotic Delusions.* Psychology today. Take a picture, it'll last longer. Even a picture of fruit.

In fact he had not taken any pictures, of fruit or anything else, for nine weeks now; it did not seem long but in fact it was, a long time to do nothing; was that what he was doing? Sleeping and eating, and reading the newspapers, sometimes two whole newspapers in a day. Making dinner, sometimes; sometimes Johnna could not come home for dinner, sometimes she came home only to sit on the sofa, still wearing her coat, purse and briefcase pressed against her like exhausted children, and eat

cheese crackers out of the box. And black coffee;
and fall asleep anyway. She loved her job, she said;
frequently; to him, to other therapists, to the
shrinks-in-training who sometimes came over for
drinks, to smile pleasantly at Grant, what is it you
do again? photographer, right.

Had he ever loved his job?

Photography, yes, that was definite; that was
art, a wonderful photograph, Mary Ellen Mark and
Joel-Peter Witkin, he could not see enough of them
but had quit taking Johnna along, she kept pointing
out recurrent motifs, kept talking about light as unconscious metaphor until he wanted to put his fingers in her mouth to shut her up. He had always
loved photography, had gone to school to learn to
love it more, and had until recently spent five out
of every seven days taking pictures of food, or small
boxes, or parts of machines. He had a colleague,
not really a friend, who shot nothing but cosmetics,
lush tortoiseshell circles and lipsticks tall and rogu-
ish as body parts, the female equivalent of the penis; he said he found it "liberating." He made
enough money from Max Factor to fly to Spain
every year. Meanwhile the rent on Grant's studio
had gone up, the jobs slowed down. Johnna sug-
gested they move into his place, it was smaller,
cheaper, she could pay the lion's share of the rent
while he looked for another studio, and in the
meantime he could find assignments taking pictures of other things.

"You mean stuff that actually moves," but she did not smile, did not seem to understand and he did not smile either, he was fed up. Fuck the nuts and bolts, the fruit, the shapes beneath light that so frustrated him that sometimes he wanted to break them, burn them, cut them up. Instead he put his props and backgrounds in storage—even that was expensive—and put his cameras away.

Rinsing out his cup and the phone rang; he let the machine get it, it was always for Johnna anyway. Outside it was raining, pale shivering lines down the glass made dark by dust, by particles and bird shit and it was dark in here too, dark with the lights on and he got his coat, hands cold in ripped pockets and going down, the elevator smelled like a closet full of wet rags. One of the neighbors struggling with her mailbox, the magazines hopelessly jammed: fat gloss stock, celebrities' faces and she glanced at him, her mouth a little open as if she would ask Can you help me? Can you give me a hand? And he pushing past her, not rudely but in a hurry, a definite hurry as if he had somewhere definite to go.

There were seven current photography magazines in the bookstore and it took him the better part of the morning to leaf through them all, more slick pages, more photographs he did not take, did not in black fact have the talent to take; what was his talent? What are your strengths, his adviser had asked him, over and over in the campus office; hot and bored, what are your interests, Grant? Why, taking pictures of fruit, of course. He ended up buying a skin magazine, some dumb porno, smiling at the woman behind the counter who did not smile back.

"That it for you today?"

"Pretty much, yeah," but she didn't get the joke; why should she? The magazine more expensive than he thought, he had to be careful; Johnna never bitched about money but with every dollar he spent he saw his savings, a block of ice melting, melting down; when it was gone, what? Walking back he went slowly, avoiding puddles, the magazine curled to a tube in his hand. None of the mail was for him, and only one of the messages: Johnna, telling him not to make dinner, she would be late with a client tonight.

She *was* late, so late he was already sleeping, waking heavy and curiously cold to the sound of the crane-shaped lamp clicking on, a medical click, breasts and panties and her copper hair in the tight braid that he despised, Heidi braid lying across her bare back like the slash in the circle that says NO; don't touch. On the black armless chair by the bed was her pile of books, fat spill of soft-cover manuals, her briefcase hinged open flat as a mouth and stuffed with sketches, photocopies, pictures in black and red and all the colors of disturbance: pictures her clients had drawn. The topmost two, heavy streaks of mucus-yellow and something below that looked like spit, or tears dried to a matte patina, clipped hard together and marked with a red pen: *R.T.*

"Johnna?"

She was making notes, the last notes of the day, busy fingers, busy red pen, and he said it again, Johnna, and she turned her head; she looked very tired.

"What."

Her panties were a fading acrylic blue, one thread of escaped elastic hanging gray and limp as a vein against her hip. Some kind of night cream still shone damp and unabsorbed beneath her eyes.

"Nothing," he said, and turned over; and was asleep before the light went out, gone at once into the house of dreams: rain, and locks, boxes jammed fast with his photographs, all the work he would ever do bent and crushed to fit where it could not fit, could never; and then all the boxes were empty, dozens of boxes, metal, cardboard, wet wood warped and splitting and they were all marked, stenciled in a way he couldn't read, a language as old and secret as the tongue we speak to one another before the day that we are born.

Dreaming, turning he woke, and in the waking felt beside him heat, blankets wrapped high and sweat-heavy, fat like a burgeoning life. His eyes open in the darkness, faint green light from the bedside clock like some poison mushroom underground and it was like lying next to a giant insect, big secret pupa in slow gestation and purposeful as swimming he moved, to the other side of the bed, the side without heat, the empty side.

In the morning another headache, Johnna gone without breakfast, and he in shameful pleasure sleeping till nearly noon; who was to know? Who cared? Waking again and the headache larger, as if worsened by sleep illicit; aspirin and coffee drunk standing by the sink, a heavy feeling in one side of his head as if the sullen blood had migrated, leaving his right side empty as a cup. Standing still, ox-dull, an animal told to stay: without initiative, without the impetus to move: it was as if he was waiting, marking time, body and mind for the one big thing, the changing moment but that was absurd, wasn't it, you could spend your life waiting for your life to change. Waste your life: but it was a waste already, wasn't it? Be honest: wasn't it? Settling for less, and less than that and that the knowledge, the wedge unavoidable sharpened to press against the shrinking skin of him, press like the glass in a broken mirror that shows you for what you are: not un-filled, but empty. Had his life so far been so little, was that what hurt so much?

And what's next?

The next big thing.

There were only three dishes to wash; when he had done that he went back to bed; he did not leave the apartment at all that day. Dreams as thin

as stale water, as unrefreshing; the same old
thoughts in the same old circles, head on the pillow
as thick as a block, and he moved it back and forth,
back and forth, compass needle pointing nowhere
because there was nowhere he could go.

"—going to try, anyway?"

Half a piece of toast in his hand, he had fixed
omelets and toast for them both. Cheese omelets,
and fresh strong coffee, the spot on his knee that
pressed the wall hurting like a burn. "What?" Shifting in his seat, there was no way to get away from
that wall, not from where he was anyway. "I didn't
hear you."

"I said, are you going to look for some studio
space today."

"I don't know." Shifting again. "I might. There
isn't much out there, you know, things don't
change that much in a couple months."

A noise, air through her teeth, not a sigh;
Johnna was not a sigher. Cup up, and lipstick on its
rim, that same brown lipstick, maybe what's-his-
name had photographed it: spring's new color is
Shit Brown. Bilirubin. He remembered his first
job, in-house photographer at a big manufacturing
company, very big, a buddy of his worked there and
had gotten him in. Just out of college and thoroughly depressed, taking grip-and-grin shots of senior VPs and motivational speakers, of unsmiling
foremen and new tools in all the shades of gray;

and brown. A red tie was an event, he could build a whole shot around one red tie. Quitting after less than a year, and he remembered sitting in the parking lot, trying to rip up his laminated name badge; it was impossible. Finally he just threw it away, GRANT COTTO in the Dumpster at McDonald's, the false fresh smile in the one-by-one mug shot a mold distorted for the smile he wore then, driving away. Eating french fries. He had thought he was free.

Now his own cup down, empty, ringed with grounds, trying to look straight at her, trying not to look away. "Still-life photography is not what I want to do for the rest of my life." Really; perhaps with your gift for understatement you could find a job in advertising, sir. "Maybe now is a good time to rethink things, maybe if I don't get—"

"You know," calm, the calm of the bystander, the helpful bystander, "it seems to me we have this talk a lot." Her cup on the table barely touching his, handle to handle like sex between insects, between beings without visible organs. "It seems to me that you could probably benefit from a little therapy. John Russell at Penn Gen, if I called him he'd—"

"Oh no," much louder than he meant and then forcing himself to downshift past that little internal voice, all volume and egging him on like a needle in the back, rage like a medicine and so *much*; "Oh no," quietly. "Don't start that again. I don't need any therapy."

"Then what do you need?" Still calm, unangry; was she like this with her clients? Raving and screaming, throwing paint around the room, and Johnna sitting there saying, You could probably benefit from a stay in the quiet room, there's a nice one at Penn Gen. Did they still have things like quiet rooms, isolation rooms? Did she put people in them, would she do it today? Would she do it to him? "Grant. What do you want?"

What do you want; who had asked him that last? After the manufacturing company job another, working as a photojournalist for a dumb little biweekly; at first it had seemed like heaven, street photography, but in the end it was just more grip-and-grin, local politicians, pictures of the library and city council meetings and he quit that too, no hard feelings: he hadn't even torn up his nametag, PRESS in red letters and another face but this time unsmiling, he knew a little better now.

But still knew nothing: next it was pseudo-editorial work for a magazine, *City Lights*, posing stiff amateur models, small-fry local celebrities and no talent for that either but he told himself he was learning, and Elaine told him too. The arts editor, chunky jewelry and a determined taste for the avant-garde as long as she was home by midnight on a workday; a gallery opening for some boring metal sculptures, drinking oily wine from plastic cups meant to look like beveled glass and afterward at her house they had screwed standing up; between the wine and the verticality he almost hadn't come but she seemed to like it, seemed to like him enough to put him onto some freelance work on the side, it was the beginning of his studio work but he didn't know that then. *City Lights* lasted a little over three years but by then he was too busy to attend the wake, he was taking pictures of fax machines and floral arrangements, he was meeting Johnna for dinner, he was fucking her standing up, too, but this time he liked it better, he was learning.

And what else had he learned, after that? How to take boring pictures, manage his books, deal with clients; Johnna called hers clients, too, was there a difference? When had he started to hate it, hate the studio, its backdrops and smell, cold chemicals and chapped hands? and in the end no closer to finding his place, his spot, the portion of life that was his: work, fruit in bright light, forget it; and love. Was Johnna love? Pale eyes and sitting there so calmly, waiting for his answer, what do you want?

"You're at loose ends," she said, but that was wrong, he *was* loose ends, that was the point and more than the point, it was the locus, the cankering heart: I want more, he wanted to say that, I want more, but what he meant had no words, it was not some adolescent wish for excitement or thrills but

the heavy hunger inside, the part of him that knew
without doubt that what was best in him was dying,
dying here in this apartment, this emptiness, this
lack. As if nothingness could have a name and that
name his, what do you want? I don't know! crying
out. I don't know what I need. As if his whole life
had been nothing but a struggle to find not the
door but what lies beyond it, where the fire lives;
not even how to get in, just to find where to get,
does that make sense? no? to you it wouldn't,
would it, you know where your room is, you didn't
even need to look for it, you were born in it. Did
she even know how smug she looked, hair up and
loose gray suit, Freud's calm daughter with a BFA
and fingers open on the table, her knee pressed
against nothing, she was free to move as she
pleased.

"Never mind," he said now, the same old ulcer-
ous burn, whoever thought nothing could hurt so
much. "Never mind, I'll figure something out," and
she reached across the table, past the coffee cups
to take his hand, three fingers: "I have to go," she
said, "I'll be late." She had never been late for anything in her life, it was apparently just a formula to
get her out of rooms but he did not call her on it,
did not even watch her go but sat instead drinking
the last of the coffee, looking at pictures in the
newspaper, looking at the ads with that same burning, aching at the back of his neck, the watery
lenses of his eyes.

And in bed that night her arms around his waist, hair like latticework, machine lace spilled clumsy and destroyed in her next motion, back and forth and his eyes closing, gaze fierce on nothing as he rode her, creaking sweat and his thigh muscles cramping, aching, pain in the instant of coming and she shifting beneath him, aggrieved: don't stop, she said, why did you stop? His cock small and wet, an apology against her thigh and she turned her back on him to masturbate, hips in brisk determined rhythm like adding up a column of figures, and afterward switched on the lamp, click-click, notebook on the night table and a client's photocopied drawing open on her slightly open knees.

What do you see there? he wanted to ask, big slashing arrows pointing at a little stick figure, the kind of thing a child might draw, a backward child. What does that mean, what does it mean to you? Pen in her teeth and arms up, braiding her hair as she considered, little figure hemmed by arrows, do you know what it means to feel like that? What if I made a drawing, what if I slipped it into your pile: would you know? Would you diagnose me correctly, would you send me to Penn Gen? Would you even know it was me?

"Grant?"

Pale eyes, and absolutely level, bright blue blanket tenting over her bent knees. Did she have these thoughts, too, just like him? Maybe everybody did, maybe everybody was—

"Grant, move over. I need some room here."

Eyes closing, again, as he shifted, from warmth to cold, moving so no part of his body touched any part of hers at all, like a drawing of two arrows moving in opposite directions, perpendicular arrows going up, and going down.

The next day more drawings, over dinner; bright red sauce and red circles, she had brought home the originals: the paper surprisingly cheap-looking, maybe they couldn't afford anything better. And felt-tip markers, red and green soaking through the paper like fluids from a bandage, an old unclosing wound. As she ate she made notes, pen and fork, fork and pen.

Cheese spilled on the table, light and pale as dandruff; he swept it away with his palm, onto the floor. Fork and pen and on to the next one, yellow smear as bright as egg yolk, a big determined sun: you had to be depressed to use colors as bright as that. Notes, notes, frowning, chewing and on to the next: this one without color seepage, must be in pencil or dry pen. When the phone rang he did not move, knee against the wall and after the third ring the machine picked it up, Johnna mouth full and annoyed, "Why didn't you get that?"

"It's never for me."

"You're closer," but even in her irritation she was unfocused, obviously taken by the drawing: fork and pen and now only pen, notes in that bad handwriting, if she were not so pure of heart he

would have suspected her of putting it on, don't all
doctors write poorly? Right. Reaching the end of a
notebook page and rising, had to hear that message, couldn't finish her dinner or her notes without knowing who it was.

The drawing lay, scrupulous the distance between it and the plate, and after wiping his hand he
picked it up, noting first the initials at the top, *R.T.*
again in red pen. The drawing was in pencil,
colored pencils, two colors barely there: gray and
pink, the colors of earliest morning, the secret colors of the brain. Close to his face as if he were
nearsighted, pink and gray and the hand that made
them subtle, it was all amazingly subtle: lines, just
lines but see how they cross, blend, lines like ribbons, like glyphs arcing, like the language the body
speaks to itself, speaks to the simmering mind, and
what kind of mind behind eyes that can see like
this? What kind of skill, this artlessness pure as
glass to sheen without covering the enormous talent; the genius? Is it genius; and R.T., what does
that mean? name, code name, diagnostic acronym,
what?

And the drawing from his hands, he had not
heard her coming: "Give me that," but not unkindly. "You're not supposed to be looking at that."

Leaning back, and his hands were shaking;
why? Like a shock, like a burn; an X-ray shadow, a
feeling in the heart. "Why not?"

"Because it's confidential, that's why not." Settling down into her chair again, propping the drawing but not so he couldn't see. "It's what we did at Maple, yesterday. I usually make photocopies, but I didn't have time." A sip of water, melted ice water and lipstick on the rim. "We ended up running late, and then I had a meeting, one of the rec therapists —the woman's just a bitch, it's incredible they even let her near the clients." Pen up again and flipping the notebook over: a note about the rec therapist? Recreational therapy. Basket-weaving, or was that occupational therapy? "Apparently she used to work at Clearwater," half to him, half to who, herself? Some other staff member? "That's where he's from."

"Who?"

"Robin," and then the pen busy, each dotted i a chime, miniature, the slim black body striking faint against her water glass; did she hear it? Gazing past her, not obvious, to pink and gray exquisite, and exquisitely sad; Robin from Clearwater, it all sounded so pastoral if you didn't know any better, if you didn't know that Clearwater was a hospital for the mentally ill, if you didn't know that Robin was more than likely mad as a hatter. Was sanity the sacrifice for such precision, such inhuman clarity, was that the toll paid at the gates of the temple of the mind and this the recompense: only this, and I will give you eyes.

After dinner she made calls, folders neat and tidy and tidily closed, the orderly mind; was order

therapeutic? From an art therapist you would expect some chaos, bright spontaneous disorder, does
it take one to know one? Some folders were
marked—MAPLE, ST. JOHN'S, M. T. BERRY—her blurred
capitals on white stickers, the folders themselves
good psychiatric blue. She had not put Robin's
drawing away, left it in fact in easy reach; perhaps
she was glad to see him taking an interest in something other than himself; why not? He was certainly
glad, more than glad and in a way he could not
name; is the blood happy in the vein? the bone in
its sheathing muscle? He tilted the drawing again,
let light run down like water, tilted it back another
way: those glyphs like angels' eyes, socketed in gray
and long pink lenses to see past the world's busy
skin to the sorrowing meat beneath, was it sorrow?
Would an artist necessarily see sorrow in everything, or did it help to be a mental patient? no,
client, and what kind of client was Robin? Johnna
met with many different groups, problems sharp
and various: affective disorders, neuroses, addic-
tions, schizophrenia; who was he, under which ban-
ner did he travel?

"Johnna?" but she was still on the phone so he
tilted the drawing again, 45 degrees and close to his
face, his eyes, tracing with vision the vision of that
mind which had in these drawings reached from its
own blackness to touch like a wand in still water
the black emptiness of his own. How many other
drawings had Robin done, how many did Johnna

have? copies, originals, did she have them here? He had to see them; he would see them. *"Johnna,"* but she was still on the phone so with acolyte hands he took up the drawing, sore knee pressed in the rising but he didn't feel it, painless in motion to the dawning circle of the crane-shaped lamp, its light bare and holy in the studying instant till Johnna came in, smiling, and took the drawing back.

"Why not?"

"Grant." Hands on either side of the sink, mirror still filmed in steam; they had taken a shower together, screwed in the needling spray. Still naked, towel around her neck like a jock and she was frowning, hair water-dark and dripping down to the basin, tiny metronomic drops.

"Grant," again, "let's be reasonable." Johnna could sound more reasonable than anyone, you couldn't acquire a voice like that, it was something you had to be born with. Put down that gun. Come down from there. Let's be reasonable. "He's not an artist, he's a client, he's *my* client and he just got out of the hospital, he's still very fragile. Besides, the whole thing violates confidentiality."

What're you, a priest? Firm hairbrush strokes and the water flying, speckling on the wall, on him still in the shower: fat pink starfish, jolly red curtains as plastic as the hot smell of the blow dryer, whipping her hair Medusa, red snakes to hide her face. "I only want to meet him."

"No," loud past the appliance roar, "I can't do that. I shouldn't even have let you see those drawings." But she was pleased on some level, he knew it, pleased with the fact of his interest and with a cunning unsuspected he nodded now, twice, the firm pursed nod of agreement.

"You're probably right," damp pink towel rubbing at his hair. "But you did, and I saw them, and they're incredible, Johnna, you don't need me to tell you that." Her gaze in the mirror and nodding too, yes, incredible, no one like Robin. "But I'm not going to bother him, I'm not even going to get in a *conversation* with him, all right, I'll just meet him and leave. All right? Is that fair?"

Eyes still focused on her face, lips long and firm as a mother saying no; "No," she said. "I just can't do it."

Anger instant; and strong, surprised himself by its red strength but he shrugged, his face disappointment only, eyebrows up and silent and in that silence left the room, towel to fall in the bedroom, and as he dressed his hands were shaking, shaking the way they had as he held the first drawing, map and passport but then he had not known how vast the land before him, black landscape, how many nuances and holes and who knew where the border lay? Did Robin know? and if he did, how was Grant himself to know it if Johnna stood between them, reasonable and watching, the dull sword of therapy drawn?

He knew where the drawings were—photocopies but he took them out anyway, defiant spread on the unmade bed, and she let him, she came in the room and saw but said nothing, began dressing as if he were not there. His head bent, gazing as if down past a drop, a funnel of color—gray and pink, yes, and then the second one slate-blue: a long plain deceptively pure, pure of shapes or nuance, empty: but no, he had studied it with a castaway's passion and knew that it was not emptiness pictured there but absence, a dark absence felt like a bone grown wrong in the body, the shift in the blood that tells in an instant the hour of death. And the third one small, greeting-card size in the scrolling center: black on white, two colors to show with the brute simplicity of pain itself a face, part of a face become part of a drying tree, grown suffering, blind remaining eyes and its lower lip hung long and moss-distorted, platform for a spider, death's little sister in her evening promenade.

Three; but there were more, Johnna did not deny; but would not say how many more, did he do one each week, others when he was alone; was he alone? Did he live alone, and where did he live— not the hospital anymore, she had let that slip at least—some kind of transitional housing, a group home, what? What? She would not even say why he was consulting her, if consultation was even the word; was it part of his mandated treatment, did he want to be there? What was his disorder, what in-

ternal blight to send him to her, art therapy; as if
Johnna could tell him anything about art. What did
she tell him? and what did he tell her?

Panty hose and blouse, brushing past him and
the hairspray smell, he would not look up, he
would not turn his head. Was Robin very ill, or only
slightly? neurotic, depressed, manic, what? If he
had been hospitalized, chances were he was not
one of what Johnna called the worried well, Grant
had laughed the first time she used that phrase,
"worried well" but prim, still, in her judgment, it's
not my business to make judgments, use labels.

Oh bullshit, he had said, trying to sound easy,
amused; you do it all the time. Schizo-affective, bipolar disorder, you use them like any doctor would.

That evenly pitched voice, her head straight on
her neck like a perfectly balanced machine, ball-
bearing socket, the sweet swivel of oil. "I'm not a
doctor," she had said, precisely.

"Then stop acting like one."

"I'm a *therapist*," as if he was deaf, and stupid.
"I provide therapy for people who need it," but
need is such a large word, isn't it, need can mean so
much. Or nothing. Why does Robin need you,
Johnna? or is he being forced to come, a condition
of outpatient treatment, outpatient commitment,
he had heard her talk about such things before.
Take your medicine or we'll put you back in the
hospital. Go see the nice lady or it's back to Clearwater for you. —But uncomfortable even in his an-

ger, this last was a lie and he knew it: such conditions were meant as a safeguard, a way to free the client to a state of semi-independence without allowing the illness to reassert, to itself force the client back to the hospital. Fragile, she had said; he's still very fragile. He just got out of the hospital: it had to mean a group home of some kind, unless he had been released to his family; or the streets. And silently his own dry amazement not only at what he knew but how much; listening, all those times, those hours spent silent over drinks and storing it away, knowledge like a tool unused and seemingly unuseful until the moment, the time: now. You need it now.

"Grant," standing over him, not smiling; not angry. Sorry? No, not that either but something underneath he could not catch, less mercury than vapor but he was angry, too angry still to name it, to take her hand. "I have to go now."

"All right," one look and no more, making no move to put the drawings away, no move toward her so that finally she turned, his gaze rising to see her go: hair up, stiff braid, stiff neck and out the door.

He turned back, again, to the drawings; color copies, surprisingly good ones but it was the originals he needed, to hold and look at them, look in the eyes of the artist himself and say, simply, Show me. Maps and legends, dark light made to shine in that darkness where no other light will do; what do you see, and can you show it to me, can you help me so I can see it too?

R.T.; Robin T. How many Robin T.'s in her clientele, how many could there be? No telling; but that did not mean there was no way to find out.

Eight forty-five and his ass was sore from sitting in the car, this parking lot for two hours now, rereading the magazine he brought, old *American Photographer* down to the ads, his hands were cold as stones in his pockets and all his thinking over, worn to a point smooth as a whittled stick and then nothing, not even a nub: is it wrong to do this? No: at once, and more slowly *no*; she's the one who's wrong, knowing what she knows: knowledge held too close will sour and worse than sour, will diminish, rot in her hands like a treat saved selfish, *mine*, *mine* and then no one's, a lump of pulp unfit to touch; is that what you want? Is it? Watching the cars come and go, blue and gray in the twilight, and it was dark, now, the lights above orange as small moons, harvest moons; two figures in suits, women walking and without conscious decision he opened the car door, pins and needles, but he was brisk, crossing to and into the building, down the hall as if he knew where he was going and he did, a little, half a memory and there it was: he remembered the bend in the hallway, elbow bend and directly past it the long room, IN SESSION on the door in muted blue and sweet as a grail; he was sweating, sharp and wet under his arms. Leaning against the wall, wanting to peer in; don't. Don't do anything but wait, not for her but no one knows that; breathing easy now, it was like being a burglar, strange how guilty you can feel doing nothing wrong.

And already her voice behind the door, close in its opening: "—for next time," and there they were, out in the hall like water spreading, two, three, six, an old man, four women, teenage girl? boy? and already past him, already gone and Johnna in his way, hand on his arm and smiling: "Grant? What're you doing here?" The old man in directionless shuffle and a woman in gray like a uniform there to take his arm, fingers like a cuff, loose, the way Johnna held him, around the biceps: come along now.

"I'm glad you came," and her head for a moment light against his shoulder, "did you have dinner? Do you want to go out?" and the thick spreading disappointment, ridiculous, did you think you would find him, did you think it would happen this way? His face like light; or wearing a nametag, HI MY NAME IS, did you really think it would be as easy as that?

"—Fleischmann's? or we could go to Hunan Express, it's just as close."

He had never particularly seemed to himself a liar, someone good at dissembling; his smile small but it was there. "Fleischmann's would be good," keys in hand, armpits dried cold and sour like the aftermath of a crash, a near-miss. "You can follow me."

Different groups, and subgroups, mosaic and maze: paging clandestine through library books, hand-books and guides written for family members, laypeople; all her books were useless, over his head. What's your trouble, Robin, what's wrong with you? Bipolar disorder, the world in pendulum perspective; was Robin suicidal, had he been hospi-talized for that? Or did he wear the gray eyeless hood of depression; or the spike and scepter, black motley of schizophrenia; Johnna had a very few of them, too. Reading, drinking coffee, reading; let the phone ring. Johnna carrying in the mail, "Grant?" and hiding the books, quick under the table and meeting her in the hall: smiling, kissing, heart beating as if he had just run up and down the stairs.

And back again, waiting in the hallway, IN SES-SION but a different time, a different group: three men, three women all very young; Johnna in muted brown and her smile more quizzical: I don't usually take lunch; but. Drinking coffee in Fleischmann's again, red beef on black rye, are you going to work late tonight? Is there another group? Flipping through her folders when she went to the bath-room, R.T., are you there? Robin; I'm looking for you. What *lousy* handwriting she had.

Driving back: "You don't have to come in," but

he did anyway, walking her to her office, tidy little cube abutting another tiny little cube, some guy in a ratty black sport coat waiting for her in the hall, file folders under his arm: firm nod, let me get my messages. E-mail, reading and half smiling at Grant, attention firmly elsewhere and the order unspoken: You can go now. Squeezing past him to the hall, the half-closed door; the computer was still on, flashing cursor small and amber like a little warning light.

He could hear her voice in the hallway.

Go on. Hurry.

LIST FILES.

Shaking hands and bent from the waist, awkward, secretive; hurry. ENTER CLIENT #. I don't know. Try one at random, two digits, four. Nothing. Johnna's voice, louder than it should have been and he straightened so fast something flashed in his back, a pulling pain; false alarm. *Hurry.* Five digits and the names spilled out, long scroll in blessed alphabetic order: R-S-T, TANAKER, TENOWSKY, TESSIEL, THOMAS, THOMPKINS, TOBIAS; Robin Tobias.

Robin.

Twenty-eight years old; medicated schizophrenic; recently released from Clearwater. Thursday evening group.

ESCAPE and the screen not yet empty before she was in again, angry hand closing the door—not slamming, she was not a door slammer—shaking her head: "Can you believe that?" pushing space on the desk for the file folders and his own idiot smile, still shaking like a swimmer freed from deep water, undertow and in the hall he almost laughed, a little laugh like a cough and the client number over and over, 41764, 41764, 41764, it had not been so hard after all. Robin Tobias, twenty-eight years old. Schizophrenic. Headache warm like hard exertion, when he got home he was too excited to read so he went back out, walking, long legs in borrowed athlete's rhythm, all the way to the cleaner's before he turned around, thigh muscles working, lungs sweeping in and out and the air in his face, clean sweat on his back, motion's rhythm and he felt so *good*; Robin Tobias, I know who you are.

Wednesday spent wondering, early up and lying watchful beside sleeping Johnna, closing his eyes in the moment of the alarm; the whole day like that, as if spent in a blind, as if she could smell his thoughts from far away. What would she do, if she knew? What *could* she do? Yell; scream. What else? Tell Robin? Warn Robin away from him? Yes. Would she? Would she? How mad would she be? *It violates confidentiality*; but not my confidentiality, I'm not *doing* anything, I'm not doing anything bad. All I want to do is talk to him, that can't hurt him. As if arguing with her, mapping out his side thoroughly and with vigor; walking around the kitchen with one hand out before him as if he were a TV lawyer, advocate for the lost; how can this

hurt him? It can't. Simple as that. "Simple as that,"
out loud and nodding to himself, knowing on some
other, passionless level that it was not, nothing in-
volving anyone so inherently fragile could be free
of complications of a scale and complexity he could
not envision, a sightless man breezy into a room
made entirely of gears and meshing wires, pressure
dials and long cabling snakes and everywhere the
signs: DANGER; MACHINERY. That same flat inner
voice like the angel of necessity: You are touching a
man's mind; like a hand to brush a naked eyeball,
open dry and terrified, the lid pinned back to admit
an access brutal by its nature, even with the best of
intentions, the truest of goodwill; and did he have
that? were they good, his intentions? What do you
want, anyway?

Just to ask. Just to see.

See what?

What he sees.

The eyeball forced open: seeing because it
must; is it like that? Is there pleasure in the drawings, relief, what? Does it hurt? I just want him to
tell me, I just want to sit down with him and

you want to use him

No.

Sun in the kitchen, a pile of grounds and half a
ripped filter, the empty coffeepot in his hands. I
don't want to use anybody, I don't want to hurt
anybody. Pain somewhere in his stomach, the highest layer of guts, intestines: water running flat from

the tap, long reluctant gurgle like a sick man's piss, warm on his hands as the pot overflowed, and he poured it all out to fill it again; I don't want to hurt anybody and I'm not going to. Not him, not Johnna or anyone. I just want to *see*, is that wrong?

Silence.

He took up one of the books, bookmark to the rule of quarters: ten years after onset 25 percent of schizophrenic clients were completely recovered, an equal number improved to the point of independence; another 25 percent were improved though still requiring an extensive support network. Of the last quarter 15 percent were still hospitalized; the rest were dead.

How many see the way Robin sees, what happens to them?

He kept reading, plowing through, not too much jargon and he was learning, a little, to master it; four, four thirty, five thirty and still reading and the phone rang, Johnna; sounding cheerful, "I should be home on time tonight," and listening he felt very dry, yesterday's rushing excitement gone as thoroughly as the blank dreams of orgasm in the moments after, when the body is just a body again, flesh and flesh beside it and nothing else to say.

Back to his book, positive symptoms and thirty-year follow-ups, neuroleptics, side effects, tardive dyskinesia; he read till six o'clock and then opened two cans of mushroom soup, a small square of beef as cold and hard as a body in the freezer turning sullen brown and wet on the microwave carousel: still dead, but less apparently so. By the time Johnna got home he was cutting bread on the breadboard; he was ready to listen to her tell him all about the stupid guy at Social Services and the idiots at the bank, listening and smiling when it seemed required and hearing nothing she said at all.

In bed her hands cool and a little sweaty, slipping between his legs to cup his testicles, work at his cock, the green clock moving from minute to minute and it seemed he could see in the dark: the tendons in her neck, the way her lower lip bent under her strong teeth, the way his own hands walked her back to settle on either side of her ribs, her lungs like bellows rich with her moving body's smell: warm, and faintly sour, a medication we take not in need but with the customary reach of habit, wanting not what is offered but instead the proscribed ritual of receiving what we have come to need for itself alone.

Eyes closed and she was sliding off him, squeezing him once in departure, already half-asleep. And the green minutes turned, and turned again; and it was Thursday, his eyes wide, and dry, and open as a trusting eye to the reaching hand that nears it, close and closer, for good or ill.

Thursday. The session ran from six to eight fifteen; he knew this, had written it down on a small yellow note, sticky on top, stuck to the inside of his pocket like a thoughtful piece of skin. It was five forty; if he would see Robin arrive, he had better go now.

Five forty-five.

Six o'clock.

He should wait till after the session, he should not seem to be barging in; no use antagonizing Johnna any more than necessary. Sitting, then standing, into the kitchen where he drank half a glass of water, one of his books and he tried to read; he would leave at seven forty-five, plenty of time.

Were they working? talking, drawing? What was Robin doing right now? Tantalizing, trying to visualize that unknown, the unseen hand and he spread the drawings around him, half circle, slate-blue and pink and gray and black and white; incantatory colors; how did Robin make his choice? Did Johnna help, suggest, guide? Like telling the sun how to shine. What was Johnna's function, in relation to Robin—and absurd, the frown on his face: jealousy? Well. Why not? She was the one who got to see the drawings, all the drawings, watch him work: and what did she do in return? Help him, teach him, give him what? Enlightenment? Signposts on the road to normalcy, life management skills, to manage his life into what? *my* life? *Shit*. Sick as he might be, Robin was a better man, with a better life, than he; see what Robin's presence, unmet, still unknown but present, yes, and see what that in itself had done for Grant: his life already changed, the gray creep of days infused, overlaid as if in twinkling gold mosaic, tile heavy with color, Robin's colors, the rushed pleasure of searching for him, speculating about him; looking—even that, even if only that and nothing more—looking at his work. He, Grant, had stopped the circular self-discussion, endless examinations like some obsessive old penitent, one eye in the mirror and praying to be saved from vanity; obsessive still, maybe, yes maybe but at least he finally had something worth obsession's selfish stare.

Seven thirty-one.

Gathering the drawings, putting his books away; should I tell him I saw them? How? I saw your drawings. Like some idiot at a gallery, pawing and gushing: I *love* your work. And then what? with Johnna standing there like a mean teacher, doctor, parent, would she even let him talk? Could she stop him? have him thrown out, what? Seeing him there she would know, she would have to, that his presence was more than brute good luck; what would she do?

A pain again, in his stomach; nervousness, a warm churn like diarrhea and he got his coat, seven fifty, found his keys. Trying to remember, how did she structure the sessions, were they the same every time? Draw how you feel. Draw a gift you would like to give to someone. Draw a secret, a hallucination, a delusion, a dream. Draw yourself and give the paper to someone else; God. Why not just cut out your heart, your wet gray brain: here. Here I am. Would he do that, give himself that way? and the answer immediate: No.

Why?

In the bathroom that same sickly plastic smell, maybe it was the shower curtain; red, red, red like a chambered heart, it made the room seem hotter, smaller, as if the walls might be warm, as if your fingers in the touching might come away damp, and sticky with salt. Some yellow cream, bright as an egg in its clear container, not glass but thinnest plastic to fool the eye; LUMINATE in lovely scrolling caps across the label, luminate, was that even a word? *Il*luminate: to give light to, to light up. To make clear; as Robin's drawings, dark illumination, subtle with anguish; was it anguish? Robin: is it pain you feel, always feel? What is it like, to see

with the clear eyes of the mad

what is it *like*?

Go; go on. Hurry up! and it was eight ten, eight eleven in the rolling green instant, what's the matter with you? What's the *matter* with you? and the dislocating sound, Johnna's key, Johnna's voice: "Shit," but not angrily, the mild voice of something forgotten and he pulled off his coat, quick, hung it on the back of the bathroom door and "Hi," as mild, "you're home early." By the front door a blue pile of folders, her briefcase, her coat still faintly cold and smelling, light, of car exhaust, of the big world outside and you missed it, sitting on the shitter and you missed it; are you afraid, will you draw a picture of your fear?

No.

In the folder, hurried open to see the drawings, half a dozen originals flipped through with a burglar's haste; but none of them, in the hallway's light, in his anxious hand open as a beggar's, were Robin's; as if he had not after all been there to see.

More reading, sitting on the bed, at the kitchen table; what will you do? Not asking aloud but there, like a rumble, an insistence, will you screw it up again? Coward. The week went by, rolling days as before an operation, time flies. He had the shits again Wednesday night, and Thursday ate nothing after noon, just coffee, wishing he still smoked; empty hands to settle to nothing, pick up a book and put it down.

But in the end it was as easy as Johnna's voice on the phone, almost a snarl in her hurry and frustration: car trouble, she was stuck at the fucking brake shop and all her sessions would have to be canceled, who knew when the fuck she would be home, good-bye. And he standing by the phone, head tilted lightly, pulse beating happy as a drum in his neck; it was five thirty. Shoes, and keys, the sun's angle in his eyes and the traffic lights green as an omen; he found a parking spot right away.

Smiling, he tried not to. Inside the building,

standing by the doors and here they came, slow, alone, a little early: a balding older man, a very young black woman and he smiled toward them, dry lips stretched across his teeth: "The session's—" and now another man, young—too young?—moving even more slowly, paralytic diffidence and the woman looked past him, Grant, to say in a voice bare of inflection, "Hey, Robin."

Robin.

Still approaching, step and step and his face, would Grant have known it from the others, would he have been able to point it out and say There; that's the one? No? Yes? Blue eyes very pale, and a red scar on the forehead; white-blond hair, dark T-shirt, soiled pants like workmen wear; and that death-row walk. Did he think he, Grant, was a new therapist, a new client, did he even notice Grant at all?

"Excuse me," and his own voice in his head specious as a stranger's, a Judas goat and he was still smiling, smiling as if he could not stop, *he* must look crazy: "Excuse me," again. "Tonight's session is canceled," almost as if it had been made to be so, a gift, a simple boon. "The therapist had some car trouble, she asked me to tell you. She—"

"Well, fuck me," the balding man said, in a calm and cheerful voice; he made no attempt to move but the young woman instantly began walking, as if his words were an unarranged signal between them. Robin said nothing, did nothing, gaze on the floor, then up, then at the closed door; then, very timidly, at Grant.

Who in this hungry moment felt as if not ice but a bridge of sand lay beneath him, dry pale sand to crumble in the time it took to say one word wrong; and so carefully, carefully not even looking at Robin, "Do you need a ride home?"

Silence; and his belated worry, would the balding man answer instead but Robin shook his head, shrugged, small simultaneous motions but something different in the pale eyes, the gaze gone almost in the instant of touch and the balding man began pushing out his tongue as if there were a bad taste in his mouth.

"I could give you a ride," very calmly, hands in his pockets fisted tight. Don't look at him. Don't say anything else.

"It's the water," the balding man said; for some reason his voice made Grant more nervous, an irritated feeling like a hair in the eye. Thin voice, like a whine, and that pushing pink tongue. "It gets into everything, and I don't even *like* to swim. Will you shut up?"

Robin in silence and did not look at him or the balding man, at the two women in lab coats who passed them, trio and noticing none. Six ten on the heavy clock, black-screened wall clock with a greasy white face. In his nose the smell of his own sweat, a sharp high odor; unconscious his step back, away

and in that movement, as twinned as if choreo-
graphed Robin's head turning, those pale eyes
looking into his, directly into his, and it was for
Grant as if he saw—what? not the drawings, not
that precisely but through them, in distance the
country from which the drawings came, the plain
burned by winds of such velocity as to scour skin
from bone, the well filled warm and trickling but
not with water, no, not with any liquid at all but
with something wet set in motion by touch; the
place where the air is black and tastes of salt and
Robin nodded, gaze gone again, one finger picking
at a frayed belt loop, picking at the thread.

And Grant's nod instant, dry clicking swallow
and "Okay," more careful than ever; the balding
man laughed, a brisk false actor's laugh: "I told you
to forget it, didn't I? Just for*get* it."

Robin gazing now at the floor between his feet
and Grant's launching step, nervous, too fast;
would the balding man follow? would Robin? but
Robin did, keeping half a step back, more than an
arm's length away; the way a prisoner walks next to
a guard, together but apart. Outside the smell of
exhaust, a car pulling away from the curb and the
sun a brighter smear, keys silent in Grant's pointing
hand.

"There's my car," and Robin saying nothing,
following, head bent at a headsman's angle, hang-
dog; beside the car like a child as Grant unlocked it
but once seated clicked his seat belt in place at

once, brisk snap of metal engaging and Grant immediately fastened his as well, a smile sudden and absurd but Robin smiled too, as if they had both done something difficult and smart and in the warm path of that smile Grant's shrug, hands on the wheel: "Do you want to stop for a coffee, or something?"

Robin's hair white in the light descending, halo, the patron saint of silence. "All right," casually, as if this was something they did often. "All right. If you want."

JACOBB's in red and white, a stylized drawing of a man staring with comic surprise through a mug with the bottom cut out: HOME OF THE BOTTOMLESS CUP! and Robin's gaze in slow puzzlement from the words to the picture, picture to the words. There were three other people in the coffee shop, teenage girls in black; six fifteen, time for dinner, not coffee. Unless you can't afford dinner, unless a bottomless cup is what you need. Faint draft from the storefront windows, a smear on the grease-yellow plastic of the tablecloth, why are you wasting your time with this shit? Look at him. Talk to him.

"I think I'll have the chocolate espresso," well isn't that interesting, who gives a shit? *Talk* to him! "Do you like espresso?"

Silence. Sun enough to turn the tips of the blond hair white again, negative radiance; the forehead scar very dark. Hands out of sight, picking at his belt loop.

"I used to drink it a lot when I was working. To keep me up, you know?" Taking a napkin from the squat silver dispenser, something to do with his hands. Maybe he should start picking his belt loop, too. "It's good for that."

One of the teenage girls left the booth and came over to them; black hair, black MAJOR DAMAGE T-shirt tied under chubby breasts. "What do you want?" in a half-accusing way, as if they had come in expressly to bother her, to disturb her chat with her friends; it took Grant a long moment to understand that she was the waitress. He ordered a chocolate espresso for himself, then nodded to Robin; who said nothing, did not look up, might have been a captive without language and the girl sighed hard through her nose, like a horse. "Make it two," Grant said. Robin brought his thumb very close to his face, then began very slowly to chew at the cuticle, eyes so veiled they were almost closed. He looked far younger than twenty-eight, as if he might be a near contemporary of the waitress and her friends, long-lashed pale eyes and that scar, red as a burn, a birthmark; it almost could have been a birthmark if not for the obvious ridge of healed tissue, someone had done that to him. Who? Or was it an accident, a car wreck, what? So many questions. Talk to him, talk to him now.

"Do you like art?" Nothing. "Johnna says—" and the gaze in motion, rising swiftly as if startled by the name and why did you bring her up, asshole? huh? "Johnna says she enjoys the sessions a lot. She, uh, she finds them very beneficial." Silence. "I like art a lot too. I'm a photographer." Although nothing I do could ever be classified as art. "It's kind of an interesting job." How do you work, Robin, how do you make the drawings? That's what interests me, that's what I have to know. Those moving eyes, the table, the wall, the thumb before his face; like teasing out a stray animal, a mistreated stray: here kitty kitty. The coffees came, too hot but Grant drank anyway, drank to keep from talking and burned his mouth, bright scald—"*Shit*"—and from Robin the smallest of smiles before he raised his own cup, slow to his lips to breathe on it, little clouds like weather of a tiny planet, a tiny black-chocolate sea.

Talk, his own voice but later he did not remember what he said, jumping from topic to topic and all of them inane and yet it was not wholly awkward, it was instead as if the whole process was necessary in some way, a step in a dance made blind but with the conviction of experience, it must be this way. Yes. When his cup was empty Robin pushed it two-fingered to the center of the table, slow and careful and this too had about it the smell of ritual: now we are done. In it the smallest residue of grounds, and as they rose, put on coats Grant told about once having his future read in the tea leaves, brown shipwreck swirl: Johnna there, too, but he didn't say that, instead recounted the fortune, travel and money, romance and a big house in a big city; what bullshit and he had to laugh, dry rueful laugh and Robin smiled, gaze down, away, out the window at the traffic and it was already seven thirty, seven forty when they pulled up in the driveway of the group home, it was not hard to find, Robin's directions brief but very clear: you turn here and you turn here, and here it is.

A house ordinary, red brick and fading yellow gutters and a man out front cutting the grass who stopped, presumably to watch them; head turned at an angle oblique, it was hard to tell if he was looking at them or not. Robin oblique, too, half a smile like half a rebus, carefully closing the car door, and Grant leaning shy, absurd: like a boy on a date, will I see you again?

And Robin in silence past the man with the lawn mower, up to the screen door where through its veiling mesh he turned to wave, just a little, just a backhand movement of the wrist but Grant in the receiving smiling instant, anointed, backing out and down the street (Omira, remember it) and all the sweet way home; like getting close enough to touch the door behind which lies what you most want in the world; the lock for next time, just to touch it is enough for now.

"And where were you?"

Stiff-backed at the kitchen table, neck swiveling like a gun in a turret to track his entrance: a yellow

third-copy on the table before her, bill from the
brake shop. "I tried to call," hands still on the bill, a
blurred spot of black grease on the side of her blue
skirt. "I left four messages."

"I'm sorry," lying pleasantly, he could afford to
be pleasant. Omira street, brick house. "I didn't,
you didn't say when you'd be home."

"That's because I didn't *know*, I've been in that
fucking garage for three hours." Beside the bill a
cup of what looked like tea; cold tea. Mascara
smeared faint beneath her eyes, more axle grease.
"What are we doing about dinner?"

"Whatever you want."

"What I want is something to *eat*," and then in
a rush, "For God's sake, Grant, you've been home
all day, why couldn't you at least fix some fucking
dinner?" Turned all the way around in the chair,
mouth pulled down and she looked mean, tired and
mean and she would be even meaner if she knew
where he had been; but she didn't know, and for
now he would not say; there was no point, was
there? Was there? and beside her, one hand on her
shoulder, bending his head like a kindly nurse:
"Don't worry," squeezing lightly. "I'll run out and
get something, some Chinese food or something.
All right?"

On a sigh, a long downbeat: "All right," and on
the incoming breath, "You just wouldn't believe it,
the day I've had. You just can't imagine."

White hair in the light like a halo, art's benedic-

tion: that little wave on the porch. Most certainly
they would see each other again. "I know," putting
on his coat again, picking up his keys. "I know just
what you mean."

She found out, of course, in the course of the next
day—one of the other therapists, one of the two
women in lab coats who had seemed not to notice,
deceptive that blank regard—and he did not work
to hide it; there would be no hiding anyway what
he had in mind. At first he was not even sure she
was angry, sitting there in her spot at the kitchen
table, her voice calm as a straight line but when he
saw her eyes he knew: focused so hard and flat and
blinkless, as if she would burn her way through him
to the truth, who do you think you *are*, what did
you think you were doing? Over and over, her voice
getting louder, I can't believe you, I can't *believe*
you, I knew you were selfish but I never thought
you would stoop to something like this.

"Like what?" Dish towel in one hand, loose and
limp, the other light on the aluminum rim of the
sink. Dirty dinner plates now submerged and the
soap like creamy clouds, good enough to eat. "How
did I hurt him? you tell me that. I bought him a
coffee, Johnna. That's all I did."

"You had no business going there in the first
place! You had no business even knowing he's a
client of mine!"

"Then you shouldn't have told me." Cold water

down the circular plane of a plate. "You shouldn't
have brought the drawings home."

Furious: "I was trying to *help* you!" but it was
the trump card, they both knew it; mea culpa, let
her scream. Trying to help, to involve—"You say I
always shut you out from my work, I was trying to
draw you in—"

"Well, it worked. It worked, why are you so
mad?" Mug in his hand, red on white like blood on
bone, HUSTON PHARMACEUTICALS and the H in HUSTON
was wearing away; fading like scab healing to scar.
Placing the mug upside down to dry, no bottomless
cups here; and inside the tiniest heat, a pleasure
small as a solar flare at vision's limiting rim. No you
can't see Robin, no you can't meet him, no no no;
did she think that would stop him, did she really
think her sanctimonious pronouncements carried
any weight at all? Confidentiality, shit; it was selfishness, the peculiar greed of the discoverer: I
found it, and it's mine. Hands off.

And still talking, her voice up and down and he
ran more water, waiting for her to stop enough to
listen, and if at last she would not listen he would
not talk; let her watch to learn, then, if she wanted
to know. Maybe Robin would even draw her a picture.

Her voice in octaves like a figure running, up
and down hills, up and down and the water kept
running, cooling the skin of his hands. He thought
of the brick house, of Robin at the screen door; he

thought of what he wanted to do. He was still thinking when he noticed that Johnna was no longer in the room.

Thursday morning and she was up early, it was barely eight when her weight left the bed. In and out of the shower, her mouth in that stern curve, and he watched her dress, deliberately watched her dress: white bra, white panties cut high at the waist; a blouse the color of old snow.

Not looking at him, "Are you going to try to see him today?"

"Yeah." Firm, but not angry; no need to be angry. Knowing she wouldn't, "Do you want to come along?"

Turning on him, panty hose at her knees and it looked strange, legs half tan and half pale, as if she were peeling or growing a skin. "*No,* I don't want to 'come along,'" the quotes obvious, response to a suggestion both indecent and unkind. "How you can even suggest it is beyond me. Why would I want to watch you undermine my treatment? Why would I want to watch what you think is—"

"Wait," one hand up, palm at her like a saint, a traffic cop. "Just wait a minute. Why do you insist on thinking that I'm going to hurt him?"

"You already have," and the panty hose yanked up, the blouse yanked down; the ugly braid a beautiful color in the half-light, morning light of the room; she was not always beautiful, Johnna, but in strange moments she could be; and was now. Still naked in the bed's halved warmth and he sat up, wanting her in a way obscure that was not desire, just wanting her to sit down a minute, to sit and listen, her hand on his through the slim dry membrane of the sheet; lightly. Listen to me.

But now she was moving, she was zipping up her skirt, sticking in earrings like pins in a voodoo doll. Lips pulled down, "Nothing I say matters to you," and gone, bedroom door and, in a moment, outer door; no breakfast, no coffee, no nothing. The bathroom still residually tropic, standing in the dwindled pool of her shower and in the water's heat he masturbated, dreamy feel of more than flesh in his hand, thoughts like pictures seen behind the heavy pebbled glass that distorts as it presents, old glass like the walls of a curved aquarium, like a scrying tube, like the antique swell of a reliquary lined dry with the blood of angels.

At seven forty he left the apartment, the day between spent in that same fugue country, not even thinking, not needing to. Walking into the clinic, air oily with disinfectant like surface scum, there was no killing that other odor beneath: pervasive as sweat and old dirt but it was not that, or not wholly; there was another smell there that he could not define, did not try because here was Robin, already, black sweatshirt and hair in a messy braid, head ducked between shoulders; but when he saw Grant he smiled, eyes and mouth, a look so shy

with hunger that Grant, ready to speak, said nothing, words gone and only smiled in return, a smile
as large as he could make it but inadequate, he
knew it was inadequate; no one should look that
happy looking at him.

"Hi, Robin," and at once behind them Johnna,
over Robin's shoulder like an instant head; had she
seen that look? that smile? No sign in her face
blank as the smooth blue folders, symmetrical and
tight beneath her crossed arms; she would obviously say nothing, was present in a professional capacity only. Grant leaned forward as if to kiss her;
she bent back as if at a striking snake, a silent cloud
of toxic gas.

"Hi," Robin said. He was red, flushing face and
neck, the forehead scar almost purple. Rolled in his
hand a tube of paper, a new drawing? Don't look at
it. Did he want to get coffee? or something to eat?

Anger coming off her like vapor, like purest
heat: "Robin's expected home."

"We won't be long," through his own anger, it
was hard to keep smiling but he did it and Robin
looking from one to another, the flush now fading
like a post-fever pallor, bright-eyed and clammy, if
he bolts now I'll never forgive you. Never. The
other clients moving past them, the balding man of
last week, the young girl, two young girls, white and
black, pretty as bookends, dirty bookends in jeans
and baggy sweats. Robin turned his head to look at

them, Johnna looking at Grant: who smiled at her, all teeth. Don't fuck with me now, Johnna; don't.

"Let's go," the smile gentling for Robin who smiled without looking at either of them, seemingly without seeing; that arm's-length walk and Grant did not look back to see if Johnna was following, or glaring, did not look anywhere but ahead and then they were turning the corner, they were out the door and his chest contracted, the long exhalation: were you nervous? Were you afraid? Of her? Guards: off with his head! and he found he was grinning, relief absurd and he even laughed a little; and Robin quizzical, uncertain pause before the car.

"Did you ever," Grant leaning to unlock the door, "read *Alice in Wonderland*?"

Robin shook his head, a very small motion. "I don't have to wonder," he said, seat belt click like warm finality. "I already know."

An hour, only an hour; the closing screen door like a rung curtain and Grant amazed, it was incredible, it was like two different men: this Robin talked, looked, even answered a question; this Robin smiled and ordered his own coffee, a strong bitter brew, drank it black as motor oil until the cup was empty, then tipped it to show the grounds: "Tea leaves," he said, and then the sweetest word of all: "Remember?" Like a password between them, no even better, it was *connection*; it was the bridge begun. Remember: see your future in the tea leaves, in the coffee grounds ringed black and small as finest gravel in the bottomless cup; in the smiles, the tentative glances; in the long careless roll of the drawing, between them on the table in the restless overhead shine; do you see it? What do you see? And nodding at Grant's glasses, a finger pointing—reaching?—at the black tortoise gleam of the rims: "If I looked through your glasses, would I see?"

"See what?"

"What you see."

Dropping him off, the laze of the closing screen and no mistaking this time the wave, definite semaphore motion—good-bye, two beats, back and forth and Grant tapped the horn, small sounds, a small smile but inside the bursting, warm unto heat, the heat of growth; not of change but the moments before change, the step before the step over the threshold: and in the heat, the light: see: here is the time to come. As if he had made, himself unaided, some principal discovery, the location of gravity, a map of God's closed and moving eye.

And back home to Johnna, on the edge of the kitchen chair and so angry she could not speak; but she did speak eventually, called names, cried; threatened, but only obliquely: if anything happens I'll. What? but he did not ask, did not even defend himself, there was no need; like a shower of shadows her anger unsubstantial, even her tears slow and curiously cool, as if they came from a place untouched by heat, some secret gland not of her flesh but of her mind; all of it as inevitable as a protest expected, rendered as much from form as need. Finally past midnight they lay in bed, opposite sides, her back to him and she might have wept again, he did not know: tea leaves—remember? and when he woke it was to her sleeping face, inches from his, her breath warm and faintly sour through her parted lips.

So: Once a week, coffee. And talk, a little, a little more; about the weather, about television; there was, Robin told him, a big television at home; sometimes the color went green but on the whole it was nice. Chocolate espresso, Robin's scar and smile, once they shared an order of cinnamon buns and Grant dropped his on the floor, black tile floor so phenomenally dirty that the butter side came back gray.

"Better not eat that," Robin said. "I once saw a guy eat a cigarette, but that was on purpose."

Do you think it will rain? Are you hungry? What goes on, there, behind that scar, those pale eyes, what did you draw today? Some questions unasked, the virtue of patience, his hands wrapped warm around the mug as spring reached summer, week by week like building blocks, like building a road; the bridge. And each week, two, four, five, Robin's answers more frequent, longer; coffee to iced coffee to iced tea, the wind-chime sound of ice in the glasses; and always, between them on the table: the drawings. Rolled into tubes uneven, casual, the Rosetta stone used to prop open a door. "I take them home now," Robin's nod, "she says I can."

"Do you put them up? At home, I mean?" Visualizing his room, Aladdin's cave papered to the ceiling with secrets, with glyphs and memories and maps of pains too subtle to have categories, to have faces or names. What would it be like to sit in that room, to look at those drawings? Bed and dresser, nightstand maybe, maybe shoes under the bed: and on the wall the garden of earthly delights.

Stirring his tea, long silver spoon like a metal tongue, around and around without tasting; head bent down in, what? Embarrassment? Sadness? So long silent Grant's mouth open to change the subject when a voice as soft as air on the cheek: "No. I just, I put them away."

Unable to fathom—the *waste* of it: "I see what you mean." Stirring his own drink, iced coffee not iced but simply cold; stale. "I know I never want to look at my photographs when they're done."

"Why not?" in real surprise, spoon poised forgotten before his mouth. Across the room someone laughed, a woman, peculiar hard laugh like a smoker's cough. "If I—I would, I would put them up. Don't you like them?"

"No."

"Why not?"

"Because they're nothing," dry, mouth down;

the coffee bitter as medication on his lips. "Everything's static, and dull, it's not even boring because if you're boring at least there's something there to bore. And there's nothing there." Ripping another sugar packet, granular spill like miniature stones shaped and irregular, thinking of all the hours, days spent trying to get the shot, the light just right: on what? For what? Nothing. He might as well have been shooting empty rooms, no not even that because there was interest in an empty room, the possibility of mystery, there was *something*. Shooting big boxes, cardboard squares, his studio a prison and he tried to tell Robin this, simple words, small sentences purely bitter: his work, nonwork, call it instead what he did not do (and thinking too of what he must do, begin to do something but this was not nothing, no, not at all: this was nourishment, call it, or call it ease; refreshment, the pursuit of water in driest land): the five-minute précis of what he had accomplished stretched to ten, and twenty, how many words does it take to delineate the pursuit of heat and hunger, of light: and in the end, here, what? Nothing. Nothing at all, and worst of all knowing it was so.

A shiver in the corner of his mouth, muscle flutter, and he stopped talking, rubbed at his face; embarrassed, now, the recitation past, long dull litany worth no empathy, not even the brass coin of pity. And looking past his cloaking fingers to see Robin very pale, almost alarmingly pale, and the scar very dark as if suffused with blood from a different source, a spring, a well inside driven by an engine not his heart: "If you feel," even his voice affected, lower, slower, "if you think like that, then why do you do it? Why don't you take pictures of things you like, like animals, or people?"

"I can't," Grant said, and in those words the pain unvoiced, smothered by technique, subsumed: since he first picked up a camera, since he first submitted a photo: he still remembered, a little girl with a green balloon and he had sent it to a shopping weekly, he had not even wanted to be paid. "I'm not, I can't really do that kind of picture. I'm no good at it." Without direction, without someone standing over him saying Take a picture of this: without that he was worse than helpless, worse than inept; he was empty. So many ways to be that way, and it seemed he knew them all.

And Robin still pale, still looking, staring almost and the woman across the room laughed again, harsh mirth and Robin's voice, so small Grant could not hear, had to lean forward across the table, across the drawing itself an arrow pointing, directing: spirit guide and Robin said—again?—"It's not your fault." Lips like prayer. "It's not your fault," and would not speak again: in his chair, in the car, on the short way home: and did not wave, slipping past the screen door, and a woman, looking out as he went in: another client? or therapist? No telling, and he too disturbed to wonder; he had hurt Robin somehow, or frightened him, done something wrong; but he had not lied, and wouldn't that have been worse? Wouldn't it?

Dragging in silent to Johnna, cool at the kitchen table, working, lifting her head long enough to say, "Take a look at this," the color copy from her hand to his and like a jolt—*this is Robin's*—the long shadings, monolithic the blacks and grays and among them, nearly hidden but not, intrinsic visibility the figure of pink, like rose quartz, pebbled pink granite: a man. Waving both hands, spread hands, spread fingers, and smiling, smiling at the viewer in a bright and particular attitude that in some way made Grant want to cry; something very sad there, ineffably so; and sweet, sweet.

"It's Robin's," unnecessarily, her voice as flat as a fact. "Working in pencils. He did it tonight." She wrote something, three sentences, he watched her hand move and saw—did he?—his name.

"It's about you," she said. "You're the one he's —the figure's waving at."

Silence. Vertical gray and black like a storm in one place, one space: and that living figure, waving, smiling. It's about you. "How do you know that?" and it was hard somehow to talk, facing away from her and he tried to say it louder: "How do you—"

"He told me." Brisk, a doctor's edges, here are the facts, here is the diagnosis. My diagnosis. "It's the most hopeful piece I've ever seen him do. I'm inferring that this means his contact with you is in itself therapeutic, it's moved him to do something he hasn't done before. Even in the group home, he—" and pausing, another note, scribble scribble. "But now he's reaching out to a stranger—a very definite reaching out, it's really atypical for him, someone from outside the controlled environment." As if Robin were a lab rat; do you hear, he wondered, what you're saying? Do you ever stop and listen to yourself? "Which is why I haven't instigated any measures."

"What the fuck does that mean?" but not with heat, a step removed. Still looking at the drawing, the copy; the original had lain across the table, careless curl throughout their talk; in Robin's hand as he slipped inside the house. It's about you. It's not your fault.

"It means I haven't kept him from seeing you. I could, you know." Was that true? He didn't think so. Maybe in the earliest days, but not now. "But you seem to be serving a definite motivational purpose, your presence in his life is a—"

"I'm his friend," loud and he wanted it louder, wanted to yell in her face, the face of the woman who had looked out the screen door, fisheyes: I'm his friend, we're friends. —And Robin's pale face averted; are we? Are we still? "We're *friends*," more forcefully. "I'm not a therapy, Johnna, I'm not like—"

But she had stopped listening, or displaying the fact of her attention: hunched like a witch over her papers and his name there, sober black ink and her handwriting like symbols from some religion dead of its own weight, and he wanted to run out of the apartment, drive to Robin's house: peering through the screen door, are we friends? Robin. You put me in your picture, you know all the things I don't, heat where I'm cold, light where I'm dark; and empty; are we friends?

Please.

He went into the bedroom and sat on the edge of the bed. He sat there for almost an hour without moving or turning on the lights, rising only when she came in: to go out and sit in the kitchen, in the dark.

The week acrawl, and Grant in the gray hour driving to the clinic, raining, hours before sunset but already dark: and hot, unseasonable through the rain: T-shirt and he was wet, the heat; and the nervous sweat of unease. Will he see me? Will he want to talk with me? Haste had made him early; twenty minutes in the hallway like a man waiting a stay of execution; stop it, walking a little way away, back. Melodrama; just stop it. He'll see you. He'll *see* you, like grinding teeth, grinding wheels moving to convince himself, he will.

Johnna opening the door, the clients moving out, straggling slow motion, and is he there? Did he even come? but here he was, last of all, head down and Johnna's hand on his shoulder, black T-shirt and three calm fingers and for Grant a moment's jealousy hot as an oven, as the air outside: *don't touch him*. Standing there stupid as a suitor, as a supplicant and he could not think of what to say, if he should speak at all: and Johnna touching him as well, one look very brief and dry; and gone, retreating back inside like a clockwork figure into its aperture, and only Robin there.

Not moving. Not looking.

And his own voice still as the air around them, false air dry with automatic cold: "Robin? Do you want, do you feel like going out awhile?"

Nothing; Robin's head still turned but he did not move, did not start to walk away. And then the nod, a very small motion: and his hand out, something there: paper; a note? No: a drawing.

"Is this, should I look at this?" No answer. Grant's hand shaking, the paper in small flutter and he unfolded it, it was folded in quarters, he spread it with his fingers and saw a simple pencil sketch: a man within a darkness, sloping walls around him like a womb, a pod, a seashell grown abnormal and in the distance another figure, a man? with his hands out: waving; beckoning.

"Is this for me?"

Robin biting his lips, rubbing at one eye, rubbing and rubbing; nodding. Biting. And then something, small as a sigh: Grant leaning forward: "What? I didn't—"

"It's you," Robin said. "You and me."

Benediction: he had not before understood the word, but did now: a mantle, a covering over the way snow covers a landscape, the way tissue covers the wound that makes the scar. His hands were shaking so badly he could barely fold the drawing closed again.

"Well," and again, almost helplessly, "well. Do you, should we go now?"

Nod; the chewed lip red. Outside the air in contrast so thick it was like breathing water, his car's air conditioner was not working right and more heat, blowing in their faces and Robin again, something too low to hear and Grant's hand sweeping hard against the a/c switch, "What? I'm sorry, Robin, this fucking thing—I didn't hear," and Robin's voice, something: you like it? "Do you?"

Head turned, the car slowing: all his attention on that strained and pale face, that bitten mouth. Slow and careful, the utmost care, like suturing cell to cell, heart to heart and the car slowed almost to a stop in the middle of the street, rain down the windows, and: "*Yes*, I like it, I think it's brilliant. I think you're an artist and I think it's fucking *great*, that's what I think."

Robin's silence; nothing. The sore lip moving, tiniest curve; a smile? Rain down the windows, so hot in the car and they were there already, he was driving past the building and had to jerk on the brakes: horns behind them, someone flying past in a roostertail aggrieved and Robin's smile, no mistaking it, a big wide smile and Grant smiling too, pleasure drenching like water and the drawing in his pocket, close to his body, close to his heart.

JACOBB'S so refrigerator-cold they both ordered coffee, hot and sweet, clammy skin sticking to the plastic of the booth, to the table's sullen laminate and Robin leaning forward, hands around his cup: to speak; to talk. Cup to his lips and eyes clouded by the coffee's steam, pale eyes as if faded from too many tears: "I remember what you said," cup down, "about being empty. I used to think I was, you know, too full," and a smile, a bitterness that was in fact not bitterness but bewilderment, a kind of sad strange wonder that things turned out this way, as if waking to find dreams real and the real world one strange dream: why is that? why should it be this way? The little drawing open now on the table between them, Robin touching it again and again, one finger in reassurance and "I did it last time, when we talked; I went home and did it. But I didn't want—I wasn't sure if I should, you know, show it to you."

"Why? Why not?"

And shrugging, not believing, not *dis*believing but seemingly unsure what Grant, a professional photographer, a maker of images, would think of this work: "I'm not an artist," earnestly, as if there might be some crucial misunderstanding. "I'm not."

No: not an artist. A seer. Oh God a visionary; oh

God what visions and at once, "I'd like to see everything, Robin. All your drawings, everything you want to show me."

And red, a flush, a blush: "You want to? I got, there's a lot of them. You want to see them all?"

Cup down, "Yes, I want to see them. Let's go now," sliding sideways but Robin shaking his head, no, I have to get permission, I need permission to have a visitor. "But I'll ask," shyly, "I'll ask them tonight. For tomorrow. Okay?"

Smile shared across the table, and Grant in the moment wanting to do more, reach, touch, a handshake ludicrous but in the end it was what they settled on, Robin's hand damp and warm, the nails dirty as a child's; his grasp firm and Grant said, "Tomorrow night?" and Robin nodded, yes. Yes.

Driving him home, driving home himself and it was a rare feeling, this anticipation, as if breathing more than air, some sweeter gas with properties exquisite, more than respiration; more than life. It was not until much later, lying warm on the cusp of sleep, that Grant realized who was who in the drawing; the little figure entombed, trapped, and the waving one, come on, this way. I'll help you.

Tomorrow night.

The house smelled like Lysol and cigarette smoke, somebody in the kitchen with a mop—big ass in blue stretch pants, he could see it from the screen —and the peculiar odor of many bodies; how many people lived here anyway? A woman answered the door, his third determined knock over the TV's howl; he had called ahead, confirming, he had tried to do everything right. He had even told Johnna: strangely shy in the telling, is there anything I should do? or not do?

"Yeah," dryly, "don't go," but in her own way she was helpful, or seemed to try to be: don't stare, don't bother any of the other residents. If the aides want you to go, go. If it seems like Robin is being affected adversely (and her stare, that one particular stone-splitting stare), if he's getting overstimulated, go. More dryly still, "You can always try again," but he chose not to think that, chose to hold instead to this feeling of anticipation, Robin and the drawings, I want to see everything. Everything.

"Yes?" and now a woman at the door, tired eyes, no smile. Sloping shoulders under baggy pink sweatshirt. "Can I help you?"

"I'm here to see Robin," smiling, he felt like a bill collector. "My name's Grant Cotto, I called?"

"Yeah," opening the door but slowly, he had to squeeze to get through. "You can stay for an hour."

The TV loud, greenish soap opera faces: a man in a Budweiser T-shirt came in from the kitchen, sat clicking through the channels. Soap, commercial, news, cartoon, cartoon, tits. He stopped at the tits. Grant found himself staring, guessing: resident? or aide? The man began to scratch himself inside his sweatpants. The woman in the pink sweatshirt called, "Robin," then in decisive motion changed the channel back to a soap.

"I was watching that," the Budweiser man protested. Even from his spot by the door, Grant saw that the man had a hard-on.

"You can watch it later. —'S on twenty-four hours a day," the aside seemingly to Grant who nodded, feeling awkward, feeling sad for the Budweiser man who apparently only wanted to jerk off in peace and then both man and sadness forgotten as Robin, white T-shirt, clean white pants, and smiling, smiling: "Hey," from the edge of the hallway, "hey, Grant. Come on in here."

Laughter from the kitchen, the big blue ass in motion and Grant behind Robin down the hall, dirty harvest-gold carpet, smoke smell everywhere, bedroom doors painted in chipped primaries: some kind of coding system probably, a way to remember: the blue door is yours. The red door is yours. The door that looks like someone painted over black with yellow: Robin, that's yours.

And inside nothing he imagined, twin bed, no nightstand, no furniture other than a two-drawer dresser made out of heavy cardboard; and the walls pale brown and absolutely bare except for a page cut out of a magazine and taped careful above the light switch: visible from the bed: an older man with no smile standing before a canvas filled with the absolute veracity of a human scream.

"That's Francis Bacon," Robin said. "He's dead."

There was no place to sit so they sat on the bed, facing each other, it felt adolescent, like visiting your buddy in his room: TV noise, the sounds of others in the hall passing and repassing, back and forth and Robin off the bed, even shyer somehow but very much excited, was this too excited? Too stimulated, Johnna? "Here," and drawing out from under the bed a cardboard container, giant's shoe box printed with little red worn-out flowers. "Here they are."

And everything else forgotten, the cover back like Scheherazade: the drawings. The box was almost full. Reaching, even Robin himself almost forgotten in that moment, and Grant lifting a layer, an inch's worth of work, looking down at the first one on his lap like a map to the light: an angel.

In waxy gold and silver, long strokes and it might even have been crayon but the lines, oh the lines of the wings and the robe, a classical angel, its head turned away and oh God that averted head, that neck, the *curve* of it, sorrow immeasurable, sorrow and the feeling not of abandonment but finality: as if everything was done that could be done, as if the pain resulting could now no longer seek alleviation or avoidance; only compassion.

Cigarette stink, and dust; tears in his eyes.

"I did that one a while ago." As if from another room. "For Alison."

"Who's—" but first stop, clear his throat; aching throat. "Who's Alison?"

"My sister."

He could not stop looking at it; he could not put it down but Robin, as if guessing what was needed, gently took it from him, showed another, the next on the pile: this of a man, deliberate stick figure in blue and black before a house, dwelling immense and blackly crooked, the distortion again in a deeper place so subtle it hurt the eye to see, it was off, *wrong*; the definition of wrongness and incredibly Robin laughed, a little laugh, a chuckle: *"That's* from Clearwater," and onto the next one: a Kali-woman with tunnels for eyes, bleeding breasts, a smile as empty as a church burned spiteful to the dirt. And the next; the next, Grant staring, sitting like a human stand for this work, this art incredible and he had seen eight, nine, twelve of the drawings, there might be a hundred more in the box and Robin was looking away from him, down at his hands, dirty nails and saying, "So are they shitty, or what?" and Grant staring at him almost wildly, are you crazy but he didn't say it, of course he must not say it but breathless, shaking his head, shaking his head: "Of *course* they're not sh—" and a knock at the door, two knocks and open and it was the woman, hand on the knob and firm: "It's time for your guest to go."

Irrational but he wanted to yell, a child's defrauded cry: I just got here! but it was seven thirty, he had been here an hour and ten minutes, ten

minutes' grace and Robin was already bundling up
the drawings, almost careless back into the box and
Grant possessed of a wild desire to say Come with
me; let's take them and go. Go where? Back home?
to his apartment, to Johnna, it was worse than absurd but this was intolerable, the woman standing
there like a jailer and Robin meekly sliding the box
back beneath the bed; and rising, standing before
Grant, would they have to say good-bye in front of
her too? Yes?

Yes. "Robin," shaking his hand, again the gesture foolish but in some way right: "thank you. I
can't tell you how good it was to see, to see your
stuff," and Robin's smile, pale gaze away but that
smile, wide, wide and "Dinnertime," pointedly
from the woman, past the TV and the smoke—
incredible, how could anyone breathe, let alone
eat?—and out the door. Robin waving once,
framed in mesh and gone; and he driving as if blind
internally, finding himself home without knowledge
of travel, hands on the wheel and exhausted,
strange to be so tired. So tired. His clothes smelled
like smoke; and behind his eyes in preservation
voracious the images: Kali and the stick-man, birds,
wings, buildings; the angel, that turned head, bent
neck; I did it for Alison. A sister, Robin's sister,
Robin's family; his life in the hospital, the group
home, so much of him Grant did not know; and
feeling again but without the wildness, feeling as

cold as the landscape under a lake frozen locked: Let's go. Take the drawings and go.

Go where?

At the table: again. Robin and Grant, two sides but nothing like opposite; smiles for each other, sliding in, settling down but something, sharp as a smell a kind of new feeling, something different between them; what? Grant again: how glad he was, seeing the drawings, he would like to see them all and still speaking, Robin still listening: and all at once this new Thursday's drawing scrolling open, now, open before his eyes. Robin's arm spreading with sure fingers the paper, anchoring as sure with napkin holder, cracked sugar bowl holding packets pink and blue; and in that movement for Grant the stroke of confirmation, things *had* moved somewhere else, somewhere different, higher: breakthrough again, as if beyond the skin that though warm is still a barrier, still both symbol and actuality, separation; but peel the skin back, gently, oh go gently: and tell me what you see.

And he did, Robin: in a voice very soft, and regular, the drawing between them a map to the country of the tale: more glyphs, long like half-closed eyes, spread like a smear of blood, of plasma viscous and serene, circling like a cyclone the central figure, small and sexless, hands open and head down: encased in lines.

Not so much story as endless episode, a moment stretching for years, for most of a life: twenty-eight years, cycle like a locust's of emergence, slow transforming, and pain, and pain, and pain. For parents, sister, the way a scream in one cavern echoes like a groan through the next: for self most of all, the pain of becoming, of *turning*: into someone different, not the son and brother, student, friend, not the one they wanted, not the one they thought they had.

"They hated it," drinking cold black coffee, his third cup and Grant before him, only eyes in motion, forgetting to drink at all. "All the relatives, calling her up, is he any better? What's wrong with him now? My mother . . ." Silence. "And the doctors—doctors, I don't know. Half the time they treat you to find out what all you have." The figure touching—stroking?—the lines, poles, or iron legs; or bars. Black and blue, and the paper itself a dusty cream, dry, like caucasian flesh left to lie forever in a light not yet hot enough to burn. "It's not like people think it is." Biting at his lip, now, lower underlip still pink with just-healed marks, bite marks, as if in the night something dark came creeping to gnaw in silence the very breath from his mouth. "People think it's one thing, you know, just one thing. And it's not. Schizophrenia, that's its name, but cancer's a name too, you know? It's not like—"

"You all set here?"

The waitress, they had not heard her coming

and now Robin all eyes, startled and then down, staring at his hands while color spread, like light in the sky, blood in water and Grant's own face taut: it's not her fault: she doesn't know, or care either. "Two more coffees," as even as possible but now Robin in motion, pushing sugar and napkins away to roll again the drawing into a silent tube, showing nothing; rubberband crawl to hold it, so, and Grant wanted to punch the waitress, ridiculous to want to but he did, stupid bitch, stupid *bitch*. Staring at them still, not even interested and Grant sliding out of the booth: "Hey," gentle, hand on Robin's arm. "Let's just go somewhere else, all right? Is that all right?"

Shaking head, no. "I want to go home," and silence all the way to the car, to the house, Grant's surreptitious gaze as if the keys to the door snatched ignorant from his hand, that fucking waitress, that dumb shit—but then in the driveway Robin's sigh: and smile, small and tentative, like health after fever.

"Sorry," past the smile already gone. "I just, I don't want people to know, you know? They can see there's something wrong with me, but they don't have to *know*."

And that preamble to again the life related, in motion: in that voice, calm, and even: more steps in the apprenticeship of pain. Head to one side as if by memory's weight, his parents frightened by his illness, a sister, Alison, bitter and now estranged—

"I called her last Christmas. She wouldn't even, she didn't come to the phone"—and mad at everything: him, his parents, the doctors, the hospitals, the caseworkers and caregivers and aides. "She was the one," squinting at the house, the slant of the gutters, "she took me to the appointments, she drove me when I couldn't drive myself. The drugs, they— I was on Mellaril, you know? You know what that is?"

Clearing his throat. "It's a neuroleptic. Right?" knowing it was, wishing he had a less clinical name, it was the only name he knew.

But "Right," obviously pleased, "that's right. I don't—it doesn't work right for me, they don't always know, they give you stuff. . . . Anyway when I was taking it, I was—not tired, tired isn't the word for it. It was as if the floor wasn't *flat* enough, you know? Like I couldn't lay down *enough*." Shaking his head as if exhausted by sheer memory; light gone from the sky, his profile now in darkness. "See, trying to treat this illness, disease, whatever, it's not like a tumor, or something you can take a pill for. It's like—like cutting out half a river, you know? Like trying to take one part of your mind out of another part. It doesn't *work*," all simplicity, the edges of anguish worn smooth but never dull. Blessed are the pure in heart; blessed are the unconscious, for they shall not remember. All the days in the hospitals, waiting rooms of clinics with Alison beside but not with him, looking at maga-

zines while the words bled one into another into
the pictures into the clammy palms of his hands;
trembling hands, and Alison pale with embarrassment, pinching his sleeve: *They're calling you,
Robin! Go on!* Made more confused by examinations that to him made no sense; by the inevitable
hospital stays, he remembered the first one: "I was
seventeen, I was just out of high school," and suddenly smiling, looking down in the dark at his
hands, and smiling. "You ever been in a hospital,
like that? —I mean to *visit*," hurriedly, and Grant's
headshake, no. No I haven't. "It's not what people
think, it's not like the movies, people running
around and screaming. Mostly they just sit and
smoke. In the dayroom. Sometimes the drugs make
you make weird faces," and Grant nodding, tardive
dyskinesia, he knew what that was from his reading:
tics and facial movements, protruding tongues and
Noh grimaces: how must it have appeared to
Robin, seventeen years old and fragile as shivered
glass, the blind obedient submitting to the act and
practice of a medicine blinder than he? and in
Grant a sudden wellspring of anger, and sorrow: *he*
would have helped Robin, *he* would not have run
away. Like the family, the sister: he could see her
now, in his mind, mouth down in a low disapproving arc, shame's frown like a—

But Robin was still talking, the porch light
clicking on in bright yolk-yellow and he was still
talking: as if all the silence within rose now to trans-

formation, sour engine of sickness and pain become fuel for the process of speech: to Grant, an outsider, one who knew just enough to listen; and say nothing.

"I sat in a corner, I was afraid to move. They gave me Stelazine," and again that smile, and Grant reminded of the way people smile on the news, shake their heads and shrug when their homes are destroyed by an earthquake, a fire, a disaster: people can smile at the most hideous things. "My mouth was so *dry*," and tongue—unconscious?—over lips, as if to erase the memory of that dryness. "They don't always tell you, they figure the medicine will make you better, it's worth it. Like the walkies, you know?"

Walkies. What—

"Some people call it the Stelazine stroll. Akathisia. A side effect," and again that slow disaster smile. "You can't sit still, you can't sit in a chair. I used to go up and down the dayroom, up and down," shaking his head and all at once, loud: "Robin," in the driver's side window, sharp voice and Grant starting hugely, banging his elbow hard against the steering wheel.

"Robin," more quietly, it was the tired-faced woman, pale blue muumuu dress and peering in like somebody's mother, break it up. "It's time to come in now." And to Grant, coldly, "He's late." As if Robin were a child, an incompetent and Robin's protest, bewildered as he stepped from the car:

"We were just out here. In the driveway," and the woman around the car to put her hand on his shoulder, gentle, Grant surprised by how gentle it was.

"I know," she said. "It's okay, I know you were out here." Turning with him to the porch, guiding him inside and the light out: click! and all darkness, his heart's indignant rhythm slowing in the drive to the dry throb of resentment, that face in the window, that look: and home, down the hall and into dark and a circle of light, Johnna in the living room, reading: looking up and the look itself entirely the same, as if he had not moved in space at all.

And escalation: that face now everywhere, in the kitchen, at the table, in the hallway outside her room: in bed, they had not made love in weeks, if he touched her even by true accident she pulled away, less or more perceptibly as the touch seemed to warrant; punishment, but if given a choice between seeing Robin and fucking Johnna, there was no choice. Staring at him, glaring at him, accusing him of manipulating a sick man's need for acceptance and warmth into a key to his own sour fulfillment, of using Robin as a diversion, a tool, an experimental device and by that subtle encouragement making Robin sicker, more unsure, more deluded than he was. Eyes narrowed over coffee, "Tell me it's not just greed, Grant. Just tell me that."

"How am I hurting him?"

Ice-cold, "It's not *healthy*," and how the fuck do *you* know? In his head Robin's voice, downcast and dry, *They treat you to find out what you have*: who's really the guilty one, Johnna, mea fucking culpa: if the shoe fits put it on. You don't know, silent in his mind, you think you do but you don't. That mouth-twist, the cast of that stare: why had he ever thought she was pretty, why had he ever let her move in?

Silence. Pouring more coffee, for himself and then her voice again, nasal, louder: "Tell me—show me a rationale that has more to it than just selfishness, plain and simple. Can you do that? Can you? I don't—"

"You're jealous," quietly, the hand around the coffee clenched and thinking all at once of coffee shared with Robin, what a difference, what a vast and—

"Jealous of what? Of manipulation? Of selfishness?" Louder still: "If you could see yourself, what you're doing! If you—"

"I don't want to talk about this with you, Johnna, it's got nothing to do with you." Rising up, away from the table, his back to her and she kept talking, louder and louder, hot in the room and her voice made it hotter. He started to wash the dishes, cool water sliding over grease, greasy plates, last night's carryout Mexican and she had bitched about that, too, he wasn't cooking dinner anymore, he wasn't pulling his weight, wasn't paying his way.

Right. What wasn't she angry about? and thinking to himself, past the anger, was there any basis at all for what she said? Be honest, was there?

On some level, perhaps, viewed through her eyes it might be monstrous: to her way of seeing he *was* using Robin, maybe making him sicker, or at least more prone to the delusions most germane to his illness (although to Grant he did not seem very ill at all, certainly less so than some people with their constant accusations and paranoia); and yet he, Grant, even if admitting to the idea of harm, would not admit even the possibility of drawing back, drawing away: so what rationale is there, can there be but greed? Greed, the faceless master in the mirrored mask, mace in one hand and the other steady on the crank that drives the wheel that speeds the engine, red-hot engine and bloodred coals: and yet never in his life had Grant's life meant more to him. He would rather—he *would* dry up without Robin, wither back into facelessness, into the restless gray arena he had struggled so long to escape.

But was Robin receiving nothing from this, was it really all one way? Or was Grant for him someone to listen, someone who was not an aide, a therapist, a doctor, who was not being paid, or made, to be there: someone who thought of him as more than a combination of symptoms to treat, or a charge to baby-sit, someone interested in him as an artist? Someone who cared; about him.

Let Robin speak for himself, with his ease in Grant's presence, his smiles when they met: even Johnna had admitted it was atypical, this reaching out; there must be a reason: reason it out for yourself. Witness the pleasure Robin found in showing Grant the drawings, all the drawings, to the bottom of the box and back: and witness Grant's pleasure reciprocal, his affirmation of Robin's talent, Robin's *genius*, that exquisite hand and eye in tandem angelic: had anyone else, ever, told Robin how very very gifted he was? Forget the illness: had anyone ever?

So, then: was it greed? Or only need, and care. Great care: on both sides? Yes; firmly. Yes. Robin cared for him, they were *friends*; and turning to say this, with calm and dignity to Johnna and she did not respond, no more talk: maybe there would never be any more talk; so be it.

And that night no dinner at all, Johnna home very late and not troubling to be quiet: door shut, briefcase dropped, water running and he in the shallow consciousness of interrupted sleep feeling, as he moved in the bed, the cold sheet of her side unoccupied, demarcation line unerased by the motion of her body at last sliding, cold and colder, into the darkness of the bed.

Hot, and Thursday's session canceled—Johnna gone that morning to a two-day conference, *Art Therapies in Focus*: think of it, rooms deadly with

the smell of jargon, art's seeds laid naked to dissection by the sword of boredom—it was ninety
degrees and not even noon. Air conditioner stutter-
ing, back seat cooler and he had called two days
ago, more than proper notice to take Robin to the
beach. The woman in charge—Maryann, sour
mouth and long pauses, as if decoding in his words
the real meaning beneath—had agreed, so grudg-
ingly that Grant had had trouble holding on to his
temper: and squeezed out times to leave and come
back, definite hours: what is this, a jail? and trying,
heroically, for mildness: "It's not like he's in a hospital, you know," and her reply curt, oh she *knew*,
all right.

Knew what? but that would just drag it out and
anyway what did it matter, none of it mattered beyond the hardening of his resolve: to take Robin
away from them all. How were they helping him,
anyway? Even Johnna, the most biased observer of
all, admitted that Grant's friendship was for Robin
definitely therapeutic; it must certainly be more so
than the atmosphere of the group home, where,
though the caring was obvious—he too could be
impartial, could admit goodness when he saw it—
the living conditions were not. Six other adults, all
with their own deeps and levels of disorders, a ro-
tating staff of aides paid, he suspected, nowhere
near as well as they should have been: Robin
needed instead of all this, a friend. And now he had
one.

Eleven thirty, right on time: pulling into the driveway, and Roger, the Budweiser man in his Budweiser T-shirt, sitting by the lawn mower. Frowning, Bermuda shorts torn high up one hairy leg, not looking at Grant: "Hey."

"Hey, Roger," taking off his sunglasses, uncomfortable squat to Roger's level. "What's up?"

"Do you know how to work this thing?" Hands tense before him, his frown very deep, the way a child looks before tears.

Sorry, the only machine I can work is a camera but Grant didn't say it, said nothing, only bent over the lawn mower, turned the cap to sniff for gas: "It's got gas," lamely.

And Maryann, blue muumuu bending over, he had not even heard the screen door: "What's the problem here?" as if he must surely be responsible.

Roger: "He's helping me."

"*I'll* help you," and Grant again suppressing the first words, fuck you too but here was Robin, shorts and a long-sleeved shirt, olive-green fishing hat spotted with grease. Plastic grocery sack in one hand, bright blue folder in the other: smiling. Red sunglasses low on his nose, richly sunburned nose: "Hi," getting into the car, buckling up. Smiling at them all.

"Eight o'clock," Maryann said, the starter cord for the lawn mower tight in her hand, like she was strangling a snake. "Remember."

"We will," Robin said.

"Remember about the sun," and something else but Grant had started the car, was backing out and away: shut up. All the windows open, Robin sweating in his long-sleeved shirt but it was necessary to combat the drug-borne tendency to photosensitivity; "I brought you some sunscreen," showing the bottle, and wanting in a spiteful way to show it to Maryann, to the specter of Johnna: See: I know about that too. I care about him as much as you do, and more.

Eyes closed behind the sunglasses, one arm out the window: serene: "Maryann doesn't like you."

"I know."

"She's scared you'll take me away."

Silence; the vacuum-sound of air through the windows. Grant's heart had begun to beat harder, a brisk peculiar rhythm; Robin's head moving lightly to the bumps and skirted chuckholes, the pattern of the road.

The beach was crowded, even on a weekday; together they carried the cooler, the blanket, bag and folder atop it. Robin's gait slightly uneven, as if he crossed different ground, Grant adjusting his own steps accordingly. There was a spot on the grass beyond the sand, a shady spot unchosen: on the blanket's ragged salmon-pink square, Robin stretching out, slow, smiling a little, glasses crooked on his nose: "I brought this," the folder in hand, to Grant's hand, "for you."

"What is it?" already sliding out as if eager for

the light, drawings: three drawings, new ones. In pencil, and more than exquisite: their very simplicity so tender and vast that the first look at each continued, one must study subtlety like this.

Each was of a man, a figure shaded hazy about limbs and torso, only the face in bold relief. The first showed him sleeping, an ease to his posture belied by the heavy clouds above him, clouds swollen as an abscess, sullen with their burden about to fall. His sleep was as a child's, total, lush, abandoned: what dreams he had did not show on his face.

The second showed the clouds massed more thickly, closer to him now, and he still sleeping but now on his back, one arm out, one knee bent up as if in sleep he sought to rise: and see how in pencil strokes thin as thread the face at ease, unconcerned by the element above, the clouds so close that the faintest wind might brush them like damp wool across his body.

The third showed the man awake, hands open, gaze at the clouds now about him to his waist and see within them not a face but what a face might seem to be to a baby in the womb, something known in the blood and tissue but unglimpsed as yet by the mind: a metaface, not wisdom but the seeds of what is wise, not kindness but the strength that causes it: and the man both embracing and embraced by this cloud, the open hands turned toward the viewer, the open eyes both self-aware and sad, as if strength, and wisdom, and kindness in the end were not enough.

And Grant gazing at these drawings, the beach, air, heat forgotten around him as if he sat in a box enclosed, sat under the face in the cloud and looking up, almost wildly as if jerked back into the day: by Robin's voice, saying, "I did these last night, for today. Because it's Thursday."

Thursday: oh. Session day, Johnna's day and the faint sour feel of disappointment, stupid to feel that way but he did; as if Johnna did not deserve to see these drawings, this man, this cloud; deserved only what she was getting, *Art Therapies in Focus*, her own focus too narrow to ever encompass anything like this.

"So then are you," clearing his throat, "are you bringing these next week?" Robin's stare, obviously confused and then understanding: "Oh, you mean to the session. No," firmly, "no, I'm not. These ones are private."

And Grant's smile, no stopping it even if he had wanted to and he did not want to, he agreed a hundred, a thousand percent: these ones *are* private, should be private. "I know what you mean," smiling, smiling. "I know exactly what you mean."

The drawings then carefully replaced in the folder, itself anchored gently with one edge of the cooler, the wind was picking up. They ate the lunch Grant had packed, chips and deli sandwiches, drank iced tea; it got hotter; Robin took off his shirt, took the sunscreen Grant handed him to do his arms and chest, part of his shoulders but could not reach his back: and half turning his head, offering with one hand the bottle. And in that offering a lifetime of care, of being always under the charge of others so the most basic need need not even be asked, articulated beyond the outstretched hand: you know what I want.

And Grant, feeling strange, embarrassed—had he ever touched another man? beyond the school-yard wrestling of childhood, of teenagers hitting and shoving in play?—took the plastic bottle from Robin and rubbed a palmful on his back, skin sticky with sweat, freckled over the shoulders; he was very pale.

"Eddie used to do that," looking over his shoulder, trying to see Grant. "Then I would do it to him."

Wiping the residue on his own arms; it smelled faintly like makeup, a manufactured cosmetic sweetness. "Who's Eddie?"

"He was, I guess he was my boyfriend."

"I didn't—" Scratching his leg, unnecessary motion. "I didn't know."

"It was a long time ago," squinting out at the sand, fat women, young women, teenagers and yelling kids; water rolling in, slow lake waves. "I met, I knew him in high school, he was a year ahead of me. My last year in high school, my—I was—" and silence, head down, hands working at the blanket, working, *squeezing*, skin over dormant flesh. "Anyway he was my boyfriend. I didn't, I never had any girlfriends. I don't really understand about girls."

"Me neither," Grant said, and meant it.

"Really?" with pleasure; and surprise. "Eddie said it was because I was naturally gay. I never thought of myself as gay. Sometimes I didn't think," that little smile, "at all. I was having a lot of trouble with the drugs, and my family, Alison said—" Hands at the blanket again. "And I met Eddie at the movies, I knew him already. And he took me back to his house." Was there wistfulness, there? nostalgia? *He was my boyfriend;* to belong, to somebody. *I don't really understand about girls;* why should you? Who was there to help you understand, about anything? Teenage Robin, no friends, no family to listen, nothing but the heavy stare of the god of illness; drugs tried one by one, in and out of the hospital and the brute need for contact, so strong as to finally overcome the fear of pain; and from then, what? Life? What life: an existence moved through like an alley, like a shadow, like a dream half-hideous and half-gone, ridden so hard for so long by this sickness incurable that to live at all he must develop his own mechanism for coping, or not-coping; and from, or despite it that core, socket of a terrible sweetness, an area unapproachable as Eden's cherubim but the one place Grant knew instinctively he must find; and learn; and be. See it there in that folder innocuous; see it in the way Robin's head tilts, the way his gaze moves across sand and water, the bodies moving through the elements: what are you thinking, now? Right now, what are you thinking?

"Where," carefully, "where's Eddie now?"

"I used to think sometimes that I imagined about the hospital," hands at rest in his lap. "Like if I made it up it wouldn't be so real. Like when you have hallucinations, sometimes." Adjusting his sunglasses, hands cautious as if handling live wires; and the bent stems relapsing into angles as soon as he released them. "I used to dream I was lying in this long yellow grass, like on the veldt, do you know what that is?"

"Like in Africa? where the lions—"

"*Yes!*" The glasses off his face, fallen in that bright jittery bound: as if his temperature had doubled, his alpha rhythms gone to spike: "The lions, I saw this show, lying in that yellow grass and sometimes I thought *I* was an animal, you know, but I was cut off from my pack, my lion pack," the unbearable loneliness of an animal separated from its heart, its reason for being. "Eddie said I was ugly. That's why he left."

Asshole; the warm feel of anger. "Robin, you're not ugly."

Shrug, head down, the green fishing hat tilted so far forward it was ready to fall, his silence like a new-built wall, a jail, an enclosure that Grant knew without understanding he must not try to breach;

and so sat, saying nothing more, simply sat and watched the water, summer full-blown around them and after long moments Robin began to speak again.

Not of himself, they were done with that subject today; but of friends: "not really *friends*," almost apologetically, "but like Roger. You know."

"I know," Grant said.

You know it's not all bad, Robin's voice softer now, it's not a bad place to stay. Roger had been, like him, resident for over a year; the aides were nice, most of them, the food was okay. There were trips—to the zoo, sometimes a movie or out on a nature walk, once they had gone to a petting farm; everyone had liked that—and anyway it was better than the hospital, where all you do is sit and smoke, or watch TV if you can; activities there, too, but not always, sometimes there are activities and you don't even know it, sometimes you even do them but you don't remember. Friends in the hospital, too, Roger-friends: like Michael, who used to play guitar in a band, a real band, but he had to stop playing because of his voices, they made him lose the beat. "He used to go around with a Walkman," smiling at the memory, a real smile and Grant watching, watching, "and every time they'd get too loud, he'd say, 'I'm turning it up! I'm turning it up!'"

—What happened to him? No—

"There was this girl, Antonia, she thought that,

that all the clowns were angels, that every clown she saw was somebody's guardian angel. It was," sweet, "horrible, it was really horrible because every time she saw a clown, even a *picture* of a clown, she would say 'Is it yours? Is it yours? Is it yours?' " Louder, "Is it yours? *is it yours?*" and heads turning, looking at them, staring at them and Grant fighting the urge to say Robin, please, Robin be quiet, conscious in a new way of Robin's crooked sunglasses, his fishing hat and mismatched clothes, shirt resumed despite the heat; and in a distant way hating himself for this consciousness, for feeling this way and not stopping at once.

"Is it yours?" and then in his own voice, normal voice, "They finally got her on Haldol, but she didn't like it. She said they made her feel like she was drowning, like she was drowning in her*self.* She said she'd rather have the clowns. But every time she left the hospital, she didn't take her medicine, and she had to come back. And then the clowns all turned into devils and she spent most of her time, she spent most of—she went—" Hands on the blanket, *hard* and suddenly rising, up above Grant as if he had grown like a giant, like a troll in a fairy tale: "I want to swim."

"Can you? I mean can you swim? I'm not a very—" but already gone, running lightly toward the water, long unbuttoned sleeves flapping lightly and the fishing hat fell off, fell to the ground by a woman in a high-cut red bikini who stared at it as if

it might spread its obvious infection through the
sand to touch her where she lay. And Grant, chug-
ging after, bent without slowing to snatch it up,
hold it and her gaze in half a stride and then he was
in the water, splashing to his thighs and Robin's
head rising up, merman, human fish inscrutable
and down again, of course he can swim, why
shouldn't he be able to swim?

Arms and legs and tireless; Grant gave up after
twenty strenuous minutes, sat on the edge of the
water, the pebbled sand. Kids ran past, sat to dig,
serious hands in the muck and their mothers behind, on the sand, spread blankets and sweaty
breasts. People left. Robin came out of the water,
head back and serene, dripping hair dark and the
sleeves of the shirt stuck to his arms like some cool
reptilian skin ready, in the moving moment, to shed
itself by itself. There was only one towel. Robin fell
asleep on the blanket, stretched out long and
Grant, watching him, thought he seemed not young
but ageless, as if time's effects must be blunted by
the pressure of his disease; eyes closed, chest moving, *Eddie said I was ugly. That's why he left.*
Drawings in hand, eyes half-focused and: I'd like to
meet this Eddie, I'd really like to talk to him. As
one friend of Robin's to another.

Robin slept until it was time to leave, Grant
determined to be punctual: hard to rouse for a wor-
risome moment, then again in the car as if drugged
by water and fresh air, slept all the way home but

woke as they turned in the driveway, roused by
some internal alarm.

Hat in hand, shirt smelly and wrinkled: starting
to say something and here came Maryann, frowning, surely it must be past her shift, don't you ever
go home? Don't you? but smiling at her, forcing
himself to smile pleasantly, leaning past Robin to
unlock his door.

"Right on time," he said.

Maryann said nothing, helped Robin from the
car, his yawn huge and delighted, waving at Grant
who waved back as extravagantly, then backed out
and away, to return to the blessed quiet, no Johnna,
nothing to do but shower and sleep, naked and serene on the cool unspoiled sheets of the empty
bed.

He could, perhaps, have seen it coming, more than
likely did without acknowledging the knowledge:
but Johnna enraged, tears continuous as lava down
her face: Robin would no longer draw in therapy.

"He won't draw for me," hands flat on the table
as if she would launch herself, burning, at Grant
who stood silent, back to the sink. "He says he
doesn't *need* to anymore, he says he has *you*." Wiping her face, bloodshot eyes, swollen nose, hair
snarled with constant pulling, tugging, at the lifeline braids. "Grant, if you care about Robin at all, if
you care about his treatment, you'll show me what
he's—"

"I can't," simply. "Johnna, think about it."

And it was true; ironic too but he would not be sharing the irony with her just now, no doubt she would appreciate it on her own later. In a reversal both honest and cruel—he was honest about that, too—he would not show the new drawings to her, the bright crayoned amazements, the subtle depths and pains of pencil and pen: because it wouldn't be fair. To Robin. "He trusts me," he said to her now, leaning perhaps a little forward and unprepared for her sudden shout, that bloodless face and those red eyes up close to him now, staring at him now: "He *trusts* you! He *trusts* you! *Nobody* trusts you, Grant, nobody thinks you care about Robin at all! Not me, not the people at the group home, not his doctor, nobody! We all—"

I don't care what you think, but he didn't say that, turned out of the room and away from those staring eyes but she followed him, pursued him down the hall to the bathroom, the only room with a lock and he tried to close the door but she was there, her face in the crack, staring and saying How can you live with yourself how can you *live* with what you're doing and on and on, deliberately impeding the treatment, sabotage, she used some ugly words. Face in the crack like a witch, it seemed her eyes did not blink at all, red eyes and that red red room, it was as if he could not breathe and the thought came to him unbidden past the dawning locus of breathlessness, panic's handmaiden: *This is how a hallucination feels.*

Calmed suddenly by the idea, he opened the door, opened it wide and Johnna pressing in but he would not run from her, would not evade her anymore: "Listen," he said, and when she would not listen he took her hands, not hard, almost tenderly, and said it again, and again, and again until she finally stopped, jerked back her hands to stand tearful and glowering before him; "Listen," gently, once more.

"Do you know," looking straight at her, messy hair, leaking eyes, her pale shrink's blouse wrinkled at collar and waist, "how many ways there are to treat schizophrenia? —No," as she moved, "just wait a minute. Do you know how they used to treat it? By prayers. By bleeding. By restraints, and acupuncture, and vitamins, insulin shock, dialysis, ECT—*wait* a minute, I said—psychotherapy, psychosurgery which means lobotomy, like in the old days when they used to try to cut out the 'fool's stone,' cut a hole in your forehead with a saw, did you know about that? Did you ever read about that? And you know something else? *None of it works.* None of it. So don't come to me and talk about art therapy, he doesn't *need* art therapy, he doesn't need you. All he needs is someone to talk to, a friend." And the drugs; honest about that too, but he wouldn't say it now.

Red eyes staring at him still, and then in a voice

incongruous, almost chatty from that Medusa face: "Do you know why I stay here, with you? To watch you. That's why. That's why I stay." And then past him into the bathroom, the door shut firmly and quietly, the clicking of the lock like the turning key in a heart closed now and forever against him. He stood for a moment, listening to the sound of the water running, an endless sound, water down the drain as he turned, slowly, and as slowly walked away.

Robin's doctor's name was Kaiser; his message was curt, but when Grant returned the call he was all graciousness, the phony candor of profession speaking to lay; as if Grant were a small grunting mammal mired over his hooves in ignorance, ignorant even of his need for rescue by those more well trained and well educated than he.

"I'm glad you called," Dr. Kaiser said. "Johnna's got some concerns about Robin Tobias that I think we need to discuss, in fact she was very—"

Calm, conversational: "Do you see Robin often?"

"What I think we need to focus on here is more—"

"Do you know how he likes his coffee? Do you know who his favorite artist is? Do you know what color his door is, at home?"

"What I want to do here, Mr. Cotto, Grant, is to—"

"Do you know what color his door is?"

Silence. Then: with cold dignity: "Blue."

"No," and surprised in a distant way by the sound of his own voice, a viciousness there he had not expected but was not wholly displeased to see, "that's *Roger's* door." Phone gently down, click into the cradle; not smiling, but able to, able too to laugh a little later, smile and shake his head over his shaking hands; how *angry* he had been, like Johnna's anger, maybe that was how Johnna felt. That fucking Kaiser, what did he know? Words, and treatments, they were all of a piece and in the end that's all they were, pieces, unconnected to the whole; they were tools without handles, they did not help at all. *I* know, to himself and not without a smile, I know what he needs.

And practical: he could be practical too, with Robin, with himself and what is most practical of all? Money. It was something of a minor miracle (and perhaps not even minor) that Johnna had been, was allowing him to keep coasting on the lion's share of her money but that surely would not last forever, not much longer more than likely but he was planning, already, he was not as stupid as that. Guilty, perhaps he should feel guilty about living with her, living off her when there was nothing now between them but an enormous muscular distrust: but he did not feel guilty: was that proof, of something? What? His bank balance was still more than half what it had been, and of course

Robin had his SSI money, not much but a little, some, enough. Still he would have to get a job, something, maybe printing at a lab, maybe some freelance work: part-time, maybe while Robin was at a sheltered workshop?—he had mentioned something like that, a kind of supervised typing job, mailing labels but it was still nebulous, there were no definite plans. The times would have to be congruent, but that was freelancing's great advantage; all of it more than possible, with planning and with care.

Because Maryann was right, Group Home Maryann with her suspicions and her stares: remembering Robin in the car, wind in his face, serene: *she's scared you'll take me away.* I *am* going to take you away, Robin, I'm going to do it soon but it takes some planning, it takes a little work. There were certain outpatient commitment laws he must learn more about but he was smart, he could read.

And did, after days spent working hard, shopping for a part-time job, shopping for Robin: new art supplies, lush brushes, expensive color pencils, a ripped-cover book on Bacon found for half price. Shampoo from the drugstore, shoelaces, toothpaste, gleeful with his shopping bags, hurrying home to catch the messages on the machine—two for him, and both responses to his résumé, he was surely overqualified for those jobs, aiming low but what difference did that make? Work was not his salvation, his definition; if he had to he would get a job as a janitor, in a fast-food place, what difference did it make?

Picking up Robin now on Wednesdays, working around the trips, activities scheduled, certainly it seemed like they were always on Wednesdays but he was prudent, he could work around anything—and smiling, polite, always smiling at Maryann: *Is Thursday convenient, then?*

And he and Robin doing simple things: picking out clothing, new jeans, a shirt patterned with red and pink tropical fish, it was hideous but Robin loved it, wore it out of the store and for every day thereafter until Grant took him to a laundromat: "The colors will fade," gently, "if you don't wash it sometimes." Tiny boxes of vending-machine soap, the water going around and around and Robin's clothes mismatched, stained; Grant bought him new underwear, showed him how to find his size.

"I lost a lot of clothes in the hospital." Frowning a little. "I used to have a *lot* of clothes."

"You don't need a lot of clothes. —Now look at these shirts," holding up two packages, Fruit of the Loom. "Which one is in your size?"

In some ways it was more fun than the trips to the beach, the zoo—Robin fascinated by the reptiles, the bird house, talking long and knowledgeably about the similarities between the two, fish shirt and crooked sunglasses explaining *archaeopteryx*, hands spread wide in the shadow of plastic palm trees, in the blue-and-green tile meant to be land and sea; himself a hybrid, beautiful and lost. But not anymore, Grant's firm resolution, not lost anymore: I'm here now. I'll take care of you.

Shopping for food, Robin pushing the cart; sitting in the car eating Popsicles, Robin's head back to catch the sun and Grant, prudent, Put your hat on, Robin, Robin put on your hat and wanting to say, each time he dropped him off, Look at him. *Look* at him, is he hurt, is he damaged in any way? No. *No*, he is not. Look at him, Maryann, Dr. Kaiser wherever you are, Johnna on Thursdays through that haze of rage: *is he hurt in any way?* No.

And now ask this, ask and answer honestly, now, honestly: is he *happy*?

Honestly.

And after the shopping, the trips and the treats, the hours spent at the group home—enemy territory, Maryann always looming around corners as if in suspicion of foulnesses unknown, ever vigilant like a Cyclops eye and he always polite or at least civil—there was always the moment when Robin would reach for the folder, smiling sometimes or not smiling at all, reach with gravity to present the work, the drawings: beautiful, grotesque, less produced than extruded; simple as a miracle, there in his hands.

And holding them, thinking This is therapy, this is therapy too, these drawings, the discussion of incidents in their daily lives, the incidents that for

Robin seemed at times to actually induce the drawings: the way he saw and thought and felt come whole and seamless from the pencils and the pens, ink and graphite alive as running blood. So: ask yourself: does none of this help him? And would those who want to stop it, would they be selfish, now? You ask. You answer.

For Grant one answer, there in his hands: that compendium of faces, postures, gripping hands, buildings so empty it hurt to see them, eyes straight at the viewer and emptier still, what would eyes like that *see*, what could they see? and how difficult most would find it, to capture an emptiness so profound. It's easy to draw what is: now show me what lies behind, like the face in the mask; draw me a picture of that.

And he could, he did: *that* was the miracle, that he kept on doing it, did not falter or cease, that was what took the breath away. Heart elusive, the feelings granted by these drawings sometimes without names or parallel but always there: wild above rule or art, who said that? Milton? Wild above rule or art, enormous bliss. He did not take the drawings home, he did not want Johnna to see them, not that they saw much of each other anyway but there was always a chance, if she was determined, if she was resourceful: as he had been, tracking Robin and now how right, how simply right he saw that was: for once in his life he had done something completely, impeccably right.

Johnna did not speak to him anymore, in and out, microwave dinners and she slept in the bed alone; Dr. Kaiser did not call again. Maryann called, twice, but when he returned the calls would not come to the phone, would not when he visited acknowledge that she had called or been called back. Festering, that was the word for what she was doing; but since she did not bring it up neither did he.

Roger did, surprising him, hot twilight and Robin waving from the screen, they had been on an excursion, Chinese food and learning how to use a money machine. Roger bare-chested, dewlap breasts and a sad, sad smile, waving at him: "Hey." Grant was never sure if Roger recognized him, really recognized him, from day to day; they had changed his meds again, Robin said, from Haldol to Mellaril, and now he did not seem to want to do anything but sit in the cracking lawn chair and smoke, and sometimes let the cigarette burn down to the tremoring tips of his fingers; sometimes it was as if he did not even feel the pain.

"Hey, Roger," smiling at him now, expecting no response but Roger's voice, dry from a dry mouth, "Hey. You're Robin's friend." Looking up from the lawn chair, same old dirty blue shorts, a cheap bright new medal around his neck. "You're Robin's friend," he said again.

"Yeah. Grant—I'm Grant." He did not say *Remember?*

"Grant." Silence. "Maryann's a bitch," he said. I know. "What do you mean?"

"She won't, she won't let me," raising up one hand as if shackled by weights tremendous, burned cylindrical filter falling without feeling to the ground and twenty more like it. "She says Robin goes, goes out too much. I want to go out," and a sigh, so deep the medal trembled on the pale fat chest, "to the, to—"

Silence again, and for Grant the feeling not of helplessness but a kind of dry regret, a sorrow that for Roger there was no friend, a holidays-only family, nothing but the lawn chair and the cigarettes every day. And when the weather changed, hot late August but in a month, two months it would be back to the TV, sitting on the couch in one position, all his money spent on cigarettes he was too tired to fetch for himself from the corner party store. What to make of a life like that? what to hope for?

Grant's hand on Roger's shoulder, squeezing it lightly. "I'll bring you some cigarettes next time, okay? Okay?"

"Kools," Roger said. "I want Kools. My dad smokes Winstons, but he can't drive anymore."

"Two packs of Kools," nodding and turning, head down as if very tired, very very tired as if he had pulled with his own body rocks enough to build a tomb. Starting his car and the screen door— Robin?—but it was Maryann, hustling Roger inside, his mumbles and her hands on his back; and then she turned and said, very clearly, "You wait a minute." To him? He didn't want to wait but did, engine idling, hot in the car but it seemed rude to roll up the windows to run the air, what the hell did she want anyway? More bitching, probably. Mary-ann's a bitch.

Out then, mouth turned down, marched to stand beside the driver's side window, leaning so she could see Grant; so he could see her. "I want to know what you think you're doing," she said.

Tiredly, "I told him I would buy him some ciga-rettes," and hard not to sound angry, annoyed and he let it show, a little, it was so hard to hold it in all the time. "What's wrong with that?"

Her face blank, eyes like closed windows and then "Oh," everything turned back on in compre-hension's light; shaking her head. "No, not Roger, I don't mean Roger and you know it. I mean what are you doing with Robin."

Sweat on his neck, she smelled like dish soap, the smell of an endless kitchen and he just did not feel, tonight, like talking to her, about this, about anything, feel like talking at all so he said nothing, only shook his head to indicate that he was not interested but that didn't stop it, he should have known it would not because she came back like a train, like an old decayed engine rumbling fast at him down rickety tracks, hands on the car window now and saying what did he think and did he *real-ize* and shaky, he's a very shaky boy. He is!

"And you're taking him over—"

"I am not," anger beneath the weariness, twitching like the first rush of a drug, amphetamine feeling. "I'm not doing *any*—"

"I even asked his therapist, Ms. Hannen, I said are you gay or something."

Are you gay or something. She had asked Johnna are you gay or— Bubbling speed feeling; it was hard to keep his voice down but he did it; for Robin, who might be listening, Robin who might see, unseen, from his room. "Is that what you think this is?" Hands on the wheel; he could feel sweat like a viscous layer, lubrication between flesh and hard plastic. "You think I'm *fucking* him?"

"You're trying to take him over." He could smell her sweat, too, swampy old-lady stink and he realized through the lens distorted, his own anger and she was nervous, she was—was she?—afraid. Afraid of him. Afraid, because of him, for Robin and it should have made him like her better or at least sympathize but all he wanted to do was scream at her, scream in her face and then drive away.

"—even *talks* like you," hands still on the window, fingers crooked as a crouch. "It's like he wants to be you. And I'll tell you something, I'll tell you what I told that doctor, and the therapist—*your* girlfriend—" as if that was the special indictment and if he sat here much longer he was going to have to do something, something. "It's not healthy for him to depend so much on one person. It's not—"

Cutting in, voice louder than hers, risen like fever and he was sweating more, his hands still on the wheel as if he might drive straight up the driveway, straight through the house to seize Robin like a prince in a fairy tale, rescue him, take him away. Soon enough. Soon enough. "But it's okay for him to depend on you, right? That's healthy, right?" and before she could raise breath enough to answer, "Why do you have to think it's something bad? why do you think I have to be using him, or fucking him, or *hurting* him, why do you have to think that? What the fuck is wrong with you anyway?"

And Robin at the screen door, pale, scar aflame and it took all Grant's willpower, everything he had not to throw open the passenger door and say Come on. Because he knew, *knew* that if he did, Robin would come: just as he was, white-faced and silent, scared as a kid watching his parents fight; and that would be wrong. That was not the way he wanted to do this; it would hurt Robin, to do it that way.

So instead, fighting himself: and hating her, there in his window, framed in the darkness and that stink, sharp and sour in his nose and he said, voice low and forced as a bone in his throat, "I am not fucking him, I am not hurting him. I'm his friend. That's all. His friend. And if you try," harsher, still quiet but harsh as that bone scraping,

scraping away at flesh, "to take this out on him, punish him for this, if you—"

"Don't worry," and she moved her hands, finally, she stepped back, still bent enough to see him, her own face in darkness. "I'm his friend, too."

And walking away then, slowly, as if everything were normal, back to the house and standing framed in the screen-door light with Robin, to whom she said something, quiet something and he smiled—a little, little but it was a smile and it was real—and they waved, both of them, Maryann behind: and Grant waved back.

And drove home, he had not eaten since lunch but felt no hunger, wanted only to stand in the shower, cool colorless cascade down shoulders and back, minutes and minutes and he felt very tired, tired inside and out as if he had been in a fight. Rubbing the towel down his back, steam on the mirror and on the sink pale bottles, pink and beige, a tube of face cream, a nail file and he looked at those things, Johnna's things, as if he could not fathom why they were there, as if they were artifacts of a time not ended but unbegun, placed in his sight with a cunning as useless as the gesture itself.

Johnna was not in the apartment; he did not know where she was. On the answering machine there was a message, John from Cade Color: they had received his résumé and application, if he would come in they could talk. He tried to remember which one was Cade Color, he had applied to so many photo labs; but found his thoughts as slow as reptile blood, moving through his brain as if he had slept in the cold a long, a very long time. He wrote down the phone number and lay atop the bed without pulling down the covers, unsure of sleep even in the closing instant of his eyes.

And dreamed: of Robin, of Maryann; of Johnna, no linear thoughts, no nightmares but all a wet amorphous feeling, a feeling of illness weary and vast: and waking in the night to find Johnna there in the room. She did not turn on the light; he did not speak to let her know he was awake but watched her, slow movements, gathering hands—something, a shirt, a nightshirt; books. Hall light on and off and in her instant silhouette he saw a shine metallic, the muted sound of keys and then the front door opening; and closing. He did not think he would sleep again, but he did.

Gray dress shirt damp under the arms, clean jeans. CADE COLOR in block primaries, big black table instead of a desk and black-rimmed glasses, blond hair John behind it reaching to shake his hand, two-second shake and your résumé, mm-hmm, sabbatical, right. Lab work, "You're looking for part-time?"

"I'm working," carefully, "on a project of my

own. It might take some time, and I want to be able to—"

"Right. I understand. Lots of guys working freelance." Black coffee mug on the desk: *Somebody's Gotta Be the Bastard.* In white script. Slides on a light table, and John's hands straying back to them, tapping one squared edge against the surface, a matte-sounding click. "We get busy sometimes, we might need to arrange your schedule. That okay?"

"Sure. Sure, it's not a—"

"Good, okay. All right. Couple forms you need to fill out," and it was that simple, black pen and printing his name, social security number, it was just as easy as that. Smell in the office like sour fixative, John joking and swearing in the hall.

Three tries to get anybody on the phone at the group home till finally someone, not Maryann answering: and Robin subdued, faint pleasure only at hearing his voice, something beneath ominous as a broken bone ready to pierce pain through the sheathing skin, the surface upon which all seems normal.

"Hey," Grant trying to sound normal too, the sense of celebration instantly quashed by this overlay, Robin's, what? Sadness? Anger? Was he mad about the fight with Maryann? but they had talked about it yesterday, talked for almost an hour on the phone and everything had been all right. Hadn't it? and trying now to remember, trying to think and sound happy at the same time: "I just, I wanted to tell you: I got a job. At a lab. Part-time, you know, like I've been looking for?"

Nothing. "Well," floundering now, deflated, "I just wanted us to go out and have a, and celebrate. A little. If you want."

Silence.

"Robin? Robin, are you—"

Like a stone falling on sand: "It's Thursday."

"Right," more mystified, so what if it was Thursday? and a sudden fear, cold little measuring fear, was Robin taking his medication? was he all right? And immediate the instinct, Don't ask. Whatever this is it isn't that.

So instead plans, trying to sound cheerful, pick you up before the clinic then, okay? Okay? "And afterward maybe we can go get a coffee or something," as if they had never done this before, as if they did not do it every week. And hanging up, the rest of the day spent trying to convince himself, nothing really wrong, nothing bad. Maybe Robin was feeling sick, coming down with something; maybe it was just a bad day.

But: pulled up and idling in the driveway and he felt it, smelled it like an odor, like the stink sickness makes: something wrong, oh wrong in the way Robin came out the door, folder beneath his arm so tight the edges of the drawings curled like burning leaves against his body, wrong in the way he was dressed: dirty painter's pants, plaid flannel shirt way too hot for the day and worst of all his face, graven: and sorrow, as if something hurt very much, very much: the pain of loss, the pain of sense. And Maryann framed in the screen, somber, hand before her mouth: crying. What the *fuck*? but Grant only smiled at Robin, a tense little smile and said nothing, just put the car in reverse, and drive, and drove.

Still saying nothing, thinking so fast no thought could be held individual, was it me? what did I do, say, what? What? and still driving, reflex turns at the proper corners and suddenly Robin's hand on his arm, hard, squeezing hard and shaking his head, no, shaking his head *no no no* and Grant pulled over right where he was, jerking stop on the shoulder with traffic close enough to feel the backwash wind and turning to say Robin what is it? what?

And that face, scar red unto purple, so dark it looked fresh, as if blood might begin to flow, seep down into those blinkless eyes and more frightened still, "Robin, what is it, what's the matter?" and Robin shook his head, free hand to cover his eyes and finally, as if there were not air enough, low harsh voice to say, "Don't take me there."

"Why not?" and then in the breath identical, "I won't, I'm not going to. Just—what happened? Did something happen?"

Silence.

They sat there for a long time, three minutes; a long time to sit silent but Grant was determined not to speak first, if he turned to stone he would not speak: it was for Robin to talk now and at last he did, voice still low but less harsh as if those first words had made through pain the way for others, slow battlefield crawl: picking at a thread on the flannel shirt, dirty and it smelled like the hamper, smelled like something forgotten under a bed, creases down the sleeves and "I'm not going there anymore. Not anymore."

"All right," as cautiously as if removing a heart from a shuddering chest, careful, careful. "We won't go there then."

Silence again. Robin's throat working, half a cough and watering eyes, it seemed he might cry, weep out loud but instead covered his eyes, again, and said, "I told Maryann. I told her I don't, I don't, it's not helping me. It's not helping me and I don't want to go."

"All right," again and then the thought, clear and instant like the touch of a magic wand, rain in a dry land, a light in blindness: Shut up. Just shut up, he doesn't need you to say anything, all he needs you to do is listen.

One hand on the folder, now, sliding it the inches from his side to Grant's: "I made these," a pause, "for you. I was, I put—I took them—" and a shuddering in his chest, his shoulders under the ugly shirt, his whole body in some terrible subtle pain and Grant still with tension, a kind of agony as if he would reach out and hold Robin the way one holds a child; but did not move, a stiffness in his flesh peculiar and Robin said, "She said I had to stay, she said she would call my—Alison. Call Alison and tell her but I, I don't want—they said I had three days, I had to wait for three days and they would call her, I don't want to talk on the phone, I don't want—" Cracked voice and rising, hands jerked high as if they were burned, burning and through the underwater stiffness Grant reached deliberate to take those hands and hold them, hold them hard as if he were grounding Robin, pulling him back from a ledge, an edge, and with all his strength made his voice very soft, and calm, and normal. Normal.

"You don't have to talk to anybody," near monotone, the barest emphasis. "You can just come home with me if you want to. Or I'll take you anywhere you want to go. All right? All right, Robin?"

But Robin could not answer, hands gripping hard against Grant's, like a raptor, like a woman in childbirth, a body in death and Grant kept talking, no linear words, nothing he could remember past the instant of speaking, just talking, holding his hands and talking in the hot car with the air dry as lint in his nose and moving mouth and finally Robin relaxed, shoulders easing as he took his hands from Grant's, set them against his knees as if readying himself for their use, again, for the battle with the world. And then a sigh, reaching to unbutton the cuffs of his shirt: "Hot in here," and almost a smile, the dirty sleeves hanging long as vestments around his pale wrists.

And for Grant a feeling he would not forget, a relief so pure it was like love, like falling in love with a moment and when he spoke his voice strangely dry, a heat in his throat like pain but it was not pain, "Yeah, it is," and rolled down his window, started the car. "You want to go and get an ice cream?" and back into traffic, smooth and easy, going the opposite way.

Ice cream, chocolate and cherry, Robin wiping his fingers on his shirt as if in some curious way regressing and Grant said nothing, used a napkin, white and green on the seat in Robin's reach. They talked very little; Grant told him something about Cade Color, shrugging and smiling, thinking Three days, what did that mean? and then abruptly Robin's nod, standing, wiping his chin with his hands, and he said he wanted to go back to the group home, calling it that for the first time. Not "home," not I want to go home. Not nervous, or unhappy or at least did not seem to be: and Grant glancing at him, red lights, stop signs and what are you thinking, pale eyes and hands quiet, what are you thinking right now? Not wanting to go to therapy anymore was one thing, a big thing but not all there was to this, certainly there was more but he would not ask, he would not press; three days. They said I had to wait for three days.

Pulling up in the driveway and Roger, staring,

peering through the front window, and Grant remembered the cigarettes, two packs of Kools and he reached down, scrabbling under the seat and Robin's door opened, heavy swing: by Maryann.

Awkward, still half-bent, and he bumped his head on the steering wheel trying to get up but Robin did not seem disturbed, or angry, or even very interested in her presence; no smile for her but he smiled for Roger, waving a little before turning to wave to Grant, shirt sleeve shivered in the motion like a chrysalis split, chimera: symbol of rebirth and Maryann, mouth turned down, down, hair skinned back by some headband, bandage, leaning through the open door, leaning toward him like a broomless witch and saying, "I called his family." Not loudly. "I told them about you."

No moment to think, like being thrown headfirst into something wet and binding but anger was a savior, anger like pressure rising, blood pressure beating past the walls of his veins, his warm brain: "What the hell'd you—told them *what* about me? They don't even know me, I never even—"

"That's the point. They have a right to know." Her knee on the seat, that soap-sweat smell coming from her and something else, a hot smell like food and her eyes were red. "He won't listen to me, he won't listen to anybody, his doctor—" and her lips pressed together, hard, tourniquet motion. On a breath indrawn, "Maybe they can talk to him, maybe if they—"

The folder against his thigh, Robin had left it there, Robin had insisted he take it home; did she see it? Did she know what was in it? "If he wants to quit therapy," quiet, through his teeth, no yelling, "if he thinks it isn't doing him any good, why can't he just quit? What's the big fucking deal?"

"Therapy," and now she was crying, he saw tears rolling down her face, sweating face and she wiped one-handed at her eyes, her mouth. "He wants to leave here, *you* know that. You of all people, you're the one who—"

He wants to leave here.

They said I had to wait for three days.

You can just come home with me if you want to.

A pain in his head, as if his brain was just being born, leapt shiny into instant usage and "—what he thinks," bitterly, she was weeping in earnest now. "You have no idea, you don't know what you're doing! You don't *know*," and then at once turning away, wiping her face hard, both hands as if cleansing herself of blood indelible. Thickly, "I did everything I could," backing out of the car, knee along the seat and the whole motion as strange as being born, a ceremonial exit and Grant put his hand to his head, rubbed hard: Robin's fears, cracked voice and then the calm, he had asked and Grant had answered, gave the right answer without knowing, without being aware—my God, what if he had answered wrong, what if— And a long shiver, tremor involuntary as if in precursor to a seizure, a state, a vision; the screen door closing on Maryann's passage, the porch light clicking off.

In the dark: and thinking, thin line of sweat down his side like a finger, like a tracing hand and a feeling in his head as if he had breathed ether, laughing gas, methane fumes as rare and heavy as the scents of heaven. Should I go get him? Should I just get him now? Things to pack; things to do. What should—and then no; positive, No. He had his own house to clean first, he had work to do. Everything had to be right.

Starting the car, folder safe against his leg and beside it the cigarettes, Roger's cigarettes; not now, Grant thought, I'll give them to him next time. One more next time to make a last time, and then no more and he was smiling, he said it out loud and smiling: "No more," and the folder pressed against him like a jealous pet, no more of this but only everything, everything coming together, not puzzle pieces but pieces of a dream undreamt for so long, so long: and now without any final effort, any executed plan it was here: now.

When he opened the door it was to Johnna, standing right by the door as if she had been put there, some prop to scare burglars and her face, what was it, a harpy's? Medusa's? Expensive-looking new suit, heavy gray and some new haircut, the braid banished in favor of this triangular swing, hair shaped against her face as if she had grown an exotic coat, a new fur skin. How well he saw, his eyes seemed brighter, it seemed he saw everything down to its heart. Sweating a little, and grinning, the folder against his body like a child, like a shield.

"The woman from the group home called me," she said. Her voice was very dry, as if she had not used it recently.

"Maryann," nodding, angling past her or trying to but she blocked him, turned her own body to block him, and he remembered, strange the suddenness of memory, her body turning during sex, fucking standing up and her body turning that same way: as if controlled by his motion, left to his right, direct and errorless and sure.

"She said Robin is leaving the group home." The muscles of her face almost motionless, when she breathed it was like watching stones scrape. "First therapy, he says he's done with therapy, and now the group home. What's next, Grant? No more medication?"

Of course he'll take his medication; stupid. Stupid: but he could not be angry, right now he felt too good. "Why don't you ask him?"

"He won't talk to me anymore." Something like a cold sore beneath that granite mouth and she kept talking, no yelling, no screaming, he had expected rage but this was something different: "If you were a therapist," that even voice, "I'd report you, I'd have your license pulled. I'd like to have you killed. But what I'd like to know first is what you're getting out of this, Grant, what are you getting out of all this? The drawings?" He did not answer. "If it were just the drawings, if I had known I would have just given them to you, I would have—"

No you wouldn't, and it was so true he said it out loud, "No you wouldn't," smiling, he was smiling, he couldn't help it and he saw her mouth curl down; she looked remarkably like Maryann when she did that, in fact this whole conversation seemed a mere continuation but what neither of them understood, hard faces, red eyes, was that this was right, all of this was *right* and Robin knew it, knew all of it; had known for how long? Long enough; longer maybe than he and now Robin is coming here: like a fire burning under heavy glass, smooth and bright the flames, their motion like the motion of the earth itself, turning to bring you the thing you want most, the only thing you need: Robin is coming here.

And Johnna still talking, about money, how are you going to take care of him, do you think you can live off his SSI, are you going on welfare? and shaking his head, not smug, not even triumphant: not a problem. "I have a job now," he said.

"You have a job," as if nothing could surprise her now. "You're going to support him. You're going to *take care* of him, is that right, Grant? That's what you're going to do?"

Tired: he realized it, standing there, tired all over. Tired of talking, really, but there was only a little more to go, only a little left to say. Johnna never got tired of talking, it was listening that was her problem. Her new hair swinging against her face, cold sore like the period at the end of a sentence, a jail sentence: relentless: "You're going to take care of him?"

"That's right." Fire: like glass and she was saying if I just knew what you were *getting* out of this, frustration like the fire that does not burn, do you care about him or what? "Do you care about him? do you love him or something, is that it? *Can* you love?"

Can you? do you? Love him, what difference did it make? Yes I care. *Yes*, I care. Taking him places, buying him things, teaching him things: listening to him; was that love? Was it? Thinking of that moment in the car, exquisite the feeling of relief: he had cared for Robin then, helped him, he would keep on helping him. And Robin would help him, too.

Robin is coming here.

"I want you out of here," calmly, not unkindly through the fire, through the glass. "In three days." Grace period: grace, pouring down like rain, this was grace, this moment: determination: this was holy, this feeling of rightness, not completion but completion's ripened heart through the haze beneficent, that secondhand surprise: a task accomplished, not only a first step but *the* first step, the step essential without which nothing could begin.

"I'm packing now," she said. "I wouldn't stay here if you paid me, not even for Robin, there's nothing more I can do for Robin now. I talked to the group home, I talked to his doctor. I have a call in to his sister—"

"Alison," he said; she seemed surprised that he knew the name, little whorl of anger in her eyes like a flaw in ice, in the dead heart of a jewel; but she controlled it, he saw her let it go.

"That's right. And when I talk to her I'm going to tell her everything I know about you, and everything I suspect, and everything I believe. And if I can, I'll get a—"

He wanted to say Robin hates his sister, but it seemed pointless; weightless; that methane feeling again, Robin is coming here. The new job, new beginning, everything starting over and memory's flex again, giving him a scene of himself and Johnna, standing here this way, fighting about something else: what? No memory for that, only their postures, her moving mouth: her stare, and his avoidance, head down and frowning but he was not avoiding her now, there was no reason to. Calmly, as if his whole body were made of glass, his mouth gentle and heavy as a paperweight, shaped as an angel's smile: "I'll help you," he said. "Pack."

"Go fuck yourself," and away, down the hall into the bedroom and he heard the sound of drawers, opening and closing like valves in a heart, opening and closing and with the folder still be-

neath his arm he went into the kitchen. Clear glass,
clear water, drinking it down as if he filled himself
from the outside with what lay as clear within and
he thought This is what it's like to be happy; this is
the way it feels: glass, and fire, and grace, as if the
rolling motion of time had brought him, finally, to
where first and always he was surely meant to be.

PART TWO
ROBIN

By being both here and beyond, I am
becoming a horizon.

MARK STRAND

ROBIN DID THE DISHES; ROBIN SCRAPED THE plates; Robin carried the garbage to the Dumpster, tied at its neck with a colored loop, red from the bread bag, blue from the waffles; he liked to leave the waffles in the toaster until they were burnt. He forgot to put the cap on the shampoo; he never read the newspaper. The whole kitchen table had been given over to his drawings; there were pencils everywhere, thin stamenlike pens, a big soft brown eraser that looked as if it had been removed with a forceps, some tiny organ the body could forever do without.

Working there, head bent, legs hooked around the chair like some antique print of a Dickens copyboy and Grant would pass him in silence, smiling sometimes if he was looking and sometimes if he was not. Cool in the apartment, he did not like it to be too hot and that was all right with Grant; almost everything was all right with Grant, living now not in a bubble, nothing that fragile; call it instead a sphere, a curve of simplicity and content.

Robin slept in the living room on two worn

sleeping bags and a quilt; he had strange sleeping patterns, up sometimes all night or up and down as if on watch; sometimes he would turn on the TV but always with the sound off; he liked to watch the people, he told Grant, have them there while he lay quiet, eyes open, or sat up with a pad to draw. Knees up, studious the angle of his neck and Grant in the next room rising, sometimes, to get a drink, go to the bathroom and there had never been a moment of strangeness, an instant out of place; he never woke to think Who is there, who's out there? They had required no period of adjustment; it was as if it had always been this way, the vast minutiae of daily life shared. What disagreements occurred were so minor they did not merit memory; problems predicted, all those dire worries—are you listening, Johnna? Maryann?—gone unmaterialized, all of it; they had all been wrong. Wrong; and the corollary, he had been right, he and Robin both right from the start. Johnna's voice in memory, what are you getting out of all this? as if Robin were a prize, an end to his means but what she did not understand—one of the many things she did not understand—was that the whole point was there was no end, only content on the journey they made together: farther in, that was all, that was everything and everything else would follow in its time.

What did she understand, anyway, what did she know? She who had not even called, to check on

Robin; Maryann, the other crusader, no call from
her either: expecting day after day to hear from
them, waiting and finally realizing that they would
never call. And realizing something further, past
the first blind alley that said they had given up, had
gone gracefully into acceptance, had acknowledged
their errors: no, it was that they had not really
cared as much as they had professed to do, had not
cared as much about Robin as about Grant's usur-
pation of their powers, their authority: that was
what had rankled, that was the infection, the dry
sore. Because if they had cared, had known, they
would have come looking, they would have seen:
because they would have known.

Because: working at the kitchen table, bent
head and vining legs and at least once a week a new
one, pencil or ink or soft crayon, sometimes small,
sometimes big: always Robin: unearthly, sometimes
frightening in their blind perspicacity: a map,
Grant thought, a map for me and as a result direct
as an experiment in pure causation found himself
changing, his perceptions, his ideas, the way he saw
the world through the lens unique of Robin's eyes.
At work making prints, Cade Color, dumb
gruntwork but it was as if, in the chemical scent,
the dark and red light up above he found more
evidence of the change, the whole world some exquisitely simple rebus and he learning, finally, the
language of its symbols: Robin's hand in his,

Robin's eyes his guide. Who would ever have guessed it could be so simple?

Pictures on the table like God's alphabet, the way the world is made and the two of them before the microwave, Robin reading off the back of a box: frozen lasagna, frowning, "It says the times may vary," and Grant beside him, reading over his shoulder, you have to adjust the heat, see, turn it up to High. See?

"The other microwave wasn't like this," carefully changing the setting. "It just had COOK and OFF." Sliding out the lasagna, icy red block onto the plate; careful hands, turning it on and then reaching down the counter for his medicine, orange plastic pharmacy bottle, child-proof cap and he never had to be reminded, he always took his medicine on time.

"People don't, you know," to Grant, leaning back against the counter. Wiping his hands on a towel imprinted with ducks and windmills, green and brown. "They get to thinking they don't need it. Or they hate the side effects—I hate them, too," dry mouth and blurry eyes, sometimes, sometimes a restlessness worse than pain but passing, always it passed. But those things not the worst of it, the worst a feeling, Robin said, like singing through a gag, like being in a sack, a membrane too heavy to split and "It's like a baby must feel," with a rare bitter smile. "Can't be born, can't get out. Can't do anything but *squirm*."

But Grant was careful, very careful during those times, making no noise, no talk, no demands until the cloud passed over, the inner door re-opened, and Robin would sit at the kitchen table again, playing the radio, drinking glass after glass of Coke and then the drawings would come like a river, sometimes two or three in as many days, all of them bright, vivid as a burn, as if to make up in brilliance what the gray days in passing had taken from him, weakness slack and formless as the spent chrysalis, husk already drying in the strength that weakness brings. Tacking the drawings to the walls with plastic pushpins themselves bright as cartoons, crayons, the kitchen become a splendor of pure color islanded by sink, chairs, appliances in timid beige and white, way stations and mercy for the sharply dazzled eye.

Living like this, together this way showed to Grant all of Robin, granting by proximity a knowledge more intimate and wide than ever possible between those who did not share a daily life. Grocery store, laundromat, sorting socks; sitting at the doctor's, Dr. Kaiser, waiting in the waiting room and Robin turning to him when his, Robin's, name was called: the need unspoken: Come in with me. And he did, standing quiet as a parent behind the examination-room door, patient and still and still Dr. Kaiser did not like him, did not overtly show it but it was there: Robin before him script in hand and Grant's smile serene: What do you know?

What do you know about it? Remembering with a cold half smile one of Johnna's friends, a doctor, sitting on the couch where Robin often sat, one of Robin's places-to-be and saying, one hand on his knee, squared-off fingers and shaking his head, "I call it the talking-to-drunks syndrome, it gets so you look forward to the end of the day so you can go talk to people whose reactions you can predict." And all of them nodding, nodding like the plastic birds that drink eternally, heads in constant bob and somewhere in Grant a burning, he would like to talk to that guy now, that doctor, talk to him very precisely and very slow: and maybe teach him something if he were smart enough to learn.

Grant, now, learning, learning every day: about Robin. Who loved to read; who was amazingly shy about some things, locking the bathroom door to pee, to shower; who had fears, their origins manifestly unshared, their ramifications everywhere: all the windows must be locked, all the cupboard doors closed tightly, all the glasses in the cupboard placed so their rims were facing down. Sometimes he started hugely, for the tiniest of sounds; but he loved thunder and lightning, would open all the windows for a really good storm, wet hands braced on the metal sill to lean out grinning in the slash and rattle, water on his face, water blackening his hair and yelling—"Yeah! *yeah!*"—in the burgeoning instant of the crash, as if it were a show for him alone, show of force. And Grant smiling, somewhat alarmed, trying to get him to close the window or at least take his hands from the sill: "The angels're fighting, huh. Or bowling. Isn't that what people say?"

"Bowling?" as if Grant had said something so foolish as to be insulting; then relenting, smiling a little, "They're not *bowl*ing, Grant, come *on*," but would not say, Grant's smile and smiling questions, would not tell what they were doing instead.

Sometimes Grant came back from work to find him sleeping, curled up like a child in a posture so fetal as to seem painful; or drowsing over a book, he had a big box of paperbacks although the blurring vision sometimes made it hard to read. He had read a lot, he told Grant, in the hospital, especially those first few admissions; to find out, he said, what I had.

"What you had?" Imagining textbooks, psych class checklists. "What'd you read?"

Shrugging, smiling a little. "Oh, you know. Sylvia Plath, and Anne Sexton, and Woolf. Artaud. Nijinsky. I had this book called *The Inner World of Mental Illness*, I wish I still had it, it was *great*. It had this cover like a whirlpool, you know, only purple and green and it didn't match, the colors didn't match up when you looked at it. And all this stuff by crazy people," and Grant suppressing that small inner flinch at the word; Robin used it naturally but it still made him flinch; Johnna's conditioning, most likely. Bad word. And Robin smiling more broadly now, head to one side in pleasant memory: "There was this one thing in it, I forget exactly what it was called, something like 'The Diary of a Schizophrenic.' I used to read it over and over in the dayroom, I used to . . . like some people sing a song, you know? Over and over. And I would read this, when I could, this guy wrote all this stuff and I was reading it and there was one sentence at the very end, it said, 'Some night God is going to come.' Some night God is going to come. I must have read that a thousand times." Sighing a little. "I sure wish I still had that book."

What happened to it? wanting to ask but in the end did not, did not mention it again; to see that week's drawing featuring as its heart a small whirlpool, half purple, half green, matching perfectly its whorls; the picture itself one great whorl of resignation, the feeling past exhaustion, the place past the edge. Robin did not tack up that drawing, and Grant did not ask him to.

Sometimes back to see him sitting quiet, holding a pencil, one of the older drawings; at times he seemed very tired, would offer only the briefest of smiles but Grant never pressed, tried never to ask the wrong question; sometimes it was a strain, but always he tried. Sometimes it was a strain to know what to do; to know what to think, but he kept the strain to himself, never hinting, even with a sigh, a frown suppressed, that sometimes it was hard on him, too. But all good things are hard, aren't they?

not even asking the question, knowing without asking that it was so. What demands passion demands price; that was the way it was.

And one day home, tired himself and a little later than normal, to find Robin—after looking: he did not answer, he had to be found—crouching, hands on knees bent numb with patience, just below the bathroom sink: one shoulder pressed against the vanity's flat pink chipboard, gazing up at the mirror above the basin. Watching.

What are you doing? —No. "What are you looking at?" softly, careful to make it softly, careful not to come too close. Those hands curled up at the wrists, aquatic creatures limp from lack of water; eyes not bright but shiny, slick, the way a glaze is slick: concealing as much as it highlights, the skin light bears to shield itself.

"Robin?" still very softly, taking half a step forward. "What do you see?"

Nodding up, pointing with his chin to the mirror: toothpaste flecks, faint film of water dried again and again to form a nearly indistinct patina. "That," on a breath, a wind from somewhere far away. "In there."

And Grant standing very still, one foot raised to take a closer step and then down his back a feeling indescribable, akin to the way he had felt watching Robin crossing the grass to him, that day, big day, decision day but he had not known it then, only known with a knowledge unassailable that something was wrong; remembering the idea, the picture sharp as pain: *something is wrong* and its wrongness measured the way the dark is measured: take its measure now.

The mirror's silver backing, the toothpaste spit, the film. *That. In there.*

As alien as the surface of a planet never named; as close as Robin's breathing, if Grant put his hand there he would feel its warmth.

All the red in the bathroom like a hand around his heart, slippery in his lungs as if he could not breathe correctly; walk away. Now.

And into the kitchen, to slowly pour a cup of coffee, as slowly stir the creamer, the room as still around him as he listened, hard, hands shaking minutely as if in the grip of some gentle drug and heard through fear's magnification Robin's movements, tiny rustling shiftings back and forth, and then, very quietly, a laugh.

Hand tight on the cup, a kind of matte sickness, a sinking somewhere inside. Hallucinations. Shouldn't his medication be taking care of that? Shouldn't the pills be—

"Oh, *no*," and Robin laughed again, a sound so strange in the heavy air and the thought to Grant as instant: This has nothing to do with the pills. Nothing.

And then abruptly it was over, ozone change in the air and Robin's movements louder, normal, running water in the bathroom and then into the kitchen to smile at Grant, a pleasant smile, and start taking out the plates for dinner: two white plates, two forks, two knives. A glass for Grant, a mug for himself, the one with the stylized rabbit, little black rabbit with antennae for ears. Pouring milk, and ice water, all of it so normal, Grant's shoulders easing and saying something to Robin who glanced back at him, back over his shoulder and in his eyes the face of the mirror, that rapt opacity and something else behind it, and then he blinked and was just Robin again, careful hands on the pitcher of ice water, careful fingers guiding the knife through the loaf of bakery bread.

And Grant like a bird taking wing, broken wing but up, talking about work, John and this guy and impossible, the turnaround time was unbelievable, and Robin listening, that warm inclusive silence that said *I hear you, you have all of my attention*, buttering the bread in patient chunks, taking up the napkins as if there were no mirrors at all in the house, no mirrors anywhere, and if there were, were surely empty ones.

Directly after dinner Robin went to bed, to sleep; curled in his nest, blue and brown and his head back, neck at a painful angle and covered everywhere with sweat, sweat darkening his hair, his scar a dainty lavender against the grayish pallor of his cheeks; breathing evenly and slow, maybe too slow, one palm exposed as if in dreams he was freed to ask for what he wanted, to show the open hand of frank entreaty: give me. I need.

What had he seen, there in the mirror?

The next morning Robin was very tired, said very little; did not take out the garbage, and for three days did not draw at all.

"So which is a better buy?"

Grocery store lights too bright overhead and Robin's squint, heavy pink jug against his thigh: comparing. "The no-brand one."

"Right," nodding firmly, "because this one, see, is almost a dollar cheaper, and you get three more—"

"Stripes," and then that rarest smile, head tilted and swinging the jug up and into the yellow cart: "The stripes means it's the cheapest one, that's what they always mean," and then laughing out loud at Grant's headshake, Grant's dry burlesque dismay.

"Smartass," pushing the cart, secretly delighted at the joke, the energy behind it; Robin had been too quiet lately, too serious, too tired. Working on the drawings but at a rate far reduced, as if somehow they hurt him, drained him: yet each as exquisite, as painfully perfect as all the others and maybe even more so, it was like comparing spirit to angel, like diamond to pearl: like windows on the walls of the kitchen, like eyes that could see all the pain in the world and turn it back like sieves bent inward, some of them were so perfect it almost hurt to look at them, to consider them soberly in a sober overhead light. Robin had taken to leaving them wherever he finished them, on the couch, on the pillow of his bed nest, on the edge of the bathroom sink, placed there in some sleeping hour of the night for Grant to find in the morning, long empty arms rendered pale and emptier in aching gray, a circle of seepage dried like a tear on the farthest edge of the paper, the edge closest to the door.

But see him now, pushing Grant's hands off the cart to push it himself, angling down the toilet paper aisle to take by himself two packages of the brand they always used, remembering on his own that they needed paper towels too. They never made lists, relying on memory, Grant's spotty, Robin's surprisingly accurate: *I don't think of what we need,* shaking his head. *I think of where things are. The empty paper towel holder; the empty carton of milk, bottle of Coke.* Lately Grant had been trying to get him to drink less Coke, there was a theory in some of the books that caffeine was not good for people with Robin's disorder; for schizophrenics, why is the word so hard to say? The books stored safely in a box marked NEGS 82–84, Grant did not want to throw them away, did not ever want Robin to see him reading them, owner's manuals, *How to Care for Your Schizophrenic. Mental Illness and You.* And you, too.

Apple juice, grape juice, papaya juice incredibly

expensive but that was what Robin wanted, they
would have to cut back somewhere else; *he* would
have to cut back, money was not Robin's department, the Department of Social Services, Social
Security, SSI benefits and all the other eligibilities;
it was hard to understand some of the forms and he
had always considered himself an intelligent man.
Reading them twice and twice again while Robin
doodled on the pamphlets in the dusty metal rack:
SOCIAL SECURITY laced with tiny snakes, little flying
forms like fleshy bees, something crawling across
the bottom of the page, he needs to bring what?
Proof of income? Yes, the social worker said. Yes,
he needs to bring all that.

"He doesn't have any income," calmly, they had
been through this before, sometimes it seemed like
they went through it once a month. "He doesn't
have any personal assets, either," unless you count
the medicine but don't say that, there's no room for
jokes here, nothing's funny.

"I know," the social worker's sigh, as tense and
bored as he. Robin farted once, a small bright
sound they all ignored. "It's just the documentation
I need."

"Again."

"Again, yes," and it was two thirty before they
got out, Robin squinting again, the light hurt his
eyes, he said, he said he needed his sunglasses
fixed.

"What's wrong with them?" Grant holding out

his hand but Robin shaking his head, stubborn, he would do it himself. Bundled in the car in a new coat, colder now, autumn tilting into winter and Robin fingering the sunglasses, careful fingerprints all over and then sliding them back on, pleased, he could see better, he said, it was much better now.

And Grant's own squint at the gas gauge, was it possible it was on empty again, it seemed like he had just bought gas. Gas and groceries, new coats, drawing paper. Phone bill, electric bill. He might have to ask, he thought, for more hours at work, could have them for the asking; but he did not want to spend the time away from Robin who seemed to need him now, a different need in a different way.

And for Grant this need a pleasure positive, this and the drawings what kept him going: and remembering as if in sleep the emptiness of his days, old days spent wanting, oh God the weariness of that wanting, how it could make you empty in a day full of motion, drained was not the word: eviscerated, but of a viscera so ephemeral the want alone could kill it, the need for what could not be named but the name of it, really, was passion; wasn't it? The capacity to feel, and feel deeply; and that was what Robin gave him, that was the gift of Robin's need, hand in hand and side by side with the gift of his sight, his drawings.

But, Grant thought, had been thinking, had been *feeling*, there needed to be something else, something more; a little more: as if the first step

had been taken, and now another needed as
strongly to be made; what? where? and how to
know? Instinct? Planning, rough chance, what? It
was one thing to feel this need, to know it for what
it was; it was another to make assumptions, plans,
changes that would affect Robin as well as himself;
he would have to be careful, he would have to go
slow. Robin was fragile; they would have to be
careful; perhaps it was Robin who would this time
lead the way. Perhaps in fact the direction lay in
Robin's new need for him, for his presence, his
listening silence that Robin filled with stories of the
hospitals, the dayrooms, the wards: his bed, his broken glasses, his books and the T-shirt he wore for
six weeks, one whole incarcerated stay and when he
came out his sister would not let him wear it home,
made him strip it off in the cold May sunlight before she would let him into the car, made him ride
back to their parents' house bare-chested, shamed
and his mother had wept when she saw him in the
driveway, hand before her mouth and his father
saying *For God's sake, Robin, where's your shirt?*
And his sister saying nothing, purse on her arm like
a cop, a social worker, coat folded over the other as
if beneath it she bore the weapon that could sub-
due him if only she might be allowed at last to give
it use. That night he slept on the kitchen floor, as
far from his family, their closed bedroom doors, as
he could be; and left in the morning before anyone
woke.

"And she said, Mom's going to die because of you, because of you she looks sixty and she isn't even forty-five." The sunglasses still on, crouched against the fraying arm of the sofa, head close to his knees; and Grant close by, close enough to touch, saying nothing.

"And she said, Dad can't stand you. I can't stand you, no one loves you anymore," not weeping, eyes wide behind the sunglasses, wide and dry as if trapped in the telling, tableau unending like an insect frozen in dry ice. "We're all afraid of you. We're all afraid of you." And suddenly a laugh, harsh as a bone breaking, a breaking heart: "And I left again, and I took her purse with me, I didn't take the money, I didn't even take it very far. Just to the store, I went to the party store to get a Coke and I gave it to the lady behind the counter, I said I found this purse in the parking lot. And she said I was the first honest person she ever met and gave me the Coke for free, she rang it on the register but she gave it to me for free. That was honest, wasn't it?" and the laugh again, rocking a little and then resting his open mouth on those bent knees, the material beneath damp when he spoke again.

"I was in Clearwater twice that year," what year? He had not said. Did it all exist for him in some perpetual moment, no time substantially different from the next? and what if it did? Why shouldn't it? and Grant found his hands clenched hard against his own knees, forced himself to open

them, to lay them open at his sides as if at any
moment they might be needed for some important
work. And still Robin's voice, a river, dry river
showing all the bones, where all the broken things
are: "—guy named Dorsett, I never knew if that
was his first name or his last name. He had a bipolar disorder, they said at first, or that's what they
told him anyway but I used to think he was crazy
like me, in fact he was crazier than me I thought.
Anyway he used to have this thing about his
tongue, it started out half joking but then he got
serious about it. Like, you can't get rid of it, right?
Your tongue? It's always there, moving around in
your mouth like it's got a mind of its own, it flops
around like a fish or a piece of meat or something
and you can't get rid of it, you can't even make it
stop moving because it has to move so you can talk,
and eat, and everything. That's what he used to say,
and he used to go on and on about it until they
tried to make him stop because he was freaking
everybody out. Even the aides." And the smile
mirthless, pushing the sunglasses back up against
his nose, once, twice, rhythmic pushing like the
genesis of a tic. "Finally they put him on this different medication that was supposed to make him
stop, or calm him down or something. And after
about a week he bit out his tongue. Not all of it,"
judiciously, "he could still talk a little, but he had a
speech problem, what do you call it?"

"A speech impediment?" in a voice very calm,

Grant proud of this calmness, it was extremely difficult not to flinch but he had not flinched and he
was proud of that. Acutely conscious of his own
tongue as he spoke. "Like a lisp?"

"Right, only not a lisp. He didn't talk too much
after that, he was embarrassed about it. So I guess
the tongue won, huh?"

Yes. No? and saying nothing for a long empty
moment, too long to speak then and Robin shrugging, mouth on his knee again, rocking a little and
pushing the sunglasses up, and up, and up.

There were other stories, told at odd moments,
driving home from the doctor's, the drugstore, putting away the groceries, washing out the tub.
Cleanser smell in his nose, blue paste and not all
the stories were sad, some of them were funny, or
curious, some of them made Grant angrier than he
would have believed he could become over the
plight of strangers, some of whom were already
dead. Stories about other patients, about doctors,
therapists, aides; stories of kindnesses shown or
tragedies averted by a word judicious here or there
and all the stories at their heart possessing an intensity, a heat so singular and bright that it formed
of its own subtle ferocity an idea that came to
Grant as obvious and certain as his next breath, so
obvious and certain that he spoke it aloud in the
forming moment before thinking of its impact on
Robin, before, in fact, thinking at all.

"Why don't you," cup in hand, pausing before the cupboard, "paint it?"

Robin's head to one side, like a listening child. "Paint what?"

"Clearwater. All of it," gesturing, the cup forgotten in his hand. "The people you knew there, your friends. The doctors. The dayroom, the wards, everything. So the people who don't know, the people who don't understand *can* understand. So they can *see*." The people like Johnna, who think they already know. The people like Alison, who think so too.

But Robin was shaking his head, gaze down and picking at his thumbnail, I don't know. I don't know. It was one thing to talk about those days, but another, certainly another to pass them bare through the filter of his art, he did not use those words but it was how Grant understood the problem, tried to understand; and tried to help, but not without a certain unease of his own, standing behind Robin like some whispering spirit, a spirit of intense and perfect reasonableness: But weren't there some things about it that you liked? Knowing there were such things, such moments all the more perfect for their rarity, knowing a lot, knowing everything. Knowing how to talk to Robin: how to persuade, from the force of his own belief that this was it, this was the step they needed, the path they had to take: but together, certainly together, he would not dream of sending Robin there alone. But together, yes, because he felt it again, that *right-ness*, that certainty of action and he brought it up again, calmly, kindly, that night after dinner; again that weekend as they drove back from a day spent at the beach, far too cold to swim so they walked instead, throwing stones in the water, gray into gray like night into dark morning, overcast: and Robin hunched into his new white coat, saying, "But I don't want to go back, Grant. I don't."

"You're not going back, of course you're not going to go back," hands in his pockets, the lining ripped and gritty with old detritus and dirt. "It's just a way to—to see it again, to see it in a *safe* way, right? Because those times are over, Robin, you know that. I'm not going to let anybody do stuff like that to you again." And the distant whisper, dry, reminding him he had no legal authority at all here; they could do what they liked with Robin if the need arose, if his behavior became unaccept-able, objectionable. But someone would have to object first, wouldn't they? Wouldn't they?

And Robin pale, nervous hands on the stones, gray stones in his palm like little bones and saying nothing, not answering when Grant spoke and he let it go; for then. To bring it up later, after dinner, in the comforting half darkness of the living room, Robin in his nest and the TV on without its sound, pictures of people living lives behind glass, a wall of glass and suddenly Robin was weeping, paper in hand and drawing, pencil pressed so it bent the paper underneath and his hand moving hard, strongly and hard and Grant saying nothing, still, still, he had to piss but did not move, did not even want to breathe as Robin drew, hand a clenched curl around the pencil, sweat on his forehead, on the bitter red stare of the scar and it went on, it seemed, for a long time; but it was not so long, the soundless sitcom was not even over before "Here," shoving the paper at Grant, "look at it. Look at it!" and then up, rising, crooked balance, and almost stumbling into the kitchen, where the refrigerator door opened, and the water ran on and on over the white noise of its hum.

And Grant, bladder aching, taking up the paper: to see: the black sun rising, tiny figures in a panic beneath and the one closest to the viewer Robin, definitely Robin staring with one eye open, pinned down like Gulliver and the reaching hand flayed, flayed to the shivering bone, to the tip of the pointing finger and slowly as handled explosives, as acids in glass jars Grant set the drawing down, as slowly rose and went into the kitchen where Robin stood before the sink, washing his hands, washing his hands, dish soap running down his wrists like viscous yellow blood and Grant took him by the shoulders, firm hands and looking straight into his face said as firmly, as calmly, as lovingly as he could, "That's all done with, Robin, that's all just memories. Just memories, okay? And you're the one in charge of them now."

And Robin's mouth moving, working, silent and his breath in Grant's face warm, so warm as if inside he was molten, memory burning like the fire that never dies and the soap dropped onto the floor, small and slick the blobs of bubbles as Robin wept helplessly, as Grant before him squeezed his shoulders with that same calm loving touch.

He did more of them, more Clearwater drawings: hunched at the kitchen table, no more copyboy, instead something of the slave in the curl of his shoulders, the heavy tilt of his head. He worked only in pencil on these drawings, cheap yellow number two pencils, sharpening them in twists of shavings that he left where they fell, left for Grant to sweep up.

Which he did, without comment; he was very careful now, had taken extra care since that first drawing, the Gulliver in extremis: not Pandora's box but the surgeon's, he had opened it unto pain and it was pain he saw in Robin's eyes, in the way he held the pencil, in the way he hunched for hours in his nest, blankets pulled around him, reading and rereading the TV guide as if in its arrangement of programs, of news and cartoons and interminable cable movies he might find what he needed, the answer to prayers never made, the kind we whisper to ourselves in the most absolute silence and could never shape into sound to speak aloud: what we want most; what we fear.

And Grant with his own—not fears, but concerns, call them concerns and the sharpest was for Robin's medication, he was very very careful that Robin not know he was checking but he did, every day. Checking: and rereading the sections in the hidden books, NEGS 82–84, as Robin slept like a camp survivor in the checkered light of late afternoon, reading swiftly the chapters about decompensation, reading that the majority of patients who stop taking their medication feel well for the first month or so afterward, enjoying the disappearance of side effects, suffering no symptoms since their bodies continue to carry a considerable amount of medication, even more if they are heavy, like an angel's kiss left sweet in their fatty tissue. But inevitably the decompensation would begin, the slide back into psychosis, the voices, the noises, the alarms in the night: the drive to the hospital, in the back seat, maybe the back seat of a police car: but that would not happen to Robin. That *would not* happen to Robin, not with Grant there to watch him, to care for him; no.

The drawings' continuance took something from them both, Grant tired by vigilance, Robin exhausted by the weight, the freight of memory exhumed, worked through; but it made him stronger, Grant believed this as he believed in the beat of his heart, the circulatory march: working with those memories, bad memories, meant controlling them, having the power to control them; how could this not strengthen Robin, how in the end could it harm?

So Grant swept the pencil shavings, took out the garbage, took over Robin's chores almost completely so that Robin would have more time to draw; to rest; to sleep; he slept a lot these days, often waking with a headache, a stomachache, complaining that these drawings took something from him, made him feel funny when he did them.

"Funny how?" Grant asked.

"I don't know," Robin said; he would not look at Grant, only at his fingers, his thumbs picked to shreds and bloody hangnails. "Just funny."

But he would not stop, sleeping when Grant was at work, drawing when Grant was home—as if somehow his, Grant's, physical presence was necessary, talisman, anchor in the house: even if he was only washing dishes, or reading the paper, or working himself in silence, some paperwork brought home from the lab. Once Robin looked up from his drawings to ask what he was doing, and Grant explained as simply as possible, there was really not much to it, "not much to any of it, really," and he smiled a little, but Robin did not smile.

"What if they're not right?"

"What, this?" Tapping the job sheets. "It'd be pretty hard to get it wrong, it's really pretty—"

"No, not that. I mean the pictures. You know, the photographs." Hands flat, exasperated it seemed by his inability to explain. "You know. If what they took isn't what's there."

"Oh. Well, then we try to fix it, offer to do it over if we can, or give them a—"

"No, no," turning the pencil in his hands, turning and turning like a crank to grind his thoughts, force them out of his head, "not if the *work's* wrong, I mean what if what they thought they were taking a picture of isn't what's really there. *In* the picture. Do you know what I mean?"

Silence. "No, I—no, I don't. Can you," so carefully, "will you tell me what—"

But Robin was shaking his head, frustrated maybe or maybe just too tired, they would talk about it some other time, he had to work now. "Maybe I'll take a picture for you someday," pencil gripped as if it might wriggle free, gripped and pointing like a planchette needle, like a tiny bayonet, "and I'll show you what I mean."

And Grant mystified, letting it go but thinking, thinking, even in his sleep the matter persisted and he dreamed, vast long complicated dreams of Robin making cameras to make pictures of what people saw inside their heads, their own dreams and terrors set down in cibachrome, instincts and hungers and beliefs and he was crying, in the dream he was crying and Robin was crying too, both of them surrounded by pictures that stuck like skin to their hands and through his tears Grant suddenly woke, upright from sleep, his face wet and real crying, Robin crying in the next room, and hurrying out he found Robin on his hands and knees, weeping so furiously it seemed he would vomit, in fact he did begin to retch and Grant knelt, arms around Robin's chest to raise him up, a little, and hold him close: strange feeling, not like holding a woman, to have a man in his arms that way: like a child, a child beaten and distraught, and "Okay," he said, "it's okay, Robin. All right? It's okay."

And past them both piles of drawings, scattered everywhere as if blown by inner winds too vast to fathom or control, all the drawings from the old box under Robin's bed, old drawings like leaves over new ones, some so new Robin's hands still bore the graphite shine, black spoor and they were all signed, all of them, ROBIN ROBIN ROBIN, every single one. And his body moved in Grant's arms, so fiercely it was like a convulsion and Grant's heart in the gallop of fear, real fear to bring sweat to his forehead but it was just vomiting, Robin retching hard and a thin spindle of fluid, richer than saliva, strung from his lips to the carpet and he was spitting, hard, as if to rid his mouth of the taste of bile, of his own sour blood.

"It's all right," helplessly, holding him close as he spit and wept and shook like a beaten dog. "Robin, it's all right."

Like waves, shock waves, the convulsing passed, the weeping, all settling into a profound quiet, a deep somnolent calm almost like a trance state and

Grant relinquished his hold—slowly, slowly, as if he were releasing Robin into deep water—long enough to fetch a washcloth, a towel to wipe Robin's face, slack cheeks, eyes unmoving behind the tender lids. Clean now, Grant dragged the blankets around him, the sleeping bags smelling faintly of Robin himself. Trembling, his hands and arms trembling as after some fierce exertion, he went to sit on the edge of his bed, hands in the towel as if bandaged, until some of the trembling passed.

And then back into the living room, in the muted light from the hallway, stepping cautious over sleeping Robin to gather each and every one of the drawings, and put them back safely into the darkness of the box. All of them; back into the box.

Robin did not draw again, did not so much as pick up a pencil for over a week; and in that time their days seemed lighter, as if some vast hurricane had passed over them, passed without more damage than a glancing touch might cause; Robin's sleep was calmer, his smile often; he took all his medicine, he did all his chores. Grant put away the NEGS box. Neither brought up the drawings, the Clearwater drawings or the others, lying signed and somehow ominous in the long cardboard storage box; instead they talked about the holidays, Halloween past and Thanksgiving coming, Robin said he would make a turkey, a little turkey for them to share.

"I made a turkey once," Grant said. Cold light through the windows, a day off from the lab. He hadn't shaved. His face itched, a strangely pleasant feel. "I got it free from work, and I thought, what the hell. But when I took it out of the oven and started to cut it, all these brains fell out." Smiling, shaking his head, memory's tumble: wet, and hideously clumped, a murder victim's organs might look that way. "I threw the whole thing in the garbage, the brains, all of it. And then somebody told me it was just the gizzards, and neck bones and that stuff, wrapped in paper. Gray paper," and Robin's laugh a brightness, a shine delighted and *"I'll* do the cooking," firmly, "I'll take care of all that." And then, still smiling, "I wonder what turkey brains would look like, if you cooked them. Like people's do?"

And that night, past midnight and Grant found on the bathroom sink a small square of paper, shiny silver on one side: the inside of a candy wrapper still smelling lightly of chocolate and exquisitely sketched upon it with the chill precision of a Dürer etching, a brain: a human brain, its lobes in lubricous elegance bisected by the diagonal tilt of a carving knife, a beautiful knife with a handle shaped like the clenched fingers of a human hand. Half the brain was shaded black; at the bottom of

the drawing itself a tiny stylized "R," its edges
curved like a modest smile.

Half-dark, half-muzzy hallway light, the silver
side of the drawing winking as he folded it in two
and Grant rubbed at his eyes, slowly, rubbed his
forehead and thought he felt behind the shape of
bone the ticking of his own gray brain, mute in
myelinated silence and as alien, as vulnerable as an
animal, a bird: a turkey bent neckless in the rush of
the falling blade.

There were other drawings like that, as simple,
as hideously complex: a burned landscape scattered
with bones, each one numbered at one end and
named on the other, names Grant did not recog-
nize: Shirley, Michael, Sylvia, Ray. A wall made of
books and all the books the same: *Getting to Know
Your Fears.* Over and over, like bricks, like cells. A
woman with huge fatty breasts strung each to each
with chains that, examined in numbing close-up,
revealed themselves to be tiny hands, all of them
missing at least one finger, some missing all but the
thumb. And they were never presented, these
drawings, never shown but only left: like spoor, for
him to find: in the bathroom, in the hallway, like a
note before his door; once he found three of them
in the refrigerator, neat next to a carton of milk.
They were not like any of the other drawings; this
too was something new, maybe another facet of
Robin's need, want gone underground in the darkening days, winter here to stay now, the light gone

at five o'clock and nothing to do but sit in silence, sit drawing until Grant came home.

His medication levels stayed the same; his appetite seemed off. Grant tried to make sure there was always fresh fruit in the refrigerator, expensive out of season but he thought it was important, he was trying to take care of Robin, trying to do his best but wondering, sometimes, what else was wrong, something there like a pale root beneath the early darkness, the long sleeps, the half smiles: something to which he could not put a name or even a feeling, nothing concrete: the shadow on the X ray, the shadow in the hall. And the doubt subliminal now raising its horned head, slit eyes in the night asking: are you right? are you sure? Are you? What did you start, with those Clearwater drawings, what process did you set in motion without knowing it was there to begin? You told him he was taking control of his memories: was he? Is he? Are you sure? You know he sits like a stone when you're gone; you know that, don't you? Do you think it's catatonia? Would you know it if you saw it, the beginning signs, tendrils like cancer in the blood, would you *know*? He doesn't eat much. He doesn't talk much. He watches too much TV, and then when you're sleeping he sits up in the dark and he draws, little tiny drawings of dead men and women with tridents and animals that smile like human beings, all those little drawings and he leaves them in places, do you know why he chooses those places, do you know what those places mean? You don't? But aren't you supposed to be the one in charge here; isn't that what you tell the social worker, the doctor; yourself? Maybe Robin knows different; maybe Robin knows something you don't.

Thanksgiving passed, turkey in slices heated in the microwave, Grant uncapping a jar of instant gravy and in the silverware drawer a drawing tucked in the tines of a fork, a very small drawing of two teeth stained to the gums with something hideous and white and very carefully he closed the drawer without taking out the drawing, did not mention it to Robin; checking again, surreptitious during dinner: gone. And Robin in the living room, in front of the TV, Thanksgiving football and his plate still full and chewing, something, thoughtful motions of the jaw and then pushing his plate away, saying nothing when Grant asked aren't you hungry, don't you want any more? Shaking his head, gaze still on the flicker and dash of the moving players, bright little jerseys and when Grant came back in from scraping the plates Robin was asleep, head on his arms, something small and white in the corner of his mouth.

And all of it part somehow of a larger transformation, the forerunner of change as the first tendrils of fever warn of delirium, as the first shivers of motion warn of the calving floe. You knew—Grant in silence, hands in fists to his temples, sleeping Robin and Christmas ads on the TV now—you knew a long time ago that a new step had to be taken: now it is taking itself, taking Robin: is that what you want? Maybe something big, bigger than you know, maybe big as the onset of disease itself, the black sun rising: do something, do it now.

At work, in the shower, trying to listen to the news but the only real news what was happening there in the living room, flesh labyrinth and sometimes for Grant the irony, you started this, you took him, you were the one. Now what? Now where do you go?

Go: or be taken.

Forced to stay late that night, too many people off early for the holidays; almost ten thirty and the car's heater working poorly, nothing but mist on the windows and rubbing his gloved hands to clear it: smear it: and the endless blinking shill of lights, lights in store windows, bright and haphazard around utility poles, and thinking This is what it must be like to have hallucinations, lights and blurs and colors, all this stuff you can't shut off, you can't get away from without shutting your eyes: and then you're blind. You're blind.

Slipping on ice unseen when he parked, slipping again as he bent to unlock the mailbox, phone bill, electric bill, a letter from Social Security (what now?), a Christmas card from his credit union; no card from Johnna, no card from Maryann; no card from Robin's family. Good.

Hallway trudge, it seemed darker than normal,

the door unlocked to his turning key and Robin
lying on the living-room floor, lying in darkness:
arms crossed, wearing only socks and underwear
and the room very cold, very cold, he had taken to
leaving the windows partly open, more and more as
the weather turned worse. Lying on the floor in one
lamp's light, scar an ominous color, purple as a jac-
aranda and his skin so cold that Grant flinched in
the touching, *as cold as if he* and the thought immediate forced away in the moment of thinking
and "Hey," gently, shaking hand shaking Robin's
shoulder. His voice shaking too. "Hey, Robin. You
okay? Robin?"

Pale eyes opening slowly, slowly, one lid dragging and Robin opened his mouth as well, as
slowly: and on his tongue like a big pill a square of
red: a drawing. One-fingered extraction, Grant
turning it over and seeing there a piece of a larger
drawing, showing only the upper part of a face in
miniature, one eye: and in that eye a look so hideous that instinctively he dropped the paper, shook
it from his fingers like contagion, like raw infection
on his hands and Robin moved, a little, tried to sit
up but fell back, cold skin, one eye still half-closed:
trying to talk. Grant lifting him to a sitting position,
that drowned-flesh feel of his cold body against
Grant's warmth, trying to talk and this time suc-
ceeding, his mouth in wrong-speed motion, a grimace like a smile and he had to say it twice for
Grant to hear; to understand.

"I don't want," head lolling back, "to draw any-more for a while."

"That's okay, that's fine," his own gibbering voice as if from far away, pulling one-handed at the blankets to wrap the nest in clumsy swirls, Robin tilted against the couch and he scrambling to shut the window, shut all the windows, turn on more lights as if light would make it warm. Robin's head sagging to one side, sagging like a drunk's: on his breath a faint sweet smell, like candy: Coke, half a glass of Coke still on the coffee table and "Grant?" loudly, much too loudly, Grant only half a step away. "Grant!"

"I'm here, Robin," trying to sound calm, dry throat and frightened, sweat on his forehead as if swimming in water gone suddenly far too deep, too cold, too full of more than moisture, and "Robin, I'm right here—"

"Grant! Grant!" trying to stand and struggling, wrapped in the blankets, and his head going back and forth, back and forth as if too heavy for the muscles of his neck to support it, so heavy it might begin to split from sheer pressure, leak soft and dribble, gray and red along the cracks: "Grant Grant Grant *Grant Grant*—"

"I'm here!" yelling, yelling right in his face, cold face an inch from his lips and then realizing with an almost paralyzing clarity *He can't hear me*: maybe he couldn't see, either. Maybe he

"GRANT GRANT GRANT GRANT"

what did he see? what did he see right now?

and Grant grabbing Robin, grabbed him hard, lolling head and shouting mouth and held him tight, tight, blankets and squirming flesh (can't do anything but squirm; who said that? who said that?) and spit on Robin's lips: contorted lips, *"Grant Grant"* and Grant squeezing, squeezing his arms and his chest, *"Grant"* but the touch was getting through to him, he was feeling it somehow past the cold. "Grant," and Grant's arms hurting, holding so tight to that cold body and when was he going to get warm, shouldn't he be warm by now, all this motion and screaming and rocking and "Grant?" Just that, his head righting: gazing at Grant and back again inside his eyes: "Grant?"

"I'm right here." His armpits wet, his back; trying to keep his voice calm, feeling as if he could not adequately breathe. "I'm right here, Robin."

"What—" Looking down at himself as best he could in the trussing blankets, looking at Grant. "Are we hurt?"

"No."

"Is anything bad happening?"

Breathing a little better now. His hands on Robin's arms were shaking badly, a tremor uncontrolled; could Robin feel it? "No."

"Did I do something bad?"

"No," strongly, and Robin flinching, as if pinched maliciously and hard: "Then why are you holding me down like this?"

"I'm not holding you down," unlocking his arms, surprising the pain in his muscles, a cramped feeling as if the bones themselves had been compressed. Robin rubbed at his own arms, shivered; yawned hard, sweet soda breath past Grant's face.

"Why's it so cold in here? I opened one of the windows, I—" and silent, rubbing his arms again. "Are you sure I didn't do anything bad?"

"Robin, I'm sure." Standing up, briefly dizzy. "You just sit for a minute, all right? I'm going to get us some tea or something." Tea, or coffee, was it too late for coffee? The stove clock in the kitchen said it was eleven twenty-two. Could that be right? Standing before the stove, eyes closed and it took a minute to notice the water was boiling, steam in a vapor line and in pouring he burned himself, invisible splash; his hands were still shaking hard. What the hell had happened in there, what had *happened*? Should he ask Robin? say something? What?

Carrying out the cups to see Robin pulling on a sweatshirt, head appearing through the fraying neck like a baby from a birth canal: and smiling a little, a tentative smile. "I remember opening the windows, I wanted—I think I wanted to see the sun. It isn't sunny much anymore." Grant sitting on the couch behind him, heavy the feel of his muscles, of his arm as he lifted the cup to drink: as if he lifted through water, through air heavier than lead. "And I laid down on the floor, I put the pencils away and I thought—I said, I'm going to call Grant at work."

Silence.

"And then what?" but softly, almost no question, tea steam before his eyes and Robin's shrug, eyebrows up in innocent chagrin: "I don't remember. It was really dark, I know that. And I couldn't, I couldn't *see*, really. Not with my eyes."

"You said you didn't want to draw anymore for a while."

Robin gazing at him as if he had not heard that; perhaps he hadn't. "Do you know," consideringly, "what angels are?"

Angels. Do you know—just answer him, just answer what he asks you. "Angels, they're like spirits, right? Good spirits. And the bad ones are devils. Right?"

"I guess," eyes closing in another big yawn. He drank; one drop of tea on his lip like a tear, like a raindrop. His scar was paler now. "Some people say there's guardian angels, you know, your own personal angel to look out for you." Another drink. "I really don't want to draw anymore."

"Robin, you don't have to do anything you don't want to. Okay? Not for me, or anybody else." His own mouth creaking open, tired all over, the day's fatigue one stone in the load of exhaustion, being scared really wears you out. "You don't have to be—"

"But I feel like I'm letting you down." Hands

open on his knees, that guileless face: pale gaze
fixed on his. "I know what my drawings—what you
think of my drawings, I know they help you. I don't
want to take that away from you."

A silence like the space between one heartbeat
and another, one turn and another, one road and
the road that leads away into the dark. Robin's
hands like wounds, white at the tips as if the blood
had fled; bled; blinkless his gaze and in that look a
light that was to Grant the next step in the dance:
the right step: it had come to him at last, this way,
past terror and fatigue, cloaked in the gentle guise
not even of idea, but feeling. A feeling, like love.
Or discovery. Or decision.

"Well, then," sweat on his back, on the backs of
his hands and his own voice very measured, very
reasonable, like the voice of a stranger coming easy
from his throat: had he really been yelling and
shaking, just a minute before? *But I feel like I'm
letting you down.* "Then we'll just do something
else, okay? We won't, we won't have drawings anymore, but we'll do something else."

"Like what?"

"I don't know," rightness like light in his eyes,
the room warming around them, like a body coming back to life, the resurrecting process inexorable
as the action of death itself. "I don't know yet. But
I'll think of something good."

❖　❖　❖

What he thought of, through the holidays, glitter and bustle from which they stayed safely away, was the idea of experimenting with altered states. At first just a shine, tail end of the light of rightness he had felt there beside Robin, the cold room coming to life again around them, it now seemed a natural outgrowth of the schizophrenic experience, itself an altered state so relentless that any small experimentations they did would surely do no harm. Robin did not cease drawing completely, despite his words; but now they came unexpected, and small, and were kept not secret but to himself; Grant had seen none of them, and would not ask to be shown; that, he felt, would be wrong.

But in some ways, although he missed the drawings, missed them more even than he expected, there was something right about their absence; they had become in some strange way peripheral to the palpable sense of a larger mystery, to the sense of change itself; like the key on a map: we are in a new country here. They would still be harbingers, signposts on the way to walk; but in themselves, he thought, they were no longer the way itself. The way was in Robin, of Robin: the way in was, finally, to go deeper and deeper still.

There had been no repetition—not yet—of that frightening scene in the living room, the dark and the cold and Robin in some place where he could neither see nor respond; but Grant was cautious, and kept watch: he wanted to be ready if it hap-

pened again, remembering like vertigo endured
that sick sense of helplessness, worse: of ignorance,
a stupidity harsh as malice, a not-knowing that
could have made everything worse. He had thought
he knew what to do in an emergency, and then an
emergency occurred for which he had no remedy;
and the remedy for *that* was vigilance: and knowledge, more clandestine midnight read-throughs of
the NEGS box books. And if, now, they were to swim
in these new waters, he would have to be prepared
even more thoroughly, heroically prepared for both
the things that might happen and the things, so far
as he could anticipate their genesis, that in themselves could not be glimpsed or guessed from
where they stood now. Read, he told himself. Read,
read, read.

Prudent, he did: a lot, as much as he could find,
amazing the amount of possibilities beneath that
blanket term of altered states. Hypnosis, dream
therapy, trance; sensory deprivation, sleep deprivation, out-of-body inducement. The chemical hydra
of drugs—tranquilizers, narcotics, hallucinogens—
he ruled out entirely: they would interact with
Robin's neuroleptics, they would hurt him in ways
both subtle and strong: there was to be no possibility of hurt here, none at all. And the human mind
was surely more potent than any drug; especially
Robin's mind, the mind behind those eyes.

December, cold and dark when he got home,
simple dinners and the evenings spent in quiet:

Grant reading, making notes: Robin reading too, or watching TV in silence, or simply lying with his eyes closed; he was not, he told Grant, sleeping when he did this.

"Just resting, right?"

No answer at first, then Robin's shrug, oblique. "I guess," he said. "I guess it's resting." Reaching for his glass of juice; they had stopped drinking Coke, both of them, Grant had cut down on his coffee, more expensive fresh vegetables and fruits but it was like being an athlete, wasn't it? though far more important, far more taxing and austere the experience, like being a monk, a mystic: a visionary, though he did not use that word to Robin, it was too close to hallucination. Instead he said *idea* a lot: we'll explore ideas, or We'll see some new things, we'll have some new ideas. He said *we* a lot, too, and was proud of it: this was something they could fully share, things they would do together. Together.

"It's like a trip, Robin," looking up from his book, *The Reality of Dreams*, six hundred pages and an index. "It's like we're going somewhere."

Sylvia Plath's *Crossing the Water* in Robin's hands, pale bookmark fingers held still around the curling paperback page. "Where are we going?"

Thinking: then the honest answer, exhilarating in its honesty. "I don't really know."

"Is it somewhere good?"

"Yes." Firmly. "Yes it is. You know I wouldn't take you anywhere bad."

"Oh, I know that," mildly, as if Grant might have announced that two plus two was four. "You don't have to tell me that."

It snowed the day before Christmas Eve: Robin went out with an empty cookie tin, to fill and put in the freezer: "There's never enough snow," smiling, nose running, jeans soaked black from the knees down. "I like to save some for later."

"I used to do that," when I was a kid. "But it always melts."

"Mine won't," shoving it behind a squared pile of frozen dinners, Healthy Dinners with a smiling heart on the package. "It'll still be good by New Year's."

Christmas Day they both slept late, woke to more snow, heavy and driving: and presents, Grant's to Robin wrapped in red reindeer paper, Robin's to him wrapped in heavy wrinkled tinfoil, marked with felt-tip marker to a black and beaded smear. "You can't really read it," black-tipped fingers, his smile apologetic, "but it says 'Merry Christmas to my best friend.' "

My best friend. "Open yours first," Grant said. The tinfoil had a strange smell, as if it had been used to wrap food; it probably had. "Go on, I want to see if you like it."

"I know I'll like it." Carefully tearing the tape from the paper, a slowness exquisite and exquisitely irritating but Grant was patient, standing silent at Robin's side to see it opened: a heavy blue sweater, soft as cashmere, marked at the left breast with two swooping initials in purest white: R.T.

"For Robin Tobias, see?" He had guessed on the size: it seemed it would fit and then Robin was pulling it on over the clothes he already wore, old T-shirt, old flannel shirt and robe, he was often cold even though the temperature in the apartment was controlled to 68. The sleeves bunched like Popeye; the blue washed out Robin's pale eyes: looking down at the initials, gently pulling the material forward to see them, plucking it out like a breast.

"Do you like it?" Grant said, somewhat worried; it had been expensive, but it was warm; and he did not like to see Robin go around in piles of clothes, it made him look—it made him look like . . . a street person, like someone for whom no one cared. And Robin was well cared for, anyone could see that.

Robin was petting one arm with the other, looking up so Grant could see his smile. "Grant, it's really nice, I really like it." A pause; petting his arm again, up and down, up and down as if he were nervous. "Now you open yours."

The foil, when removed, smelled distinctly of meat: chicken, Grant thought, old dry chicken and now his hands smelled too. Carefully setting the foil aside, he opened the box, a Healthy Dinners box bulging slightly at the middle, and pulled out a little object wrapped in layers and layers of blue toilet paper. Unwrapping as Robin watched, bright eyes and blue paper and then uncoiled like a stripped mummy, finally revealed: a doll, a little pink plastic doll with short yellow hair half on end with static, dressed in a napkin stiff with glitter and safety pins and glue; the face near obliteration beneath the marker makeup job, heavy blue eye shadow, heavy pink lips. On her back something like butterfly wings, made of a carefully notched paper plate, colored lavish and sumptuous with glitter and with gold; behind the wings a stapled-on ribbon, bright red Christmas ribbon still gently scarred by its shape unraveled, the factory prefold.

Eagerly, "It's a guardian angel," reaching for it, the tremble of his hands. "See? Your name's here, on the back—" turning the doll around to show beneath the wings GRANT COTTO, stick-on Day-Glo letters from the drugstore, the kind kids buy to decorate a folder, a schoolbook. "The ribbon's so you can wear it, if you want. Or you can keep it somewhere close by, and it'll—you know. It'll guard you. It's a *guardian* angel, see?"

"I—oh, yeah. I see." The doll depending from its ribbon like a body on a gibbet, gold and glitter, yellow and pink and blue. "You made it all yourself, didn't you?"

"Yeah," smiling; proud. Turning the doll over and over in his hands, but gently, as if she were a living thing, a creature capable of pain at a touch unguarded. The crackle of glue on the skirt; the distant smell of meat. "I made it for you."

Grant took it from him, ribbon around his index finger, holding it dangling like a Christmas ornament, the ornaments Robin had made for their two-foot desktop tree: stars and crescent moons, squat little spangled snowmen round as balls of dough; no wonder he had gone through so much glitter, Grant had been vacuuming it out of the carpet for weeks. The doll swung, its hair still spiked with static, its war-paint face turned away from him; have we been properly introduced?

"You have to name her," Robin said. "She needs a name." A pause, then, "Will you take her to work with you?"

Imagining: the people at Cade Color, John and his crude loud humor; imagining the little angel hanging from the swing-arm lamp, hanging there for everyone to see. "I don't think so," slowly, trying to think where to put it, where to hang it now. "I mean, it's just work, right, it's not where I live." There was a swing-arm lamp in the bedroom, smaller than the one at his desk. With Robin following, he hung the angel there, the ribbon fitting neatly over the socket housing of the shade, low enough that, the light on, it shone full on the dress and wings to make of them a light distinct, pure gold: and Robin in admiration: "She looks really good there, Grant, *really* good!"

And Grant turning to Robin, one hand to squeeze his shoulder, bunched with fabric through the sweater's skin: "You did a great job on it—on her. It's a great present, Robin, thank you."

"Everyone needs to be guarded." Smiling, at Grant, at the angel in her circulating swing. "Even you."

It snowed all day, hard snow, nothing picturesque; they ate Christmas dinner—turkey breast, instant mashed potatoes runny with too much milk —and watched a Christmas special with the sound off; Robin fell asleep before the television, still wearing his sweater, Grant on the couch reading *Inner Journeys*. Your mind and you. His mind and me; our minds together. Snow still against the window; thinking of Robin leaning out in thunderstorms, thinking of driving to work in the morning, driving through the cold as if through a foreign country: and in its own way it was true, work *was* like another country, far far away and the people there were nothing, really, to him, John and his mockery, his dirty jokes, Dave and his coffee machine, Grace and her productivity fetish, what difference did any of it make to him? *This* was life, here in this apartment, this room: a journey in mind, a book in his hand: Robin on the floor, sleeping; an angel in the bedroom, to guard their every move. Wasn't there a prayer like that, a psalm? *They will guard you in all your ways.* Yes. In all our ways, our journeys: no matter how difficult, or how very far we go.

The New Year: a paralytic cold, no overtime; snow on the ground gray and heavy as lead. Grant and Robin sitting on a blanket on the living-room floor, blinds drawn against the chilly white light of a Saturday afternoon.

"It says here," Grant's finger marking his place, *Dreaming Real*, "that changing your sleep patterns can put you in touch with your dreams better, you can remember them more, stuff like that. So what we're going to do is keep staying up. For twenty-four hours, stay up, and then try to sleep for twenty-four hours, or at least keep lying down. Do you think you can do that?"

"Sure. I guess." Pinching one sleeve of the blue sweater, aimless scissoring fingers. "I used to sleep for days at the hospital." Pinch pinch pinch. "But I was on drugs then. We're not going to take any drugs, are we?"

"No," firmly. "We're going to do all this with your brain. —Our brains, I mean." A pause. "We're not even going to drink coffee. Tea, it says we can have tea. But no coffee." It said a lot of other things, too: Robin asked a lot of questions: what if we don't have any dreams? fall asleep anyway? have nightmares? But he accepted Grant's explanations, some of them from the book, some of them popped instant from Grant's mouth; but he had read, and read, he knew what he was talking about, he knew what they were doing. After this it would be forty-eight hours, then catnaps, as many as they could take: and write everything down, how they felt, what they thought, if they dreamed. If the dreams changed at all, from more sleep, or less; document that change, keep track. "Like explorers," Robin said. "Like Lewis and Clark. Finding a new world," and Grant deeply pleased by this confidence, Robin's confidence in himself, in Grant, in the two of them as a unit. See—to that inner eye, Johnna's eye, the medical eye always creased in condemnation—see, it *is* making him better, it's something he needed to do, get away from that institutionalized mentality, the idea that only doctor knows best. Doctors like Kaiser, looking without sight; therapists like Johnna, who thought they already saw all there was to see. An open mind, that was it, that was what Robin had: despite the schizophrenia, the sometimes side effects that slowed him into hands-clasped silence, despite the years of confusion and pain, his mind was open, wide open, ready, *happy* to think new thoughts. They should all—Grant's smile now as proud as a parent's—be so open as Robin; as me.

They had been up that morning at nine thirty; by evening, eleven, Robin was ready to sleep, head sideways, leaning on his shoulder; they drank tea, played cards, left the windows open. Played music till one, then took turns with the Walkman, loud

pop music, nothing slow or sad. Drank more tea.
Grant's eyes burning, Robin's scar brighter, he said
his hands were cold and hid them up his sleeves:
nothing up my sleeves! and that started them
laughing, silly laughter, stupid droll jokes and they
laughed till they were tired. Very tired, propped up
by the window and "Let's count the stars," Robin's
face very close to his, his breath sweet and hot from
another cup of tea. "Let's count all of them and
give them names." A pause. "Did you name her
yet?"

Name who? Her. The doll. Lying, trying to
think, "Yeah, I did. I did." Cold air in his face, his
brain like an old machine, wet gears, missing parts.
"I named her Angela."

"Hey, that's a *good* name!" with real pleasure,
and scrambling up to go: and back, holding Angela
by her ribbon, holding her in the draft from the
window, and they both sat watching the doll swing
in the air, dark air, her wings shiny and fragile,
suddenly so fragile in the cold; fashioned, like her
nameless sisters, brothers, those sexless creatures
from every myth in the world, to fly the ether, *ethe-*
real, breathing airlessness, vacuum, able to fly past
the concept of height itself: *up. Up.*

"She's really nice," Grant said.

"She likes it here," Robin said.

And the angel, Angela, swung gently, and
gently, the cold reflected dark upon her wings.

* * *

They did not have spectacular dreams; they did not dream, in fact, at all, or did so at least without remembrance; the spiral notebooks were empty, there were no notes to make. Long sleep after such long waking left them unrefreshed; tired at work, Grant making one small blunder after another, burning his wrist on the coffee maker, knocking and spilling, tired. Home to find Robin half-asleep at the table, a frozen dinner blackened to plastic on the microwave carousel. Neither had the energy to clean the mess; Grant ate half a package of supermarket salami, Robin ate animal crackers. Lions and elephants, bears and camels, pale brown and nearly shapeless and "I went to this zoo once," Robin said through a mouthful of crumbs; the crackers were stale. "From the group home, you know? Like an outing?"

Salami between his teeth, ropy and faintly bitter; maybe it was stale too. "Field trip," he said.

"Right. Right. There were like eight of us, and the aides, you know, and we went into the bird house, the aviary? And one of the birds on the branches, you know, behind the bars, kept looking at me." Pineapple juice, a little glass bottle in his hand, the yellow label peeling. "Looking and looking, and finally when we were ready to leave it said to me, 'It's cold. Flying is cold.' "

Flying is cold. The greasy feel of the salami against his fingers; he coughed, wiped shiny hands together; knew better than to ask whether the bird

had been a parrot, or toucan, or whatever other
bird could be trained to talk; it had not spoken
aloud, he was sure of that, or if it had could not
have been heard by others. Flying is cold; well. "It
probably is," he said.

"Do you want any of these?" Pushing the package toward Grant. "I'm going to lie down awhile."

"No, go ahead. I'll clean up here," closing the
crackers, folding the salami wrapper shut and he
thought about that, the bird at the zoo, the zoo
itself: eight patients, and how many aides? Two?
Three at the most? Spring or summer, hats and
shorts and maybe nametags, some people wander-
ing off, maybe, or maybe getting agitated, nervous,
scared by the crowds; going someplace else to eat
their lunches, brown bag lunches in a sturdy
totebag carried by one of the aides. Sitting on the
grass, smoking; some of the people might not eat,
or be able to; they would all be stared at, no matter
how far away they sat, how isolated from the main
picnic grounds: look at them, people would say,
instant the stigma, the recognition that something
is wrong. Look at them, bread on the grass, crumpled plastic and the aides, coaxing maybe or maybe
stern, or just tired from a night of yelling, or side
effects, a bad long night and a day at the zoo. And a
talking bird, Robin's face pointed up, rapt, Grant
could see the expression as if he had been there,
had in fact seen it himself: everything of Robin,
there in his eyes: and: Flying is cold.

Shaking his head, disengaging from thought to think of Robin, now, to look in the living room. Box of crackers in hand forgotten to the touch, and Robin not in his sleeping bag, not in the living room at all and Grant called his name, "Robin," not loudly; no answer. "Robin," with more purpose, remembering the crackers long enough to set them down, heedless anywhere; where is he? Not in the bathroom; not in Grant's bedroom; he could not be in the kitchen that Grant had just left so "Robin," more firmly, and back to the living room to see what he had missed before, not in his nest, no, but there beside the couch, almost beneath it: eyes closed, hands narrow on his chest as if replicating a sarcophagus, prayerful, silent and his scar vivid on his skin: "Robin," very quietly, not meaning to be heard but his eyes, opening, rapt again and words, something, sounds from him that made no sense and Grant bending, one hand out, gently, gently: not calling his name, not trying to touch him but simply to be close enough to touch if that became needed, wanted. Bending, awkward stance and that red, red scar, Robin said something else and it occurred to Grant, standing there, formed perfect as dread the notion that he had not checked Robin's medication, had he, recently at all. Had he? All this reading, and planning; and tired at work; but not tired now, frozen in this bent position, had he checked it? When, last?

What if.

Knowing with perfect logic that no decompensation could yet have begun, still the idea was strong enough to bring to mind another, the inner picture of Robin without medication, nothing, that mind in all its naked whorling extremis and pain: signs and wonders: what then? Three worlds out of balance: his, Robin's and the world created by them, both its facets—the day-to-day and the dream—fractured in that nakedness, that whorl: all of it dependent like a card house on one particular card, that daily medicating benediction; fragility and impermanence beneath his feet, a house built not on sand but air; the ether. Flying is cold.

And Robin murmuring, almost half a smile and "Nighttime?" lightly, a whole world recognizable and suddenly like a slap Grant thought *He's dreaming*; and out of the posture painful, shuffling quick through the books on the table to find the red notebook, his notebook; to open it; to write it down.

They gave up sleep, then gave up deprivation; not working, Grant said, tired-eyed and more than tired, this just isn't working at all. Robin, head down, mumbling into one hand cupped around his mouth as if the words were stones, bones, seeds to catch and plant in some fresher, more friendly soil; mumbling without looking up, no smile, crumpled somehow and colder than the ice on the windows, the ice outside in the air to chill in touch's instant the unsuspecting lungs.

"What?" but gently, he was extra gentle with Robin these days; a strain—he was tired, too, worn out from the double burden of being both participant and director, and carry as well that other burden of their daily life; who was there to take care of him?—but necessary, given those eyes, that hunch and slump; that scar that never now seemed to pale. "I didn't hear you."

A long minute for breath, then soft, soft as that breath expelled: "I don't want to do that anymore. I —it gets so I can't draw at all, not anything. Not even little ones." A sigh into the cupping palm. "I don't want you to get mad, though, Grant. I know you have stuff you want us to do, you want to get—"

"Robin, listen, forget all—no, *listen*," hand out, up, emphatic, Robin's face before him stilled and tense; and sorry? Sad? "If you don't like it, if you're having a hard time with anything, we'll stop. Okay? We'll just stop. Because it's you that we have to—"

watch

"—take care of, okay? I'm not the artist here, it's you. So if you don't want to do the dream sleep anymore, we won't. Okay? Is that okay with you?"

The smile manifest as warm relief, it was okay with him; there would however be no dispute if it was not. This knowledge a power Grant could not admit to accepting, but there were more things unacceptable, things he did not want to try to name: to admit: but there they were, like a small black spot, a stain in the middle growing larger like waves spread by breezes, little breezes; but what happens if the wind picks up, what happens in a storm? Remembering that wretched helplessness, Robin staring in the mirror, Robin writhing blind and in his head the cold reminding voice, *Aren't you the one in charge here? Aren't you?*

What if a plant nurtured in darkness finds within itself a taste for night? Whose fault, then? and whom in charge?

Nighttime? Robin had said, that pleased dreamer's voice: it had not been a dream. Grant knew this now but carried the admittance like a rock; it was not in the end Robin's reluctance to continue that kept them from doing so, but Grant's own squeamishness, his urge to skirt these darker waters, crawl back like a child from the twisting branch unsafe to bear his weight. No dream at all but some kind of trance, but not from the illness, no; no. And his own notes trailing off, jittering hands and he remembered each moment with the hyperclarity memory brings, sometimes, to minutes of high shame; or fear, though fear trails its own dilutants, its own clouds and fissures like drugs to blur the recollection and the blood in the brain itself, black adrenaline surge to make ten feet a thousand, one scream twenty in the middle of the night.

But he *knew* what he had seen, heard: that milky smile, rolling eyes and Robin's body bucking,

once, there on the couch and reaching hands wild
for something, something, it all came like lightning, like a heart attack avenging, and Grant had
dropped his notebook, spiral red and stupid pen in
hand still like a useless medical syringe, nostrum
petty now before this, whatever it was, what was it?
What?

Robin's voice, speaking: moving mouth as if full
of blood, or nubby bones: moving strongly and then
    the voice changing

and a smile exquisite, tender, tender, something brown leaking wetly from his mouth, lower
lip loose unto grotesquerie, unjoining in the smile
and

"It's *cold* here."

"I *like* it."

And then the vomiting, huge and hot and unexpected but instant beside it the return to normal,
normal, Robin's eyes wide and *there*, all of him
back now and all of him in terror, grabbing for
Grant to roll without balance from the couch and
into the slick spread of his own vomit, a cry of
disgust and more, heavy, as if he had been eating
for weeks, rich foods, heavy foods in chunks and
spatters and finally subsiding, drenched and hitching air in his chest; "God," thick through his nose,
wiping helplessly at his mouth and face with hands
as fouled, "oh God, Grant," and weeping then,
loathing's weakness in the way his hands lay limp as
dead against his wet smelly body; and Grant weak

too, hands shaking so hard it was comic, finally, bent to wipe and they both had to laugh, shivering laughter but it was something to do, something positive and between them they got Robin into the shower, their clothes into the wash; and Grant alone in the kitchen, hot water in the sink and wiping his mouth, wiping his mouth, wiping his mouth to pain and past and seeing there on the tremble of his fingers tiny crescents, lines etched in dark brown vomit beneath his nails.

Robin had slept for two days after that, long days during which Grant fought at each instant the urge to run home or at least call, call, once an hour, and hurrying past John and Grace grinning together, leaving the lab and he wanted to turn on them, himself at bay and What the fuck's so funny? What's funny? And said nothing, sat at his desk, worktable, checking a job number, light a hot circle and for an instant he thought he could smell that vomit again, rich in rot as any humus; a garden: what grows there?

And back home in a literal sweat, *hurry*, to see Robin sleeping, there in his sleeping bags, his blankets and nest: real sleep, not trance and maybe dreamless or if not then harmless dreams alone, pale face and pale scar, cold hands curled and his posture suggestive, now, of something, something white and sightless and cool to the wondering touch and Grant thought, Like a chrysalis, that's what it is.

Spun living tomb; to hold that which becomes.
What?

And Robin turned, there, in his sleep, a motion
very small: and sighed: and Grant for a moment
imagined him gone and the room as empty, no
blankets, nest, no sleeping bags, no books and notebooks and no one, no other there; and shivered like
a child, hands open, and turned quickly gone so as
not to wake the sleeping dream.

Hypnosis, they found, was silly, or at least silly to
them; you are getting very sleepy, half the time
they could not do it without some overlay of hilarity
and then the hilarity relentless in ascendance,
Robin making faces, Grant waving an imaginary
watch and so they abandoned it before, properly, it
was begun; there was after all a measure of accom-
plishment in the recognition of a dead end.

Next, Grant thought, judicious to himself in the
shower, a morning's half erection reduced by the
distracting power of thought, next we'll try sensory
deprivation. Not a tank; he had thought of that, the
salty womb where one pays by the hour, rejecting it
for many reasons, not all of them obvious. It would
not, could not be in water; their own little tub was
insufficient and anyway might prove dangerous if
he was not right there beside Robin; and how could
that be, without violating the parameters of deprivation? The darkness cannot be entered other than
alone.

Soaping his scrotum, his shoulders, the backs of his knees, if not the tub then what? A darkroom, he thought, and thought for half an instant of the main darkroom at work, his own small darkrooms scattered through his past: this room, this bathroom was small enough to work, to light-proof: cardboard at the tiny window, towels beneath the door; a blanket on the floor to provide not stimulus—no blankets in the house could provide that, they were all too worn down, too nubless and old—but a layer of protection from the floor itself; and lie there in the dark; yes. Yes.

And where will you be? the question answered in the asking: the hall closet. Take out the box with the boots, the old shoes, take out the carton filled square with some old gift, Christmas gift to himself and Johnna, some kitchen toy they had never begun to think of using; pyramid outside the door and he inside with his own blanket, his earplugs, his bottle of water. For a moment the image became so strong that even in the hot spray he shuddered, but it was a small shudder more of excitement than anything else; not fear, he told himself emphatically, drying off brisk and rough. I'm not afraid. Robin's not afraid, either.

Robin's smile accepted; Robin's first offhand suggestions were better than Grant's plans. "The bathroom, sure," nodding up from his perusal of the newspaper, the back page; the weather page.

"That way I can pee if I have to. But what're you going to do?"

"Hold it," Grant said. "Or use a coffee can, I don't know."

"We should wear blindfolds, too," Robin said. "Probably."

Probably; yes. There was beneath the careless square of the paper another pile of paper; drawing paper; Grant did not mention it, tried not to let his gaze move that way but Robin was aware, aware of him and said, very gently, "I did a couple yesterday. You can see them, if you want."

If he wanted. This apartment, his job, all his waking thoughts and energies, his imagination and his money and his time: like a laser, focused on this one thing, this passion-fed engine that in these few months—so few, really—had changed everything: and all of it built on the drawings, Robin's art: and Robin. You can see them; if you want.

They were both the same view, from differing perspectives: a long hallway ending in a door. From beneath the door was not light but the suggestion of the possibility of light: as if there might have been a light in the room beyond but that light not yet fully illuminated, on maybe but under a cloth, a scarf; a bushel? The first view showed the door and its light as terminus, a destination not perhaps to be desired but recognized as unavoidable. The second, viewed a foot from the door itself, showed through its cracks, grains, its splinterings and sore slivers that beyond it everything was light, everything: light so particular and vast that the burning eye could not fix on it for long. The same dull hallway, the same ugly door: hell, and heaven.

"We can do it tomorrow, if you want," Robin ruffling the newspaper at Grant, small sharp noises to get his attention. "Grant? We can start tomorrow."

"Oh. Okay. —No, wait," trying to stop looking, to put down the drawings; to think concretely. "Tomorrow's the social worker," that office again, that woman; her forms and all their forms together and it always took much longer than expected, no matter how long they had expected it to be. "Thursday I have to work. Friday's a half day, let's do it then."

"All right," serenely, folding the paper closed. Beneath the other sections, sports and food and local news, lay a fat black pencil, thick as a finger and pointing at the drawing, lay down before it, of the hallway and the door that led to darkness: to the feel and smell and surety of hell. Robin did not see it, or at least Grant did not see him if he did, and with one swift minute movement rolled the pencil one turn over, one turn only, to point to the other hallway, the doorway into light.

On Thursday night Grant had a dream, begun as an ordinary sex dream, himself standing up in a hallway preparing to fuck a pretty blonde woman wearing a dark blue dress he had seen Johnna wear on many occasions, semispecial occasions, it was not like her usual serious shrinkwear at all. The best part about it was a deep neckline into which if one were nimble, and dexterous, both breasts could be scooped for viewing; and touching: he was touching them in the dream and the woman was smiling, eyes closed and smiling, her immaculate ass pressed tightly against the orange smudge of the hallway wall.

"I don't understand exactly," the woman said; Grant's erection so pure, now, it was painful, painfully ground into her thigh. "But I believe you need sunglasses, or something. It gets pretty hot in there."

"Blindfolds," he said. "We're going to use blindfolds," and then all at once they were done fucking, she was smoothing down her dress, she was directing him to a room where he might wipe up, wash; there was semen all over his legs, on his pants, dark gray pants on which the stain seemed enormous; and with a feeling of adolescent shame he made his way into the room

which was filled entirely with light

and Robin was there, bent over a table, bent drawing but not (he saw as he approached, smiling, the smile dead on his mouth in an instant) his Robin at all: oh God not his Robin, this cold bright face and

"Look"

he wanted to run but

"*Look* at this"

and the paper turning toward him, a feeling like gas in his lungs, napalm, liquid fire and the paper in his own hands now, inescapable

and he was running out the door, he had dropped the paper, running in a terror that was nearly comic for his flapping pants and his jouncing flabby cock shriveling more with each bound, running and running and he saw that he was bleeding, from the nose, the mouth; bleeding slippery viscous plasma from the palms of both his hands.

And woke up then, consciousness instant and aware as if wakened by a burglar with a knife to the throat, a gun to the temple: the little black hallway the bullet rides. Here you go. Shaking, he rose from the bed, turning on slow the friendly light— how would it shine?—and moving into the hallway, the living room to check on Robin.

Who lay on his back, in the middle of his sleeping bags, the nest in disarray; sleeping normally, peacefully, silently; without a smile, or a frown. Beside him was a small rectangle of papers, a pencil diagonal atop; new drawings, Grant thought, knew.

And wanted to go and look at them; turn them over in the half dark, silent the motion of paper: and did not move: and did not move at all.

Robin cleaned the bathroom, hands and knees on cleansered tile; scrubbing the tub, industrious as if in concoction of a potion, a plaster, a voodoo drink:

the gathering of hairs, effluence, the body's shed ephemera; what the gypsies knew. Each hair contains the soul entire; like a hologram, who said that? Grant had read it in a book somewhere, it sounded like part of a poem. When was the last time he had read a poem?

Sitting at the kitchen table, filling out another form, a long form from the social worker; it seemed these forms must be generated, regenerated quarterly, either that or they were lying to him for some dumb reason of their own, maybe they had lost the damned thing. NAME, AGE, SEX; for God's sake. Robin blurring past, rag in hand, sponge. Smiling. ADDRESS. DATE OF LAST HOSPITALIZATION. LENGTH OF STAY: Forever; and never again. NEXT OF KIN: None. I am his next of kin, he wanted to write, print his own name neatly, GRANT COTTO, that's me. He left it blank, then, scowling, went back and printed TOBIAS, Parents. And the sister, don't forget the sister.

"We can use these," and rags in his face, scarves, something bright, "for the blindfolds. Okay?" Leaning back a little in the weary chair, faint flesh perfume: Johnna's scarves, one blue severe, one ugly purple paisley, found who knows where and Robin's smile almost too bright: "Okay?"

"Sure," Grant nodding. "If you want to, sure," and Robin gone again, Grant himself setting aside the pencil, rising for coffee, thinking. Thinking: He sure is excited about this. More than usual, even more than me. Thinking: and not thinking, the mind unconscious roaming, roaming, associations linking like bridges, like arms across water, like hands in the dark. Excitement; eagerness; a manic eagerness, almost? No? Then what: something deeper, older, colder—*the dream-Robin, not-Robin: cold*—cold from what? Where?

From beneath the surface, said the connecting mind; from underground.

Transfigurings begun subtle as a seed—when? when? remembering only the disasters, the face in the mirror, the thrashings, the convulsions on the floor, the arc of spattering vomit; why are all the bad things brightest? why? and are they more than that, are they in fact, must be in fact a pattern, and seen as a pattern in clear emergence; something else is going on, something beyond—how far beyond—what he or even Robin with his more intimate knowledge, everyday knowledge of the space beyond the norm can, by its nature or theirs, understand, anticipate; control.

Who's in charge here? The mocking mind, now. *Who? You?*

Coffee in hand, not remembering the moment of pouring, of stirring; dry: is this what it's like to have blackouts? Voices in the head, his own voice warped by irony and self-delusion: shit. Shit. Robin was singing something, the same phrase over and over like music-box music, scarves on the table where he left them, curled coy as an unopened letter, a love letter from someone you hate. Scarves; and the forms half-finished, and a roll of silver foil, shook foil opened to seal the bathroom windows into darkness, into night.

Thursday night, trying to sleep, sleeping poorly; was Robin sleeping poorly too? He did not go out to check, to see; kept struggling toward sleep, remembering it seemed in each approaching instant the dream of the hallway that had frightened him so much. Scared awake by the alarm, heart thumping and the memory of another dream, a dream unremembered and maybe better so: today was the day.

He had read a lot about sensory deprivation—a few of the books called it sense dep—or what he supposed was a lot; it was hard to tell, hard sometimes too to assess the quality of the books. Inferior road map, perfect guide? There was no knowing, you had to judge for yourself; he had to judge for himself and for Robin too. Read enough and a picture will come clear; and it had done so.

So. Driving home from work, one last book finger-marked and Robin meeting him, solemn at the door: "I got it all ready." Scar pale, but a certain pallor about his lips, almost a yellow color; ivory. "We're all ready now."

"You know," continuing, that same too rapid pace, "I used to be a little afraid of stuff like this," as Grant shut the door, set down the book (*Inner Peace: Finding a New You Through Sensory Modification*; some of them called it modification, maybe "deprivation" scared people away). "I used to think I didn't want to spend so much time left alone with myself."

Sweatpants, bare feet; the blue R.T. sweater, the Christmas gift and in his hands the scarves, blue and paisley purple. "The bathroom's all ready," he said. "We can start whenever you want."

"Robin," putting out his hand, conscious of a care used in other situations, extreme situations; why did he think to use it now? "Listen, we don't have to do this right now, we can wait a little bit if you—"

"Oh no," earnestly. Earnestly. "I want to do it, Grant, I only told you about being, about being scared, you know, because I thought, I thought you would want to know. But I'm not scared now. Not with you, you're going to be right there. Right? So I don't feel scared at all."

"Well. Okay," and he did not want to show doubt, did not want to feel doubt; why should he doubt, now? what was the big deal? They had done other things, tried other avenues that in the end had hurt neither of them or the drawings, Robin's capacity to draw, either. So what was he worried about? "Just let me take a piss, all right, and we can get started."

Careful into the bathroom, water bottle and box

of tissues, Robin's sleeping bag on the floor and careful not to dribble on it inadvertently; shaking off, and seeing the mirror covered, too, covered in foil. Shiny side in. Did Robin think it would reflect light, somehow, and needed the covering? What did it matter, anyway? He was trying to be thorough, he was doing a good job.

"See," opening the closet door in the instant of the flush, Grant's reappearance and Robin eager, even anxious to show him the emptied closet lined with a blanket taken from the bed, identical water bottle, an empty plastic milk jug—"It's easier than a coffee can"—and there on the outer doorknob Angela, wings bent to accommodate her new post, Robin's one finger to set her gently swinging; smiling a little and Grant smiled too.

"Well this is great," Grant said. "You did a really great job, Robin, thanks." The closet itself smelled like dust, warm musty flavor and for a moment he did not want to go into it, did not want to sit down and shut the door in the dark. "You need anything else? Or do you want to start now?"

"Now," Robin said at once. "Let's do it now."

Into the bathroom, Robin stepping delicate and sure onto the sleeping bag, sitting down to rearrange the space—bottle, tissues, a small drawing pad (and how had Grant missed that, before? pad and pencil)—and hold up with two hands the blue scarf: ready: bind my eyes.

"See you in a while," Grant smiling through the

surge of uneasiness, a sudden footless feeling that made him want, almost want to say *Let's not do it now, let's wait.* But that was stupid; what was wrong here? Nothing. Nothing. "I'll be thinking of you."

"Me too," and the hands now across his lap, Zen posture, each finger curled just a little and Grant tied the blindfold tight enough to hold, loose enough, as he demonstrated, to easily remove.

"See? You can get out of it anytime you want, okay?" Eyes sealed again and now he moved past the door, closing it almost to upon the sudden sight of Robin's face revealed, eyes bare in a gaze of such naked strangeness that Grant stopped at once, *what the hell* but then Robin smiled, a smile determined and pulled the blindfold back into place, pushed one hand as determined at the door.

Trying not to sound anxious, to transmit an anxiety surely only he felt: "Robin? You okay?"

"Sure," faintly muffled through the now closed door. "I'm fine."

"Okay," towel in hand, pushing it into the crack beneath the door. "I'm going in the closet now."

And did, sealing himself past the nervousness, eyes doubly blind; it was small in there, and hot; he sat. Waiting. They had not set a time limit, it was to be open-ended and he close enough, he had assured Robin over and over, to hear if there was trouble, problems, anything; to hear if Robin called out and wanted to stop.

So.

Think about how this feels; this is an experiment in consciousness. Pay attention.

Dark. Hot. Smells like a heat register, furnace dust, like an old shoe dry with old sweat. His back hurt a little. He changed position. He scratched his balls, wanted a flashlight, got a drink from the water bottle. The blindfold smelled not like Johnna but Johnna's perfume, it could be anyone's perfume, anybody could buy it. Time seemed to be moving slowly, but that was the one thing all the books had agreed upon, that time would seem elastic: half an hour seem half a day, it was a common occurrence. What a weird look Robin had had; nervous probably. Probably. He changed positions again. He could see dots before his blind eyes, what were they called? Phosphenes? Phosphors? He should know; he should not be so ignorant. He should read more. The research he had done for these experiments was the most reading he had done in years. He had used to read a lot; hadn't he? What happened?

Was Robin afraid, in there? No.

Was he afraid, in here? No. Uncomfortable, it was not at all pleasant to sit here, was pretty boring in fact, he was gaining no insights. Maybe this was a dumb idea. Maybe it was all a dumb idea, all these experiments, maybe none of it would help Robin with the drawings; maybe he, Grant, had been wrong about it all from the start. Another step needed making, that he knew: like pain, or an erection, or the feeling of needing to sleep; it was that cellular. A step made, but not these steps, maybe all of this was wrong (and maybe *this* was the insight, maybe he ought to be paying attention to *this*). Perhaps Robin should have been calling the shots, should from here on in; they would talk about it, soberly, seriously, when this was over; it would not be much longer now.

His neck hurt, a pinched feeling at the back of his head; he realized he had been sleeping, head on his chest sleeping and for how long? Time; a watch, they had forgotten about a watch. Someone was supposed to time this, someone outside but they had no one outside so they should have had a watch. Shit. How long had it been? No way of knowing without ending the process; shit shit shit. Stupid; he was stupid, he should have known.

Dark in here.

What was Robin thinking?

Finally he could not stand it, not the darkness, cramped small boring darkness but the feeling of being stupid, of planning his head off and yet neglecting an essential, like diving the trench and forgetting to bring extra air, like climbing Mt. Everest barefoot, great idiocies made greater by the moment of realization, that crystal instant where one's own stupidity rises up like the jinn from the bottle to point the slow accusing finger in the balance of the fall: it is not enough to be stupid, one has to know about it first: and two thoughts—stiff-legged and rising, himself like some poorly made construction, you can't stand up in a closet—colliding with such enormous force that he was back down again without thinking the motion, back on his ass, his stupid ass and thinking:

What the fuck do you think you're doing here, playing with a schizophrenic's brain?

and: Robin's face, that look, that strange look and he was *afraid*, that's what it had been, scared shitless, scared into such agonized panic that he could not even speak out, call for a halt, for help

and he was out of the closet, yanking off the blindfold and almost falling as he tried to stand upright and move in the same instant, move with purpose; before anything else he had to know what time it was: how long?

In the hallway it was dark; it was night.

The bedroom clock said one forty-five. They had been in the dark for almost twelve hours.

Slowly through his vast alarm, they had never meant to be in there for so long, never so long. Switching on the bedroom light to give light to the hall and it seemed hideous, as bright as the light in his dream, bad dream and his hand to the bathroom door, slowly: the turning of the knob seemed not loud but excessively quiet, had Robin done something to it, something to make it quiet? Had Robin tried to get out? Carefully, carefully, so as not to overwhelm with sound or movement, the light from the bedroom still too bright and as softly as he could he said, "Robin," softer still. "Robin, it's me. It's time to stop now, okay?"

Fetal slump, there at his feet: he had almost stepped on him, right on him and oh Christ, scattered drawings like skin pulled wet from the flesh it covers, the leap of adrenaline so fierce he was dizzied, put out one hand and oh *Christ*: Robin curled in a ball, mouth open like an imbecile's, chin slick: beneath the blindfold (and Grant's hands shaking so he could barely move the soft false silk against the pale face) Robin's eyes half-shut, pupils hideously huge: and dull; dead eyes. Oh Christ, oh Jesus God.

"Robin," gentle with terror, breath hot as exhaust past his beating heart, beating so he could barely breathe, "Robin, it's me. Okay? It's me. We're all done now," like a lullaby, a litany to the dead (stop it stop saying that) and lowering himself, graceless as a drunk from his trembling crouch to sit, half falling where he was, where Robin was, atop those drawings (the drawings; of what; not now), atop the shreds and clawed husks of tinfoil— the mirror bare now, bare and dark and with shaking arms hold Robin against his chest, he could smell his own sweat, fear smell as potent as piss from a dog and "It's me, Robin. Robin, it's me."

Over and over. And over.

It took him until dawn to get Robin to speak, and when he did it was one word: "No." Softly, mumbled as if through a mouthful of blood, saliva, the crunched sweet bitterness of bones: "No," still not all there behind the eyes, swimming back and forth, back and forth, who knows what he saw when again he closed his eyes.

"Okay," Grant's whisper, his arms were numb, past even the memory of sensation. "Okay."

Robin's head back down, against Grant's chest, heavy like a child's; and silent, maybe even asleep and Grant's own head bending, sagging, his frozen arms and the burden they bore: and then he was sleeping, too, cramped and sorry, walking in the hall of dreams that told him nothing, that spoke nothing to him at all.

He did not want to talk about it, Robin; Grant did not want to press, did not want to bring it up even in memory, even to himself but in fact it was impossible to escape, these consequences, these indictments after the fact: for they were indictments, each moment together, each meal shared, each sentence spoken showed Grant over and over how desperately foolish he had been; who's in charge here? Who is in charge here?

"I don't want to do anything else for a while,"
Robin in his sleeping bag, drawn up to the throat:
slow his words and meaning never, palpable the
meaning in that dead smiling face. "It's too much
like being catatonic. Out of it, you know?" in the
same flat dull frightening way, and smiling, he was
smiling way too much these days, smiles like plank
boards stretched chipped and loose over something
worse than utter darkness, something so wrong that
Grant found himself blundering through his days in
a formless fog of anxiety that worsened, day by day
by smiling day until he found himself weeping at
work, bent over in the darkroom and crying silently
into his cupped hands, mouth open as if he would
howl: what have you done? What have you done to
him?

Stop it. Sweating, wiping snot with the back of
his hand. Stop it, what if someone sees you, just
stop it now. The chemical smell bitter as medicine
against the roof of his mouth, breathing in, breathing out and all of it heavy: with fear: with a kind of
inner wriggling torment that Johnna would say—
and what would she not say, if she saw him now,
saw both him and Robin together; remembering
the things she had said brought a special and particular pain to the back of his head, a feeling
Johnna would call guilt. For standing unheeding in
the black shadow of madness, the reality of Robin's
illness versus the dream chase, these alternate real-
ities: remembering something Johnna had said—

had she?—"You don't dabble in schizophrenia, it's like dabbling in cancer."

This is not cancer.

Sweat under his arms, under his hairline like a line drawn in red: here is where we cut. He drove home too fast, cut off a garbage truck, cut off a bus, the side closest to him festooned with the yard-high face of a movie star, an actor: *The Last Loverboy* in festive sans serif, coming to a theater near you. When was the last time he and Robin did something as simple as go to a movie? sit at home and watch TV? Quests, quests, grim reading and notations and Robin there, patient on the floor, drawing: and now, of course, not drawing at all: had not so much as asked for a pencil, had not volunteered the drawings he had produced there in isolation: and Grant—aware of his own cowardice, exquisitely aware—did not ask to see them; sleeping dogs; sleeping demons. Robin, asleep behind his own eyes and this was—wasn't it?—supposed to be better than the group home, this was supposed to be *helping* him.

He was definitely not helped; he was if not decompensating (check the level on that medication, please; are you sure? are you sure you can do that much and do it correctly?) then certainly regressed: back to a state of such perfect blank calm that all his actions, even simple things like brushing his teeth, or folding the newspaper, seemed informed less by presence than absence: not-there; stranded on a plateau where not only were they deprived, both of them, of Robin's drawings—Robin from the catharsis, the pure release and pleasure of drawing, Grant from the insights gained and granted and, yes, the pure pleasure of looking at what Robin had done—but of the sense of connection they had shared without even thinking of it, without consideration, without expecting it would ever change. Now they were separate, apart, each in his own particular sorrow as if behind glass walls, heavy glass that distorts, that changes the image for the viewer as well as the seen: and Grant weeping again in the shower, red walls like some fisty womb and he had not cried like this in years, years, he felt fifty years old, a hundred, as if every sorrow of humanity had first passed like arrows through his shrinking flesh.

Things did not soften; days went on; once Robin laughed at something on TV and it seemed to be a real laugh; the next day he soiled himself without realizing, sitting reading the weather page in the newspaper, and Grant, watching without appearing to watch, seeing to his disbelief a spreading wetness at Robin's crotch, and, as mortified as if he himself had done it, said nothing; for hours; until the ammonia smell became too much to ignore and gently, gently, he pointed it out: "Robin," with great delicacy, holding out a pair of clean sweatpants, clean underwear discreet inside, "I need to do the wash now, can you change into these?"

And Robin smiling, equally gentle, stripping where he was (and a redness at his crotch, Grant could not help but see it and thought *Oh shit what now* and the words diaper rash in his mind without the thinking; he had never seen diaper rash in his life) and handing the pants to Grant, his nose wrinkling: "Here," without commenting on the smell. Pulling on the other pants, careless blue to cover his legs and the underwear falling neatly to the floor to lie there, white, a rebus, a trenchant comment, until Grant bent without comment to retrieve it and carry it away.

Eating canned spaghetti, no more fruits and juices, no more steamed vegetables; he would not touch it, Grant like a parent with a child: but he was not a parent, Robin not his child. Eating tortilla chips with ketchup and pepper for dip; eating bread and butter mashed into a ball. His sleep patterns seemingly altered for good, skewed to some rhythm only he, Robin, could guess; it seemed he never slept for more than four hours at a stretch. His weight fallen, a little, his cheeks and chin more prominent; it seemed he blinked his eyes more now; his scar almost perpetually pink, as if the tissue lay fresh and freshly wrinkled across the newly covered wound.

The most telling change of course was the need for light—understandable, perhaps the most so of all the new inexplicabilities, just another wretched souvenir of those hours in the dark—demonstrated through small ways, warnings Grant thought later; like leaving the bathroom light on all night long, curling like an animal in the sun and following its path across the floor; carrying a penlight in his pocket; nothing too drastic, nothing too strange until the evening when Grant, back too late from work, heard as he trudged slow and tired the hallway the sound of: what? Yelling? Robin, yelling? and he ran the rest of the way, giant steps and at the door, keys in hand but in panic pounding, useless shouts and calling "Robin let me in, Robin let me *in*!" until: the keys, hurry: and he was opening the door, slamming it open to see

Robin in the midst of the blinds, all down, yanked from the windows, torn from the walls: a bundle of slatted plastic pathetic now as broken bones and Robin before the darkened windows, all the lights on and yelling, almost past comprehension like a prayer, a chant come straight from the body itself: a howl:

"I need it to be *light* in here I NEED IT TO BE *LIGHT* IN HERE"

stepping on the blinds but without consciousness, crying out and bending, bending in half as if shot through with pains, arrows, needles and

"I NEED IT TO BE *LIGHT* IN HERE"

and Grant moving toward him, slowly, slowly stepping into the circle of debris and hearing his own voice, how long had he been speaking, that slow monotone: shock's calm: "We'll make it light, Robin, okay? Okay? We'll make it light. Okay?"

"I *need* it to be *light* in here!"

"We'll make it light, okay? Robin? Okay?"

Eyes wide open: does he see me, Grant thought, does he see me now? "Robin," not daring yet to touch him but to reach, just a little, the crunch and snap of slats beneath his feet like walking on glass, shattering, shrieking and

"I need it to be *light* in here, Grant, I can't *see*," and then the tears, wet face and not so much coming to as coming back: here, to this room, to Grant there before him breathing as if he had run for miles; which in some ways he had and "Grant," crying hard, looking around him with bewilderment large in his eyes, sharp and in a shaming cry, "Oh *shit*, oh *shit*," seeing the broken blinds, the screws torn from the walls, the cords spent and looped like stripped veins and he slumped, half falling, where he was, face in his hands and Grant beside him, bending to say what is always said in tragedy large or small, "It's okay, it's going to be okay, Robin, don't cry. All right? Everything's going to be okay."

And a knock, some noise tentative (for how long?) and Robin unmoving but Grant turned his head like fruit on a stick to see in the doorway a woman, older woman in a sky-blue sweatsuit: one hand on the door and staring: "Is everything all right in here?"

A feeling weary as rage: suddenly so tired he could hardly open his mouth: no, nothing is all right, *stupid* but Grant smiled, as false a smile as he had ever manufactured. "We're fine, everything's all right. Okay? Can you shut the door, please?" and for a moment it seemed she would not move at all, would keep standing there staring, but she did, finally, to close the door in a motion prim and quick and exact, exact too the misfired click of the self-lock as the door swung improperly to: then open again, gentle toss of keys, his keys: and closed again for good.

On the smell of tears, and urine; broken plastic sharp as glass; and Robin's weight against him like a split and emptied chrysalis of pain.

Passion; this was passion.

His hands were bleeding, lightly, in lines across his palms.

Things can always get worse; and they do; they had, now, and Grant was back to reading at night, clandestine, NEGS box down and what do I do now? What? Robin sitting on the floor, making balls out of bread. Robin sitting on the toilet for hours at a time, literally hours, his ass ringed painful in red when he finally pulled himself upright. Lying to the social worker, lying to the doctor: "He's fine. He's a little tired today, that's all."

Robin's stare, not empty so much as profoundly uninterested: the examining room, his physical health was fine: "Little underweight," the nurse said, PAUL on his crooked nametag, hairy arms helping Robin on with his shirt. "He been eating all right?"

"No," obscure relief to tell the truth about something, sitting there in the chair extraneous, never knowing what to do with his arms, his hands: holding now the nervous curl of a waiting-room magazine, *Time*; I can tell you about time, if you want to know, of course now I know more than I used to. "He doesn't want to eat much more than spaghetti, you know, and bread, all that starchy stuff."

"Mm," making a note; the nurse had not shaved recently, or maybe he was one of those guys who have a five o'clock shadow by noon. "Meds working out all right? Any symptoms, any signs like, you know, TD?" No, Grant said, nothing like that. Robin buttoning his shirt, paying no attention, Angela in hand and doing it wrong; reaching without thinking to do it for him, Robin smiling at him as if from the deck of a ship floating farther and farther from shore: bon voyage.

"Wish we could try him on Clozaril," the aide said; sighed. Another note on the chart. "Wish we could try all of them on Clozaril. Can't get the money, though, you know it? 's like anything else, they say it's cheaper to do it the old way." Shaking his head. Another note. "You want me to put him on the updated waiting list?"

"Sure. Please," bending to tie Robin's shoe and then straightening to lead him out, into the waiting room, the script renewed in hand and making another appointment, the receptionist sounded like she had a cold, writing them in with a leaky blue pen. Dots and spatters, dribbles down the page pristine. "We'll see you then, Robin," she said; she was, Grant had noticed, always careful to speak directly to the clients, not in that over-the-head grown-ups' talk to the caregiver that Grant hated, knew Robin hated as well; or had hated; who knew, now, anymore, who knew anything. He had to make sure Robin's seat belt was fastened, had to prod him into going to the bathroom as soon as they got home.

Mail in his weary hand, his days off were more tiring than going to work: bill, bill, junk, grocery store circular, bill. Nothing good. Robin emerging from the bathroom, into the living room: with Angela, in the sleeping bag, in the sun. Eyes closed. Not asleep.

Grant came to stand over him, careful not to block his light. "Do you want some lunch?"

"No."

"Want something to drink? Coke?"

Angela's head turned in pantomime: no.

"Want to watch a movie with me, or draw, maybe?"

Firmly, one eye opening beneath the clouding brow: "No, Grant, I don't want to do anything, I just want to lie here awhile, okay?"

"Okay, sure," and receding, watching the angel recede as well beneath the covers, Robin's eyes closing in the kiss of the sun and a posture of perfect and counterfeit peace. Grant into the bedroom, opening the book again: *Surviving Schizophrenia. Decompensation and Your Family. What to Do Next* and half sitting, half slumping on the bed, a feeling in his back as if he had walked for miles, miles, without rest or refreshment, a feeling in his head as if somewhere very close by, *very* close by, was a brick wall higher than his vision could reach, the bricks themselves dark and faintly stained and smelly, and damp to the pondering touch. He read until it was time to make dinner— soup and canned vegetables, peas tumbling like green pearls from the white-lined can—and bread, don't forget the bread, soft and unbuttered, the better to roll into balls, my dear and in the end it took him more than ten firm minutes to wake Robin enough to eat.

No drawings; little motion, few words; how much worse, Grant thought, does it have to get, how bad before it gets better? Before it gets beyond me? Manuals, and reading late, and working with one eye always on the clock: is it time to go home yet? to, what? Nothing, really, essentially; just Robin, sleeping in the same clothes, sleeping in the sun, Angela clutched in his hand. Or sitting up, looking not out the window but at the window, as if he expected visitors, as if he expected something to come in.

Grant too felt himself expecting: something: what? He no longer fully trusted his own perceptions, felt like a motion tectonic his own filters slowly warping; he was seeing things differently now. The books made less and less sense in the context of his experience: but if he did not have the books to guide him, what did he have? The doctor, whom they rarely saw? The nurses or the aides, the social worker to whom he had to lie, put up a good front, a good false front so they would not, what? Take Robin away? His behavior was not hurtful to self or others, it would take more than that but still Grant worried, silent fear under his skin like the worming motion of disease; he felt tired all the time now, he felt empty: felt afraid when he looked at Robin wide-eyed as a squirrel in the middle of the night, looked at him now in the well-lit silence of this endless afternoon and he wanted to go to him, sit by him and say To be truthful, Robin, all of this is beyond me, I'm out of my fucking depth here if you know what I mean; I wanted us to experiment but this, here, this is one experiment I want to stop, I don't know how but I want it to stop, okay? Is that okay with you? We'll keep it light, we'll keep all the windows open but it really has to stop, now. Because I don't know what to do next, I don't know what to do.

But he did not say it, said nothing, felt dumb as Angela there with her drooping paper, her spangles graceless but thank God for her, too, she seemed to help, she did more good, Grant thought, knew, than he himself; too bad she can't cook. Too bad she can't talk. Too bad Robin can't, won't, lies in that ditch (but a well-lit ditch, trench, gutter all the same) with Angela and will not speak; too bad *you* don't know, can't guess, can't decide what to do.

Are you making it worse?

I hope not.

Hope is not enough, not enough, not enough

and he realized he was rubbing his thumb, thumb and forefinger together with such slow concentrated violence that he had rubbed away a drift of skin, tiny tatter already curling and he did not for a moment even feel the blood, a little blood and no pain there, no pain at all.

Robin was not looking; Robin's eyes were closed and remained closed even when they heard it: the knock on the door but his body reacted, a flattening, a kind of curl along the spine and he put himself into himself as firmly as a crab in the shell it inhabits, pain and grace and safety in the motion and Grant rose, wondering who it was, who was knocking: no one he wanted to see. One of the social workers? No, they were required to call first. Who then? Johnna? The other one, from the group home? Or maybe a friend from the group home, and he actually smiled, a little, felt that little curve of his lip and wondered at it, opening the door in that unguarded square of wonder and saw there: pale hair, flat face, one hand clenched on a purse strap as if she had just arrived in time for her own mugging: and a look to her jaw and eyes strangely, strangely like Robin's.

Like Robin's.

"You're Grant," she said, as if this were information he lacked. "I'm Alison Tobias."

Robin's head rising up from the sleeping bag, the hand holding Angela beginning a jackhammer shake: all there behind his eyes, all present, here and terrified; terrified. In the instant before the smell Grant knew that Robin had pissed himself too; apparently Alison knew that smell as well for her face folded into a well-worn wrinkle of deep disgust as she said, leaning past the door, the obstructing angle of Grant's body, "For God's sake, is he still doing that?" and then, more sharply still to Robin himself, "Go on into the bathroom and clean yourself up."

Rising, Angela in hand, sleepwalker stumble and still in the sleeping bag like a dream unshed he almost fell, caught by Grant's hasty arms and righted, Grant's own eyes wide as Robin's beneath the umbrella of panic contagious, but Get a hold on yourself, Grant to Grant as he pulled the sleeping bag free of Robin's legs, saw the wetness and the tremor there, get a fucking grip and, as gently as he had ever spoken, with all the force of feeling and of care, "Robin," one hand on his shoulder, such a careful touch, "go on in the bathroom, okay? And then go into my room, and wait for me in there. All right?" and in that instant, those words, she was past the door neatly as a knife; she was there, she was in.

Robin did not answer, perhaps had not even heard: hearing nothing past that whiplash voice, sister dear from the dear dead past and Grant knew like a slap, an instant pain that his own trembling came from rage; a liberating realization and he hugged Robin, firm warm one-armed hug and as Robin stumbled off, still clumsy with fear, Grant turned—all this in seconds, slow literal seconds like the moments passed in car-wreck time where everything happens as it never does in life, slowly enough for reflection in the very moment of the crash—turned to the woman still standing where she entered and said, "Don't talk to him like that again."

"He's my brother."

"He's my friend, and this is my house," congestion making his voice slow, blood throbbing hard in his throat, temples, his chest expanding; he felt both invincible and clumsy, as if he had suddenly become a giant in a playhouse, a one-room playhouse with furniture made of twigs. "If you have anything to say, you can say it to me."

She did not answer, instead turned her head smooth as bearings to look around: the room itself captured for him in her gaze: the blinds still broken, slats snapped in drunken angles and hardware cracked from the walls, newspapers and open packages of chips, crackers, snack foods left out to tempt Robin to eat something other than balled-up bread, Grant himself in wrinkled shirt and wrinkled jeans and the final touch of vinegar benediction, the piss smell hanging over it all.

"I talked to your girlfriend," still in that same posture, as if to move would be to invite contamination, imply an acceptance she would die before granting; she got a lot out of a little. "Your ex-girlfriend. She seemed to think you didn't know what you were doing." She did not need to look around the room, at him, again. "I wanted to see for myself. For my parents, they're worried about him."

"What about you?" coldly; is Robin listening? She said nothing. Why had she come? To see Robin? hurt him? take him away? Panic again, that beating-blood feeling now in his throat but he said nothing, only stared, stared at her: I asked you a question, *bitch*. Your turn. We can stand here all day.

Finally she seemed to realize this herself,

shrugging a little, head to one side the barest inch: "I told you," she said. "I wanted to see for myself."

Picturing Robin listening at the door, crouched as low and small as he could become; that deep eye-rolling quiet and Grant said, "What else is there to see? The bathroom? Want to see where we eat?" keeping his voice reasonable though cold, he did not want to frighten Robin further, he must not let himself lose control of the situation; of himself; there had been entirely too much harm done already through loss of control, harm to Robin and he would not, would *not* see it happen again, here today. With her. "Are you done?"

"No," as coldly. "I'm not. I promised my parents—" always *my* "—I would check everything out. And I want to talk to Robin."

"Absolutely not," as the words were leaving her mouth, he had known she was going to say that, there was no way. No way. "I don't give a shit what Johnna told you, you don't need to talk to him; you can talk to his doctor, you can talk to the people at Social Services and if you—"

"I did. I called them and I—"

"—to talk to him, call him on the phone. Or send him a letter, I'll give it to him." Robin, are you listening? see how I keep you safe? Nothing bad will happen to you, I swear, I swear to God nothing bad is going to happen to you here. "But you're not going to talk to him now."

He expected more defiance, a stand-making

speech; but she did not argue; but she did not leave, either, only stood there staring at him, hand still on her purse, he had an impulse absurd to wrench it from her, say for God's sake put that fucking thing down, will you? Those eyes so subtly like yet fundamentally unlike Robin's, she could have used a little dose somewhere down the line, a little humanity, a little Clozaril, something. She did not move; he did not move; Robin, somewhere in the bathroom, presumably did not move either. Light, through the windows; he was getting a headache, adrenaline backlash and finally she said, without relaxing her position in the slightest, "Then I guess I'll have to talk to you."

"All right," trying not to let out the breath that wanted to go, long exhalation of—relief? Maybe. Disappointment maybe too but she was shaking her head, looking around and "Not in here," positively, "I can't talk in here, I can't stand that smell." A pause. "We can stand in the hallway or something, or sit in my car."

He did not want to leave Robin alone, did not see a real way out so "Wait a minute," going to the bathroom door, knocking as gently as if the door itself were some extension of Robin's body, some embodiment of his terror: "Robin?" softly. "It's me. I'm going to take"—he did not want to say *your sister*, or use her name—"I'm going to take her outside, okay? so you can come on out if you want to. Or stay in there, whatever you want to do. All right? I won't be long, okay?"

Silence.

"Robin, are you—"

"I hear you," right by the door, so close and real and somehow so terrible that Grant flinched back, the jump literal in his flesh as if he had been touching fire; or the cold so cold it burns, something from which his autonomic nervous system demanded he withdraw; and he did, backing away, back to the living room to Alison Tobias and her posture of universal dislike: "All right, let's go. Not for long though."

Don't worry, her face said; she herself said nothing, walked out into and down the hall with a stride longer than he had expected, he had to hurry to catch up, his motion matching hers and down the elevator (opposite sides) to the outside, slanting sunlight on her cream-colored subcompact with its political bumper sticker, its briefcase and blue ring-binder manuals in the back seat. She opened her own door first, firm click of the lock between two fingers to let him in. It was a bench seat; they stayed as far apart as possible.

"Look," at once, freer now to let his hostility show, "you have a hell of a nerve showing up here like this without calling, without even bothering to let—"

"Me?" but she was not rising to it, not really, she was exactly as she had been upstairs; of course she had had more time to prepare for this, she had been thinking about it apparently as she drove from wherever it was she came from; she lived, he thought, with the parents, wherever that was; Robin had never brought them up, ignored as best he could the continuing fact of their existence, or at least did so on the surface: there were deeps, obviously, which could not be ignored or Robin would not now be crouching in the bathroom, his face to the door like a rat in a monoxide box scrabbling for air enough to live; no. "What about you?" she said. "You take him out of his art therapy class, you—"

"Wait a minute. He did that on his own, it was his—"

"—out of the group home, and you bring him here to live with you. And your own girlfriend thinks you're probably more than just a little bit on the—"

"My ex-girlfriend, for one thing," but this was getting nowhere, just louder so he tried again; the quicker you can shut her up, the quicker she'll go. Shut up and go; and in a voice reasonable again, but cold, cold, "If you think a minute, you'll see that Johnna—my *ex*-girlfriend—obviously has her own ax to grind here, he fired her, he walked out on her therapy—which incidentally wasn't doing fuck-all for him and if you don't believe me go ahead and ask his doctor, it's in the records that he didn't even—"

"I told you," around her own deep breath and

see, now, the color in that face, flat poison color; he was getting to her, a little and at last. "I talked to the doctor. I talked to the social worker, I was trying to check you out without actually having to come out here."

"Then why did you?"

"Because I told my parents I would."

"They're his parents too, aren't they?" and before she could respond, fire back: "They don't know anything about him, *you* don't know anything about him, not the way he is now, and you care less, right? Right? About your brother who you're supposed to love?"

Her whole face one knuckling curl of some emotion so intense it shut him up, for the moment, took whatever words he was going to say next and with a distaste so deep he could smell it from her, its scent as actual as blood: "I don't love him," she said. "Not anymore."

Staring at her, their backs to the doors at disparate angles and "I can't do it anymore, you don't understand. You've known him for how long? Six months? a year? Well he's my *brother*, he's *been* my brother all my life and I just can't anymore, I'm fed up." The sun against her face and she blinked, strange little rabbity motion and for that one moment the family resemblance was so strong, so horrible and clear that Grant became in that instant weak with a pity so intense it might have been Robin sitting there; and even as he told himself Be careful, look out he felt sorry, *sorry*, sorry unto death for this woman whom two seconds earlier he had felt like throwing out and down the stairs; in her pain she was Robin, his Robin with claims on him deeper than anyone else in the world.

And then it passed: she said something he did not hear and then, "Have you ever sat with him in a restaurant, or a movie or something? a store? A doctor's office, I'm sure you've been in plenty of those. Do you see the way people look at you, when he does something weird? Not at him: at you. First they stare, then they look away, then they *move* away like it's catching or something." I don't care about other people, he wanted to say, but did not; shut up, he advised himself, let her talk herself out. Go on, talk.

"It about killed my father," she said, talking somehow through him, as if he were attention itself in the abstract, "both of them he almost killed. They're old, they're afraid. Afraid of their crazy son! Afraid *I'll* go crazy," with a dark secret bitterness, layers and layers, speaking to him and yet only to herself, or maybe somehow to Robin as well, invisible Robin up above them hiding in the bathroom; protected, and terrified, and safe. "There's nothing crazy about me," she said and in those words he heard all the advice in all the manuals, the handbooks, the pep talks for the family: there is a chance that if one sibling is schizophrenic another will be as well, just a chance, not a very large chance but present, still, like the executioner at the back of the room, never raising his ax, never even allowing it to be seen but they had been through it once already, the family, they knew what it was like; there was no need after all to let the blade be seen. Robin himself had once told a story, Alison with him in an examination room and the doctor, some doctor unremembered saying *Well there is that genetic basis for schizophrenia* and Alison reacting at first dismissively, then coldly, as if she had been accused of perpetrating an act both ridiculous and lewd, then with a mounting and un-reachable hysteria as if the idea itself were alive as a virus come to eat her unawares: and shouting, screaming at the doctor: at Robin: at the room and her parents by whom she had been bequeathed the hideous possibility, the defection in her genes: "There is nothing wrong with me! *There is nothing wrong with me!*" and turning on Robin, specifically on Robin: "*You're* the sick one, you're not anything but sick," and listing instantly a long range of accusations, stories told and half told as if she would in the telling reduce her brother to a collection of symptoms, mannerisms and behaviors; fist in his mouth Robin had wept, the doctor had taken Alison outside to calm her down, to talk to her alone; they had talked for a long time and when Alison opened the door to the examining room Robin had shrunk back, struck by the hammer of instinct, fear: had shrunk back when she said *Come on; let's go.*

Let's go.

Shut up; let her talk.

Sun on the windshield. A car passed them, loud radio, a truck, a pair of kids on motor trikes with long waving poles on the back, tiny neon flags snapped atop. "I told them I'd check up on it, after that therapist told us what happened. So why don't you just explain to me, all right, what's in it for you?" head at an angle, staring at him as if through glass, the sterile protection of a microscope. "Are you his boyfriend or something, is that it? You're lovers?"

"I'm Robin's friend," with dignity like ice, no purchase, no surface for her shifty feet; all pity gone and he stared at her with everything he felt at that moment, that one particular moment, held nothing back and let her see it all: like a laser, like fire, like a knife pointing straight and particular at one particular heart. "I'm trying to help him. I *am* helping him."

"Everyone says that," with her own peculiar smile, seemingly unaffected by this display of his contempt. "All the doctors, the therapists always said that, the counselor in *high* school said that. In junior high! Everyone always wants to help Robin, poor Robin, he has so much *potential*," like a snake, like an evil charm, her breath faintly bitter, both hands empty in a static crouch on her lap like animals ready to spring: at him: at Robin up above. "Everybody always wants to help him, but nobody ever does." Silence in the car, all his defenses gone or unevocable, nothing left but the bare-wire determination to see this through, shut her up, get her gone and out of here without harming Robin, without frightening him further: staring at her and thinking like words said aloud Fuck you, and fuck your parents and fuck Johnna too for siccing you on me, you freeze-dried bitch. You'll never ever *ever* see him again if I can help it, we'll move if we have to, I'll get a court order, I'll do something. Something. Anything.

As if she had heard him: "Well, I'll tell you what, Mr. Cotto. The worst thing I can do to you is let you go on ahead with whatever you have planned, whatever it is, whatever rehabilitation you have in mind—and let me tell you he has been through it *all*, I know, I was *there*—and you know what? That's just what I'm going to do. So you go on ahead," leaning not forward but giving the impression of advancing, coming closer, coming on, "and do whatever you have to. But if you ever once call us, if you ever try to get in touch with either me or my parents," *my* parents again, she had them now and was not letting them get away again, "I'll bring legal action against you, and maybe criminal too. So you just keep that in mind."

She was crying.

Tears down her face, running like water squeezed from a rag, wrung but no other, outer manifestation, he did not even know if she knew, as if the tears were water from heaven, pigeon piss, the draining weep from some faulty overhang; her voice, its timbre, her gaze did not change in the slightest nor did she move to wipe the tears away.

"Just keep it in mind," she said. "Because we can't do it anymore, you want to do it, go ahead." Tears; that mouth; her hands he saw had nails chewed so far past the skin line that her fingers looked in consequence deformed, some subtle defect revealed only at the limits of her touch. What must she feel like, every day, to gnaw and worry at her own skin, her flesh that way? My hands; my nails; my parents. My brother, Robin.

"That's fine," he said; a final feeling in the air, it was time to get up, go. "That's fine. We don't need any help, we won't ask you for anything. Or your parents. We won't—"

"Good," she said, and started the car, seeming almost as if she would drive off at once and leave him leaping to the curb so: out, turning back toward the building and looking up at once like a learned response, a Skinnerism to their window, where Robin crouched: even from here Grant could see he was weeping, his mouth one great O, a Munch howl, a cry from the heart, and upstairs, quick as he could move Grant was upstairs, opening the door to go to him, crouch beside him where he knelt by the window, Angela in his fist, staring at the street and the emptiness left by the little cream-colored car.

"Alison," sobbing, snot on his upper lip like some rare extrusion, rhythmically squeezing small Angela and weeping as if his heart would burst from the sheer physical pressure of the agony within, like rising water in a well too small, like vapors' relentless expansion to split steel: "Alison's gone," to Angela, to Grant, to himself, "Alison's just gone."

She won't bother us again but he knew that was the wrong thing to say, absolutely the wrong thing and so said nothing, only crouched there, pins and needles in his legs and in the reach of his comforting arm, Angela swinging in the motion of Robin's grief, tears and words inexhaustible, indistinguishable, inextinguishable as the black and empty fountain of grief itself.

Now: the silence. If before Grant had believed Robin was in a trench, a rut, a gutter of his own devising now he saw entrenchments unencountered: like a wall, a series of walls, a prison built brick by brick and engineered so cunningly that by no device could it be opened, no key found to part the lock, never; never. Robin refused outright to even listen to talk about drawing, he would not read, he would not speak at all beyond small islands of words in the white lake of his silence; not stubborn or recalcitrant, it was as if he no longer remembered why he should, why speech was necessary or desirable. Chores, his old small duties were out of the question; even the ones he once enjoyed, the newspapers, the small tries at cooking: now he would barely eat, Grant had to nag him, gentle with fear and exhaustion: Come on, Robin, you have to eat something.

"I don't want to," he would say, squinting a little in the light he must have, almost all the time now; he did little sleeping but when he did slept mostly in light, cat-curled, that face with its lines looking older, that hair longer but clean, still clean, he was still able to keep himself washed, teeth brushed, clothes occasionally changed; he had stopped pissing himself too which Grant took to be a hopeful sign: he needed a hopeful sign now, especially now when: "I'm not hungry, Grant, really. I don't want any pizza."

"Don't make me eat this shit alone," still trying not to nag, not to be frustrated or angry but Robin was losing weight again, he needed to eat, he needed food to balance out the pills; thank God he was still taking the pills. "Come on, this stuff is like glue, it's like cardboard, look," but Robin was no longer looking, eyes open but unseeing, he was slipping away again and back in the kitchen, uneaten pizza in hand Grant hurled it into the sink, strangely quiet slap of wet against wet and he put his hand to his head, rubbed the flesh there as if he might in his search for solutions strip back down to bone, the firm clear cradle of logic and thought itself as logical, as thoughtful as nature could be: he had once heard the human skull referred to as a strong bone box and he needed, now, the tools to open that box of Robin's, not in experiment, no, that was done, had gone too far already, the golden eggs lost forever maybe but he had at least to try to repair this damage, he had to do something; since Alison's visit (the way a plague, say, is visited upon one) things had gone even farther downhill; this had to stop.

This had to stop.

"Remember Lewis and Clark?" Standing over him there in the sun, there in the fitful embrace of the day's last light; arms folded on the sill and looking up at Grant, smiling a little: "Remember?" Grant said again.

"Remember the Alamo." Angela, dirty in the draft, this way and that way and this. "Remember the *Maine*."

We can't keep on like this. "Remember," but he had to let it go, there was no use and very close somehow to a state like tears but not tears (and Alison, there in the car, her whole face wet but her eyes in some strange intrinsic way dry, dry, dry as a bone; *remember*?) he rose, went back into the bedroom, did not look at the box marked NEGS or the books inside but sat instead, head in hands, and tried: to think.

At work John noticed the difference, the change in him or said he did which amounted to the same thing: sitting there at his table, the shine from the light table like some streamlined crystal ball beneath his hands, tell your future for the next fifteen minutes: "What's your problem, Grant? You know you really look like shit."

Thanks, asshole. "Nothing," eyes averted, shoulders tight, drinking coffee that tasted as if it had just been dredged out of some basin as dirty as it was old, "nothing really. Not sleeping a lot I guess."

"Your roomie giving you shit again?"

He had told John, told all of them that he lived with a temperamental roommate, it seemed a good defense if Robin should ever have called; but Robin never did, never had, now never would, would forget how to use the telephone, forget how to talk at all if something was not done, why was nothing done? *Who's in charge here anyway?* Whose idea was this anyway

but John was still talking, saying something, gesturing with his own cup and Grant found he was nodding, nodding, he was drinking and nodding and getting up out of the chair; he had just agreed to some time off, a couple days without pay of course but it'll make a whole hell of a difference, Grant, I know it will. "Anyway we've got the slack in the schedule now, it's no problem, take three days if you have to," and he was still nodding, like a motion once learned and now inescapable, out of John's office and into his own, the room that passed for an office, his own light table still on. He set the cup down somewhere, out of his way; there was a message on his phone, an old one dealt with hours ago. The whole room smelled subtly of photographic paper and dry decay, as if the entire building would one day go in one puff of faintly corrosive dust; his car smelled like mildew, like old oil, like the dirt in the courtyard of the apartment building.

The mail was all bills, there were grocery store circulars, there was a neon flyer stuck to his mailbox, all the mailboxes: CHURCH HALLELUJAH, it said in black across the heavy orange face, the cheap dry feel of the flyer itself. Nondenominational, it advised in smaller, primmer type; All Faiths Are Welcome.

He shoved the flyer with the other junk, slow into the elevator where a girl and boy no older than fourteen, thirteen maybe, maybe even twelve were kissing with the kind of smug passion that delights most in public viewing and the more miserable the viewer the better; the girl had tiny little tits, barely there under her skintight tank top; the boy had a truly amazing raft of pimples all up and down his cheeks, his chin, that girl must really love him if she was willing to get that close to so much contagion. They were still kissing as he left the elevator, slow walk and slower ponderment, when was the last time he got laid? Johnna; and he had to smile, even at this distance Johnna did not look all that good although their sex had not been bad; he remembered her hair, the feel of her breasts, the sounds she made and all of it somehow sad in a dark way, as if through this new lens of his, these new and broken filters he saw the way a bee sees, saw kaleidoscopically, saw more than he was willing to admit: it had all been pretty pathetic after all or maybe (there were always two sides, weren't there, to every story, every memory; it takes two to tango, to fuck, to fight) it was just his warped perspective telling him so. Certainly he had changed, changed a lot in this long association with Robin, this attempt to see things differently: regressing, maybe, back to the old flat state only now with a new hideousness, a new empty feel: this is passion, and where it goes; and how it ends. See? Did you think it would be like this? You wanted to feel, didn't you? Feel *this*.

Hands cold at the fingers, Robin asleep on the floor and Grant into the kitchen to stand by the counter, sorting listless through the mail: junk and more junk, set the bills aside and the church flyer, there, bright as a burn against the countertop, listless his gaze across it, reading it seemingly without meaning to: CHURCH HALLELUJAH. All Faiths Are Welcome. Even the faithless, even the tired, even the ones who cannot see past the pain in their own heads, their own living rooms, how about us? How about it? How long had it been since he had gone to church, any church? A long time, childhood maybe? Had his parents ever taken him to church? They must have, it was something people did with kids. He dredged for the memory, could not reach it; looked at the flyer again.

Robin, in the living room: asleep. Hallelujah.

"Robin," quietly, this was stupid, "Robin, wake up. Robin? We're going to go out for a while."

Impulse; why not? All the filters are cracking, are warped nearly unto uselessness: go with the flow, try something new. Things have to get worse before they can get better, like a fever, like a boil, like an abscess in the secret breathing chambers of your heart, body, you have to let it ripen before it can eat you alive. So go: take a chance. Why not?

"Robin?" louder now, going into the living room: that sleeping face on the floor. "Come on, Robin, get up."

The dying sun through the window like the space past benediction, the drunken slant of the still-broken blinds, a spot on the rug shaped like a kidney: Robin's hands fluttering, in sleep, para-sleep, his mouth open just a little as if breath were currency enough to take him where he must go, needed all the while to be: to exist: and Grant's hand on his arm, shaking him gently, waking him: touching him the way a father touches a son, a mother the child of her breathing, bleeding, aching body: Robin, Robin get up.

PART THREE
SASKIA

*I heard many things in hell. How, then,
am I mad?*

POE

IT LOOKED LIKE AN AA MEETING, A GATHER-
ing, a convocation of the suffering, the soiled and
the tired. It'll be fun, Grant had said, sleepy Robin
down the elevator, his head against the moving
walls like a man on the way to perform his own
painless dissection, you'll like it. We don't have to
do anything, we don't even have to talk to anybody,
we'll just watch.

Robin's drowsy frown, why can't we just go to a
movie but the words lost ultimately in the descent
of the elevator, the opening doors; it was good,
Grant thought, to be moving again, to surrender to
the act of motion: the air of discovery faintly re-
vived between them, a new and shared adventure,
an *experience.* In its own way it was miracle enough
to have gotten him out, down, moving again,
enough for one day maybe but yet there was something changed, indefinable but as real as respiration, in and out, a difference in the way Robin
moved, the way his feet hit the ground, the way his
eyes slid back and forth as if through ether in the
private heavens of his skull; but at least tonight he

was aware, and awake, moving on his own power, Angela in one thoughtful pocketing hand.

It had rained, brief showers to leave the ground, the pavement not wet but damp, the way the air smells in a beach house in the autumn. They found the building without difficulty, the ground floor some vague Pentecostal meeting place, the basement stairs shielded primly from Pentecostal view by a large black signboard with removable white letters now spelling out SERVICE 6:30 WHY THERE IS LOVE EZ. 4:7; why is there love? *What* is it, first? but no time to think of questions like these, down the stairs with Robin before him, hair drifting like underwater in the breeze of his descent, Angela closed in his thoughtful fist like the ticket to enlightenment, a token, a benison, a bequest; don't lose that, sir, whatever you do.

A basement room (but well lit, of course, absolutely it was well lit by the greenish stare of fluorescence, their half-heard white noise buzz); why did all these things seem to take place in basements, church basements; well this was church, wasn't it? Folding chairs, a tape player, a truly hideous crucifix with the Christ painted thin and red and white, gory hands and feet, nobody could bleed that much and live but then that was pretty much the point, wasn't it? They took seats near the back of the room, cigarette smoke and mashed plastic foam, something sticky on the nonslip tile floor itself brown and beige, like spilled coffee, maybe that

was the idea. Robin sat bonelessly, his back one
pale curl, hair close about his cheeks and chin as if
he were hiding, maybe he was; let him alone, Grant
thought, just let him be. At least he's out of the
house, at least he's here.

Perhaps twenty, thirty people in the room now,
filing in, loud and quiet, a woman in a waitress
uniform, hasty coat thrown over; a man in a de-
signer suit. Two girls dressed so much like hookers
they could not have been hookers. A woman and
child, the baby plump and still as fruit in its plastic
container, a padded carrier with some kind of re-
tractable handles.

And it began, or seemed to, without warning or
discernible form: loud music from the tape player,
who would have guessed so much power from
those little speakers, huge booming gospel with the
treble too harsh and high. And a man from the
crowd, a surprisingly humble-looking man in a
plain gray suit with the high crown of receding hair
began to speak, his voice moving without effort
through and above the music, through and above
the smoke and the sighs and voices of the crowd,
forty now maybe or maybe forty-five.

What he said was consciously lost on Grant,
who did not listen, did not want to listen, did not
particularly care beyond the effect of this experience on Robin; who at least was awake, was paying
attention, was fondling Angela in one calm and
thoughtful hand and all without squirming or with-

drawing or being scared, or wanting to run away;
did he want to run away? It had been a long time,
longer than Grant felt able to reckon, since Robin
had been someplace other than a doctor's office or
to see his social worker, they did not get out much
anymore: light was everywhere, light was free, light
was at home and at home in his nest pulled up to
his perspiring chin *he* was at home, and safe. But
tonight he was here, and presumably listening; he
looked as if he might be listening anyway.

"—for the love of God," the man was saying.
"Gray is all the colors together, black and white
and everything in between. And red, here," flipping
at his tie, tossing it up toward his own nose the way
young boys do, "red is for the blood of angels."

Robin's lips moving, Robin saying: what? and
Grant leaning closer, wanting to hear but not to
seem as if he were prying, eavesdropping, *listening
in*: "Angels' blood," Robin's whisper to himself, to
Angela, "isn't red at all. It isn't even a—"

and the rest of it lost, the man saying something
about blue and the infinite mercies of God and his
angels, every angel a soul waiting to be born or
something along those lines; Grant shifted a little
on his seat, Robin was certainly paying attention
and maybe he better start paying attention too,
who's in charge here after all? Don't miss a word;
you may be sorry, you may definitely be sorry about
it someday.

A woman two seats to the left of them was

weeping, it seemed a little early for that but there she was, weeping, her hands to her mouth; a young woman, maybe twenty-five, short hair and braless and weeping into her hands: praise God. Praise God. A believer? They all wanted to believe something; Grant wanted to believe lots of things: that Robin would start talking again, start eating, start drawing, that he would get better and better until maybe one day, in defiance of all the doctors, the aides, books, everything, all the collected wisdom forever and ever (and amen, since they were here, why not) maybe one day be well enough to go without the doctors and the aides, the handbooks, maybe even the medication; oh sure, tell that to a diabetic, tell that to the guy with hypertension whose blood is a glittering fountain beneath the earthly crust of his skin, the science of tectonics and don't you ever say anything like that to him, you understand? Himself to himself, you understand me now? He has enough problems without that, hope, hope is shit. Hope is shit and don't you ever forget it; he cannot live without that medication, not any life you want to see him have.

And now the man, the minister was speaking of desire, a desire to help everyone in the room, everyone, God loves us all. All. As if this were a switch pulled, a compartment entered, the talking began: one by one, rising up like time-lapse flowers, help me, heal me, pray for me; hallelujah but not exultant, not in praise but in defeat: hallelujah,

I am dying: help me, heal me, make me whole. My heart is sick. My kid is sick. My daughter has AIDS, my son is in jail, my husband is screwing his sister and I can't stand it I can't stand it I can't take it anymore

and Grant with his mouth shut, staring in amazement and something like terror, even Robin (staring, as well, next to him, utterly transfixed) nearly forgotten in this litany of hopelessness and loss, Jesus God there were some problems out there, weren't there, weren't there just and his own problems with Robin, his own difficulties and sorrows and worries were just another drop in the bucket, weren't they, just another thin and viscous drop in the overflowing bucket of blood.

And from talking now to testifying, it got very loud very quickly and then the ecstasies began: the moving, the shouting, the talking in the tongues and Grant, taken very deeply aback now and almost to the point, the locus of departure, of flight, of escape turned to Robin to say *Let's go* but in the end said nothing, shut up: shut up shut up because Robin was listening hard, Angela in hand and bent forward at the waist like a man at a prizefight, a big game, an important and life-defying event: he was not menaced by the noise, the hysteria rising like glue in a tube, he was unafraid and he turned to Grant on his own to volunteer a remark: with a smile, a bright smile totally out of (and yet deeply in) place: "It's like the hospital," he said, "only everybody's having *fun*."

And in the midst of this vortex of yelling and music, the groans of the inarticulate, the gray-suited man with his hands in the air as if calling down an air strike of blessings, God's irrevocable ordnance to rain down and down and down, in the clamoring and hectic midst of all of this they saw, noticed, became aware of a woman, standing as apart somehow as they but in no way still, perhaps ten feet from the music-holding table at the front of the room. She had maybe just come in; Grant had not noticed her before and she was certainly worth noticing. Young and dirty, dressed in two patterned dresses the patterns of which (green and gold, red and sickly blue) did not even come close to matching, or even to clashing interestingly, long blonde hair bound in a matted half braid and little twitching hands, jittering and curling like the paws of a sleeping cat, a dying insect, an animal writhing unconscious in the hunger it cannot control. Staring at her, just purely staring and Grant thought of energy relentless, the human embodiment of what light must be and suddenly as if in some way she had discerned his thoughts and was anxious to prove him right she jumped, literally jumped up and onto the music table, careless of balance, and yelled out—hoarse voice older than she looked— "Hey! *Hey! I* want to testify now, I want to say something! I want to talk about Clearwater Hospital now!"

and Robin's whole body jerking upright, one long sustained tremble stilled in the electric second and Angela in the spasm of his fist, eyes wide as if the woman had just called his true and secret name aloud and boldly for all to hear:

"I want to talk about it, it's a mental hospital, it's for *sick people*. You understand?" leaning close, too close to a woman in the front row who leaned away, whether consciously or unconsciously it was somehow patently offensive to the blonde who leaned farther still and promptly fell off the table to rise not so much nimble as like mercury, water, fluid in a tube rising from the heat and she stared into the woman's face, the man next to her, the minister in his gray suit forgotten by everyone, stilled by her emergence, her wild restless avidity: hands in the air as if creating in that space the dimension of pure theater, the theater of painful dreams and more painful wakings; and saying with her mouth one long Kabuki snarl, "Why do you call us schizophrenics? You don't call people with cancer 'cancers,' do you? They used to call me twice a week but you know what I did? *I ripped the phone out of the wall*, that's what I did! I'd do it again, too. I have a statue of Santa in my front yard, I have envelopes from every hospital in the country and Clearwater, holy *shit*. Do I ever have envelopes from Clearwater, do I—"

"Praise God," the minister said, obviously shaken, blown off course by the force of her attack. "Praise God and he will heal."

"I don't *want* to be healed," and she turned that smile on him, the way a wolverine might smile, the way the knife smiles in the middle of the night. "I *like* being this way. I'm not a *client*, I'm not a fucking *patient*, I'm not *patient* at all! You know who Prokofiev is? *The Fiery Angel*, you know about that? Shit. You call yourself a priest and you don't know about that? Hey mister, in Clearwater they got hot and cold running Jesus freaks and every single one of them knows *all about*—"

"Well praise God," less certainly, hands poised in some weak ineffectual benediction and searching Grant supposed for some way to shut her up, not even the best or easiest or most final but oh boy there was not going to be any shutting up here, not until she was ready; anyone could see that and see her now (and see too from the side of his eyes Robin's face as mortally transfixed as a man beholding the circumstance of his own birth: *pay attention now*): arms akimbo, head to one side like a clever trick-trained dog in the instant before it surrenders to the silent-growing hydrophobia within and bites your hand off at the wrist: her growling voice and "Mister, in Clearwater we got no less than four Jesus Christs, *four* of them, one more than Ypsilanti and except for Eddie Christ who only listens to big band they *all* know *everything* about Prokofiev.

They're *all* fiery angels, you know it? And they all take Stelazine and they're all on waiting lists and they all can see the future in the palms of their hands! So don't come to *me* about healing, I don't care fuck-all for healing, I like to be *just the way I am* and if anybody has a problem with that they got to catch me first! *Fuck!*"

The music still on, her hands on either side of her head as if without such ballast it might pop straight up and off: Robin staring, staring, consumed and for Grant one pure and calming second, epiphanic, what his father used to call the light-bulb minute: if this, if *she* was not a catalyst, what else could have the name? *Look* at him, his face, the way he held Angela: all there, alive, burning in the minute as he used to burn in the drawings, *look* at him now. Nothing hiding, nothing lost: all light; pure light.

And the minister saying something about surrendering to God's plan but she was done or at least done for now, done listening certainly but as obviously unwilling to wind down as the minister was rapidly winding down the services, they were for all intents and purposes (*her* intents and purposes less obvious or sure) over anyway: music off and one last hasty and unambitious prayer in which perhaps the two front rows joined and then "Donuts," someone said, a front-row woman in a red T-shirt that said FAITH MAKES THE DIFFERENCE above the static smile of an ironed-on child, "donuts and coffee, we can—"

and the blonde shrugging, the way a child shrugs to show she does not care two cents' worth anyway, and moving then toward the door, her walk as peculiar as the rest of her: a strange swaggering, almost a stumble as if she were permanently on the edge of some fine and endless line, a half-ragged gait that in its pointed pelvic hitching, its balance-less glide was more erotic than anything Grant had ever seen. I have to talk to her, he thought, I have to get her and rising up, himself strangely clumsy and moving as if on a drawn line, close enough to take her arm (although he did not; smart enough to know that much anyway): and said, "Excuse me. Excuse—"

Turning to him, on him and suddenly he was in the tunnel of her gaze, he had never been looked at by anyone the way he was regarded by her: brown eyes, big eyes circled in lavender, gray ash smudge as if she slept as little as Robin (and by the manic dance of her probably less, if he was any judge and he was, a little, by now), watering a little as if both-ered by the smoke, or more likely her own inner burn: staring at him: "What?" she said. "Who are you? Do I know you or something, are you a doc-tor?"

"No," embarrassed, no, *abashed*, he found he was trying to talk to the ground, his head canted down and he forced it up, forced himself to smile a smile that felt particularly painted on and "No, I just wanted, I heard what you said and I—"

"I can't hear you," she said, in her voice the buzz of annoyance; thinner up-close and the smell, she obviously hadn't washed in a while, hair or body; God, look at those eyes. "Are you trying to ask me out or something? because I don't go out with anybody unless I can kick his ass. Although I could probably take you," looking him up and down and he thought for a stark moment she might be about to try, "I took biology in school."

"No," again; stupidly; what is wrong with you, get to the point; she'll walk away in a minute and for that moment he felt intensely and horribly as he had when he was fourteen, trying to talk to girls, find the magic word to catch and keep their attention. A fine thread of sweat at his hairline and "That's not, I just wanted to ask if you—you see my friend, we came here and we were—"

And amazingly Robin's voice from over his shoulder, the voice of the guardian angel, angel guide and "Come drink coffee with us," he said, and even more amazingly came forward to reach, and take her hand: dirty little jittering hand in the fold of his own and "Come with us," he said again. "What's your name?"

"Saskia," she said.

The memory of another coffee shop, sitting with Robin, infinite caution and care and that exhilaration; remember? Almost like falling in love, the airless burn, the feeling of excitement intense and superceding; remember? Sitting in the booth next to Robin who sat opposite Saskia who did not sit, would not sit, stood to drink her coffee and glower at the waitress who was pretending not to see her but staring, staring every backhand minute. Eating a cheese pastry with the heedless voracity of a child, crumbs on her cheeks and chin, the hand delicate on the napkin, dabbing like a princess.

"Four years," she said in that whiskey voice, "I'm fucking twenty-nine years old, four years. This time. You do the math. You figure it out."

Robin stirred his coffee, smiled; he had been smiling ever since they left the church, smiling in the dark outside (the dark; and Grant's own disbelieving smile, *smiling* in the *dark*). Angela on the table like a crooked centerpiece, she and Saskia had met; Saskia had approved.

"I don't have to," Robin said to her, calm, a calm he surely could not have conjured, summoned a day ago, an hour ago. "I already know."

"*You* know," she said, musingly, not displeased. "Did you know that my palm prints tell other people's future?" Loose and dirty fingers spread wide like a mask before her loose and slanting grin. "Each of my fingers tells a different fate, all my fingerprints are different from other people's."

"Everyone's are," Robin said, not disagreeing. "That's why the cops always want to—"

"Have you ever heard," that smile again, "of dermatoglyphics?" White teeth in a smile ferocious, the remaining square of pastry torn in two. "You know I tried to teach a class in it, at Clearwater. *That* went over big." Frowning mouthful of cheese, "You know they need people with no imagination to take care of people like us; it keeps things balanced. If you like balance."

"Do you like it?" Robin again, Grant sitting back, saying nothing, only watching them, observing the way one might observe some principle of nature, some tectonic circumstance like comets to the earth, like dinosaurs mating, like borealis leaving the sky to burn like phosphorus along the trembling ground: do nothing, intrude not at all; only watch. Learn, if you can; listen. *Listen*: through the beating of your heart, the smell of her, those eyes and their mirror, Robin's eyes: wide, giving off his own light. "Balance," Robin said. "Do you like it? Do you have it?"

"I hate them," with real bitterness, her eyes for that moment unfocused as if to liberate an inner sight, memory's light, the parade of degradations small and large, privileges denied, injections given, shit wiped damp and spotty with the rubber fingers and the rag. "Fucking idiots, half of them couldn't get a real job so they work with us. They don't understand, all they want to do is wash their hands, *you* know that. *You* might even know it," to Grant, that turret gaze swung like a gun barrel, what ordnance there and ready? "You seem like you might. Or, you might be an asshole."

"Oh no," Robin's gentle defense as Grant's face filled softly and fully with blood, his crossed hands crossed more tightly on the faintly greasy surface of the table. "Grant got me out of the group home, he helps me out with doctors, you know, stuff like that. We live together."

To Grant: "You help him out, huh?" and not waiting for an answer, the last of the pastry in her mouth, crumbs on her lower lip and directly behind her the waitress with the coffeepot, strange dry odor as if the coffee within had been cooked for days: "Refills here?" but without enthusiasm or even false politeness, stepping obviously back, one step, two to stand hip shot; and staring. For Grant, though he was not its object, he was peripheral in the safest most anonymous way, there came that familiar prickling feel, anger and sorrow and if that was what he felt what must they feel, Robin and Saskia to whom that stare was as constant as respiration, their daily path the line between eyes averted and every gaze a freak show, hey look at this; where discourtesy called itself kindness, the eyes turned away from the spectacle of illness, two dresses, matted hair, dirty little handmade angel on the table and the waitress was looking at that, too, looking and finally saying not to but at Saskia with no real attempt to modulate her disgust: "You have to sit down and be quiet, this is a restaurant."

Grant, louder than he anticipated, the instant
words like marching feet from his open mouth:
"Hey. Why don't you just—"

and Saskia turning her stare to him for one instant, itself imbued with such murderous contempt
that he withered almost literally, subsided with the
precision and force of a chemical reaction as she
pointed that stare at the waitress and said, not
loudly but with great force, "Fuck you and I'll sit
and stand where I want to, *fuck* you."

"Listen here," the waitress said and then
stopped, apparently strapped for continuance, the
coffeepot still in hand and Robin surprising them
all, rising up with Angela in hand and sharply, in
real distress: "Just stop it, all right? Just *stop it*,"
and pushing out of the booth, out of the restaurant
and Grant rising, throwing money onto the table
and turning to Saskia, wanting to say *Come on* or
Let's go but fearing a reprise of that stare, of the
words that might occur and so simply following
Robin, Robin who had been so happy, Robin who
had been enjoying himself for once, for once—and
there, out on the sidewalk, he had not gone far
after all. Leaning into the closed door of a bakery,
HAGELSTEIN's in silent curls of neon and his body
just below that silence as if by the force of need
alone he would press himself inside it, and Saskia—
she moved so quickly, water, mercury, Grant had
not even felt her passing—already beside him, saying something into his ear. As Grant reached them

she stopped speaking, looked at him as if she were Robin's friend and he the newcomer, uninitiated, unwelcome in these deeps and arenas: I know, that look said, what I know, and *he* knows; and you don't.

"Robin," softly, not trying to get past her, not trying to reach for him (although a part of Grant wanted very much to do both); "listen, Robin, what do you want to do now?"

Indistinguishable; a sound into his arm, bent head pressed to his sleeve like an old woman crying, weeping into a rag. Saskia's eyes very bright suddenly, like a pet, a wicked bird: dismaying to Grant on some level subterranean and her mouth at Robin's ear, whispering, words like a breath and then out of the doorway, past them and down the street, not hurrying but moving with such awkward speed that looking once toward Robin and back to the street Grant had lost her: like something strange glimpsed from the corner of the eye bewildered and then gone: gone.

And Robin moving from his space, that cloaking angularity of door and sleeve and window and he was smiling, in the dark and bereft and *smiling* and Grant thought of magic, true magic as hideous and remorseless as electricity, as the pulse enormous of light: and saying to Grant, "Let's go home now, all right? I want to go home now."

"All right," Grant said. "All right, sure. Let's go," and from the doorway down the silent side-

walk, past the restaurant without either of them
glancing at it once, past the church (dark inside, no
Pentecostals, no basement dwellers left to emerge
in amazement) and to the car to drive home as if
through one serial darkness as small after all as a
room, sweet and drowsy as dusk in a nursery, the
hands that gentle and hold you, the swaddling feel
of the blankets and the dew in closing eyes: there is
nothing bad here, there is no way to be hurt. Only
safety. Lights on the road like the orchestrated
flickerings of a hundred candles, a thousand tipped
faintly green, Robin's head calm against the window, Grant's hands on the wheel and between
them both Angela, her skirt much the worse for the
evening's excesses, hair tumbled to baldness on one
side and her whole small body canted permanently
sideways as if blown forever by a wind as wide and
consuming and possessive as the open gates of
Heaven itself.

Catalyst; cataclysm. Armageddon. The smell of her
dirty hair, the way her face had looked when she
leapt atop the table, when she whispered to Robin;
her eyes, those eyes. A schizophrenic like Robin,
but where beneath that blanket, that gray circus
tent did her own turns and thrashings fall, which
ill-made label had they devised for her? Something
special, Grant thought, stirring coffee in the silent
morning, Robin still nested and presumably asleep,
it must have been special, it must have been some-

thing achieved like lead made from gold: new
words, for this one, new devices, new treatments
and plans. Maybe that was why she said she hated
doctors so much: under the pressure of her difference they had perhaps evolved some differences of
their own, although that presupposed imagination
and Grant had yet to meet any true imagination in
the mental health system; of course that was most
of the problem, it was a system for mental health,
not mental illness. What had Johnna called them?
The worried well, yes. So much easier to diagnose,
to treat; so much more sensible, amenable, so
much less mad. Not that he dismissed utterly the
possibility of imagination in the doctors, the aides,
the therapists who like Johnna seemed ruled
equally by concern and didacticism; it was just that
he must judge by what he saw and what he saw was
not imagination. They had their rules and proce-
dures, their ways of conducting the business of
care; but then there was Robin, with his drawings;
and then again there was Saskia.

She had been in Clearwater, she said; she was
twenty-nine years old, she was apparently in no
continuing treatment at all; she did not wash, had
eaten as if she were truly hungry; was she sub-
sisting without medication, was she living on the
street? Probably. A lot did; deinstitutionalization,
that was called. Smart, he mocked himself, the coffee cold and brown. You know all the words, the
terms, you know who to blame, you know a hell of

a lot more than you used to. That's why she can come in and in two minutes do more good than you have in months and months. And months. Pat yourself on the back a little harder, smart man, stupid man, and if you're so fucking smart for your next trick you can figure out how to get her to come back.

But she took care of that: she was smarter than he, infinitely smarter and quicker, more adept on her mental feet: she was supposed to be the crazy one, wasn't she? and yet here she was like a flawless magic, nothing up her sleeves and crouched by the outer door, grinning in the afternoon rain: on their way out to the grocery store, the cash machine, the sidewalks gray and she there in a tangle of limbs and plaid shirts, crooked static elbows and knees and those eyes bright as bullets, her filthy hair wrapped in some complicated crown and "Hey," to Robin who stood unsurprised and hugely pleased, reaching with his hands to raise her up. "Hey hey hey. Got any cigarettes?"

"No, I—no. I don't smoke." Still holding her hands and Grant behind them both, amazed, there was no other word for it: by this connection, its almost insupportable ease: how had she known? He had been with them every second, hadn't he, except for a second or two. Dumb smart man on the sidewalk with a sagging plastic sack of returnable bottles cutting painlessly into the flesh of his bent fingers, staring at them both as they stared at one another in the damp wind and the slant of the rain.

"Oh so you're the guy," smiling at Robin, "the one crazy man in the world who doesn't smoke. What did you do in the dayroom then? Watch the TV? Soap operas?"

"I don't know. Draw. Read," smiling, shrugging to make Angela jitter, Angela who hung from a button on his jacket, the rain creating slow ruination, her true nature emerging slowly in the interstices. "Talk to myself. Talk to God."

"Bet he didn't answer. Want to see where I live?"

The bottles in the back seat along with Robin and Saskia (and Angela, whom Saskia took as seriously as she took Grant and with less suspicion and intrinsic dislike), the wipers back and forth and Saskia's directions having as little to do with the landscape around them as her asides to the conversation, or the conversation Grant was hearing: of course he was handicapped, wasn't he, by the hardwired habit of linear thought, he was not in this game at all, at all.

"Left here, *turn* here—*left* I said!"

"I did turn left, I—"

"That tree. Do you remember it?"

"With the little gate around it? the fence thing? In the exercise—"

"Yeah, yeah yeah yeah. Grounds privileges, shit. I had to get the whole—*here*, right here, stop stop.

Stop," with a glare Grant could feel through the
headrest. He stopped: four corners: a party store, a
mailbox, an empty lot, a gray brick two-story house
with a red Toyota in the driveway and two snowmo-
biles up on some kind of plywood platform.

"Turn here," with the dignity associated with
giving orders to monkeys, making demands of dogs.
Stray dogs. "Just turn here and go down to the
middle of the block. A blue house. Did you know,"
her tone changing instantly, eager and sweet, "that
bird?"

The name of the street was Regent. Most of the
houses were bungalows, old houses, the kind of
neighborhood where everybody had been living in
the same homes for a long time and would probably be living there for a long time. And his eyes in
motion and stopping without being told, stopping
before Saskia could say "That's it," pulling up beside a house that was maybe blue somewhere underneath its outer layers, its concatenation of layers: there was not an inch of the house that was not
decorated in some way, for some holiday, in no
order and without apparent conception or design.
Half-grim plastic hilarities, red hearts and Easter
bunnies and blow-up Halloween skeletons all
now blown baggy in the wind, harvest cornstalks
withered anxious by the long alternating circumstances of heat and cold, peeling Santas and green
wreaths and brown reindeer hanging from the windows, the porch, tied like hostages to the backyard

gate and presumably the fence as well, though
from where Grant stood it was beyond vision; the
whole house was somehow beyond vision, it was as
if the house existed at the core of the sense of holiday itself, where any aberrancy can be tolerated
and bad behavior be excused, where for one day
rabbits talk and skeletons dance and anyone can be
your valentine and there is truly and completely
peace on earth.

"Ho ho ho," Saskia said as if she could read his
mind; maybe she could; was he that transparent?
How boring he must seem to her, little linear man
with his linear mind and everything the way it
ought to be, no surprises, no terrors, no alarms in
the night; no fracturing beauty, no pain. Nothing
like that at all because all that was Robin's province
and hers as well, the land of the schizophrenic, the
undifferentiated landscape as alien as any moon
through which he could walk, could visit, could
learn the landmarks and the signs and maybe even
be allowed to stay awhile: but could never live,
could never after any amount of time or suffering
or brute effort become a native, or even pass for
one. An outsider, perennially outside, unafflicted
with the natives' logic, Saskia's logic, pure Z logic
that not only accepts its permanent estrangement
from what is normal living, normal people's normal
lives, but has chosen, fiercely, to revel in it, rejecting both the semi-hope of early illness, where a
cure, a return to the normal seems possible, and

the bleak blank despairing emptiness of the chronic patient who has forgotten where the lines are, forgotten where the last long step across had come: this was the triumph of Z logic, each intersection, each branching and each revelation of difference: we are not as you, that house said, every inch of it, every tatter, every twist, *I* am not as you: and fuck you, all of you, every last staring one of you and every stare you ever have. Because this is my house.

"Come on," Robin mildly to Grant who stood still gaping (as tourists will, he thought, and despised himself briefly) and then up, past cornstalks, past Christmas angels whose laminate eyes had been so long worn blind that they were on the verge of again achieving some cyclic sight, past the threshold into a darkened house that smelled so strongly of urine that for a moment Grant literally lost his breath, gagged into the catch of his cupping hand: and then Saskia was swearing, kicking her way through the aggregate mess—newspapers, newsmagazines, grocery sacks of clothing or rags— to an unseen background where he heard a door slam, her curses again in rising volume and intensity, her face now dry with a pallor that seemed to herald some kind of dire epiphany, a seizure or a stroke, no one could look like that without eventual disaster: "—fucking *dogs* is what it is, that fucking bitch Regina, bitch cunt and her bitch cunt dogs and she lets them piss in here, my mother hated

her, my mother *hated* her," with such white-faced
passion that Grant stood absolutely still, absolutely
without motion as he had stood during the most
extreme explosions of Robin's pain: but then Robin
was there, saying nothing, opening a window,
kitchen window to let in the breeze and the rain
and calm to the front door to open that too, hold it
open and miraculously Saskia was beside him, her
smile as well miraculous although it seemed as if
she had forced it somehow through her own flesh,
some inner pressures at work in ways that Grant,
the outsider, could never guess.

"Well shit," she said, "there's plenty of that. You
want a drink? Get one. For me too."

The refrigerator was new, almond-colored, very
clean: Robin took from it three immaculate cans of
Coke which they all opened and drank standing in
the living room, amid the junk and the piles to the
ankles as if in performance of some fine though
faintly solemn duty; and then Saskia was sitting,
shoving a clearing with ass and elbows and pulling
one of the bags to her, upending it so a compressed
cube of clothing fell out and into her lap. With one
hooking finger she fished from the cube a blouse,
long prim sleeves, blue and white flowers: "You
think," to Robin who stood, can in hand and head
at the angle with which we behold the miraculous,
"any of these will fit Angela?" .

* * *

They ended up staying: to drink Coke after Coke, to piss in the big blue bathroom (guest towels dusty and untouched, one big beach towel that apparently served for Saskia; no pills, medications anywhere to Grant's swift half-guilty inspection and what, he asked himself, did you expect? look at her), to sort through the bags of clothing—"Regina gets it from the Goodwill, I think, for five bucks a bag or something or maybe for free 'cause it's for a *good cause*": dresses, some mismatched shoes, old panty hose stretched like skin discarded, a raveled green sweatshirt that said SHIT HAPPENS—"to me!" comically to Robin and even to Grant; thank you, Mrs. Dives, for the crumbs from your table. She kept the sweatshirt, kept a couple pairs of socks, a strapless bra, all the rest bundled back into the bags that Robin then stacked neatly by the door, then onto the tired sofa where he perched enchanted, watching her move and chatter in her balanceless way, her dirty hair, her gaze coming back and back again to him; and across the room, less sturdily placed in a wire-backed lawn chair Grant not enchanted but in some simpler way amazed, watching her and in a private and attenuating perception watching her effect on Robin as well.

They ate the dinner she prepared, heavily salted macaroni on paper plates; there were no less than thirty boxes of macaroni in the cupboard; Saskia's bored explicating shrug, "Regina thinks I'm

too stupid to fix anything else." Robin ate very little, Grant cleaned his plate, the macaroni weirdly
tasteless despite all the salt, clumsy on the fork,
drinking more Coke and Saskia's voice the thread
and counterpoint, cocked head and moving fingers
and eyes, eyes, eyes. Viewed not as habitat, now
that the piss smell had dissipated, the house itself
was not uncomfortable and clearly as much a nest
for its lone occupant as Robin's pillows and sleeping bags in their own living room (and no broken
blinds, either) were for him.

She talked as she ate not about the hospital, as
Grant had expected, but about her mother, using
the salt and pepper it seemed on every bite: a pair
of little glass leprechauns, one black-hatted, one
white, both grinning. "She died a couple years ago.
Regina's her friend. They wouldn't let me out of
the hospital until the day of the funeral, they
dressed her in some shitty old dress of Regina's and
then makeup, makeup all over her face. I wiped it
off," without a smile but Grant could visualize the
scene entire and thought she must have been smiling then, a kind of triumphant teeth-baring smile,
there she goes again the relatives would have said
in mingled discomfort and dislike and the unseen
Regina furious maybe or maybe only silent, silent
and in tears. "This is my house. Regina got the car,
I can't get a license anyway. You got a license?"

"No," Robin said. Macaroni congealed on his

plate, his head at a dreamy incline. "I don't want to drive anyway."

"I remember," the saltshaker in motion again, down down down the crystal rain, "holding my head and telling her Mama something's wrong with my head, something's really wrong. And she gave me aspirin," without bitterness but not without a certain anger, the wronged feeling common to the misunderstood; but then in swooping reversal that long crocodile grin, " 'Course she had her hands full with the old man." Wiping her mouth. "He was a crazyman, just like me. Runs in the family. Runs in the family, that's what she used to say."

They sat at the table for an hour, two after dinner, and Robin would have stayed the night, mutinous as a child when Grant insisted it was time to go: "You have a doctor's appointment tomorrow," successfully resisting that caretaker's urge to say *we* have an appointment, resisting many other urges as well and some of them so subterranean that even he did not really understand, did not want now to take the time to understand and anyway he was not and never would be the issue here. Never. He was the facilitator, the caregiver, the friend, yes, the friend on the outside, the one who dealt with the regulations and the consultations, the one who made the meals and paid the bills; and the chauffeur, don't forget that; I don't want to drive anyway.

Surprisingly Saskia agreed with him, prodding Robin with one admonishing finger: "He's right,"

she said. "You need to go to the doctor, get your
meds. Even if they're all fucks, which they are,
fucking crazy bastards like that old Johnson guy,
remember him? Dr. Johnson, they used to say it
like he was holy, they built the building around him
I think. What a *prick*," and Robin's smile, wide,
nodding, Angela nodding in twinned motion and
Saskia's grim wreathing memories, her Clearwater
was his Clearwater although perhaps a little less so,
at least it seemed to have affected her with more
permanent pain or maybe that was because her
case had always been more extreme and therefore
more prone to extremities of treatment; or maybe
Robin was equally pained and he, Grant, was simply unaware; anything was possible. Anything, and
Robin's laughter, Grant had missed something
(again), some bit of business and Saskia was laughing too, flat rising giggle behind her hand on which
a tiny scrap of macaroni had dried, head back and
one of the twists or braids of hair had come loose
and now lay against her neck and cheek, dirty
blonde with real dirt, who knew what she would
look like clean? Not prettier, maybe, grime might
be her glamour, a matte protective layer to heal by
covering the lifelong evidence of her illness, her
excesses, intended, self-inflicted or not; or contrari-
wise she might be more beautiful, Botticelli bitch
scraped pink and clean and long damp billowings of
hair around her face, down her back, across her
breasts—and Robin was standing up, then, touch-

ing her hand and saying, "You come and see us, all right? Okay?" and she was nodding, sure, sure, neither of them looking at Grant who to his own shamefaced amazement realized he had an erection, thinking of Saskia not only clean but cleanly naked, pointy little breasts and long hair and those eyes rolled back in mute ecstatic orisons, it was just, he told himself, that he had gone without for so long, he had not fucked anyone since Johnna and that was a long time ago. A *long* time ago. Of course he would not want to have sex with Saskia, it was wrong in too many ways to number, not the least of which that if anyone was going to fuck her it ought to be Robin who now bent to say something into her ear that did not make her smile, only nod: and then Grant was thanking her for dinner, the normal thing to do, the tourist thanking the natives for a lovely fire dance and ritual sacrifice. On the porch, a long-deflated Easter bunny now sagged like skin in the renewing rain, its pink color strapped and mildew-mottled and Saskia was saying, "—from a gas station, my dad brought it home. Blew it up on the lawn with a bicycle pump and my mother kept saying That's enough, really, that's enough but he wasn't happy till he blew it right the fuck up. *Up*," and just behind Grant's car another car, a small dark blue subcompact and in it a woman watching them, an older woman in some kind of red and blue slicker, its hood pulled back and away from the disapproving face; maybe this was the unseen Regina, come to clean up or check up or whatever she was supposed to do. She did not move nor did Saskia acknowledge her; a simple slam of the door and Robin first with Grant following down the slippery walk to their car, sat inside long enough for the defrosters to work on the foggy windows and Grant saw the woman from the other car leave it to enter the house next door. The nosy neighbor, then.

Robin fell asleep on the way home. Grant played the radio softly, softly, a station with a song that seemed without end, all electric violin and a bass line beneath that went on and on, like a heartbeat, like a river, like the endless flow of medication into Robin, into Saskia (hidden maybe?— maybe), into all the ones for which it was more than a lifeline but less than a cure, into hospitals like Clearwater like a colorless ribbon to bind if never heal the swollen, sluggish river of endlessness and wounds.

Cursing from the traffic, the stairs and not the elevator; just back in fact from the doctor's, Robin dreamy and silent on the sofa and he sorting the mail with irritable haste: and then like a cat, a curious nameless beast he heard the scratching. *Her* scratching, not knocking at the door like a, like a (say it) normal person would and once in she walked around the apartment with the disinterested interest of a police officer, an investigator, poking into everything, seeming dismayed by the order or maybe that was only Grant's discomfort; the rooms took on a different cast filled with her presence; she changed things. Robin on the sofa watching her, simply watching, hands in lap and smiling a particular smile, one not often seen; as if he observed a change in the weather, a change in climate: a shift, a drift, a drop.

What engaged her interest engaged it utterly: she liked the books about dreams and altered states, liked them as much as Angela but less than Robin's drawings, all the drawings, he showed her everything. Both of them on the floor, half-wrapped in his nest and all the pictures spread before her, surrounding harvest of beauty and unspeakable pain but to her, Grant supposed, nothing was unspeakable, no holds barred, no doors closed: once you were in there was nothing you could not say, nothing to which you could not refer, no subjects too agonizing or severe for comment or discourse. There on the floor in the murmurs and the silence, heads bent in agreement and consideration they were together in a way Grant for all his care and his own agonized moments, his own upheavals and remorse could never approach, an acceptance not denied but simply not possible: the way a fish, say, might watch the slow recursive swoop of birds above, swimming as well as he but in an element he could not master.

In the kitchen making dinner (chili, dumping

canned soup and beans into a pot, chopping peppers and onions with fast ominous flicks of the carving knife, a knife too big for the job) and hearing
without listening (he was not listening surely, he
was not eavesdropping, he would not do something
like that to Robin) their words and small sounds,
their occasional laughter: he was *happy* for Robin,
it was incredible that Robin had been able to con-
nect not only so deeply and well but so instantly
with anyone; *instantly*, that was the surprise here, a
matter of days or more sheerly hours as contrasted,
say, with the weeks it had taken Grant to effect
even the most tremulous bridgings, the thinnest ice
of trust and no matter how hard he had tried in the
end she had been able to achieve quantum levels of
closeness and access that he, now, *he*—

And Saskia yelling something about adult children of psychotics, of alcoholics and "I'm an adult
monster, how about that?"

and Robin's laughter, easy, instant, the laughter
of agreement, two people with one idea and the
sizzle of peppers in the pan, flashing in the grease
and burning, smoking and burning

and Grant careless with the spatula, slapping it
in the pan and "Shit!" as a large popping dollop of
grease landed on his wrist, burning him, burning
even under the splash of cold water and Robin into
the kitchen saying "Are you okay? Grant?" and his
snarl: "I'm *fine*" which he instantly tried to check,
make easier by saying, "I burned myself, that's all,

it's okay," but Robin's eyes downcast and he left the kitchen, left Grant to think as the water ran down his arm, barely touching the burn at all: *Why you simple shit, you're jealous of her. You're* jealous *of her. Of them both. Third wheel, fifth wheel, oh you asshole can't you do anything right at all?*

And in that larger shame, a burn much like the burn on his arm but bigger, oh, and infinitely deeper, the scar born as well in the brief conceiving moment and Grant felt the water run, without ease or absolution, cold and colder down his arm until he felt nothing there, not the burn, not the sense of his own flesh; nothing. Cut off.

On the stove the chili had boiled to a skin, the peppers sullen and half-translucent in the ruined smolder of the oil. He scraped the frying pan clean and started over.

She stayed the night. On the sofa. Presumably on the sofa but Grant's own door closed and resolute, resolute as he had been all evening, through dinner (a long wild discussion of the mental health field, two insiders and one arriviste despairing and decrying, Saskia mocking in particular the idea of gender differences: "Estrogen is an antipsychotic? Stand by for menopause!" and himself trying to mumble something somewhere between conciliatory and knowledgeable and earning her mockery for that, too: "Oh no," her mouth pulled down, "he read a book"), through the longer examination of Robin's art (at least they could all agree on something) and the well-lit midnight, Grant fetching bedclothes for Saskia and leaving them there, together; alone. Still alone together in this exceptionally well-lit morning but as he had all night he would not listen for sounds of talking, of (say it) fucking, would not sniff for spoor; the penance of silence; lay off, he told himself, and did.

Water running in the bathroom and that had to be Robin, washing up (washing his dick?) (shut up) and out of his room in sweatpants and T-shirt to see Robin still asleep in the nest, Saskia's blankets and pillow snarled on the couch: they had not slept together then (and a little mean gladness, instantly suppressed but unforgivable). Quietly making coffee, the water running and running and then Robin was awake, and then it was the three of them, in the kitchen, together: Saskia a tangle of wet hair and yesterday's clothes, Robin's smile instant and shy: and Grant pouring three cups of coffee, three mugs unidentical on the counter, lined in a short and staggered row.

The Holiday House, Robin called it; and the time they spent there was very much like a holiday: not a vacation, there was not that sense of planned aimlessness to it, of pleasure structured and enjoyed, but a holiday where there are rituals to be once again undertaken, certain acts and gestures to be performed and all of it overlaid with a sense of time: time the fourth participant, the unseen watcher whose presence influences everything.

For Grant, the only one whose life intersected on a daily basis with the real world, the one whose standards and attitudes were in many ways in conflict with both, the Holiday House would always as its true and secret name be known to him as Saskia's house; where Saskia lived, had lived for years and years, most of her growing-up time: growing up crazy, with that mantis smile. Schizophrenia had come early to her but not unannounced: in the blood, she said, her father's blood, her father as crazy as she and "I used to be scared of it, you know, scared of him," sitting at the kitchen table, idle fingers on the black-hatted leprechaun, turning it this way and that. "He'd do some weird fucking thing and I would think, is that going to be me, too? Am I going to try to smother the cat like he does? Am I going to go out for drives and not come back for two days or not at all until the cops bring me home, is that what's going to happen to me?"

The leprechaun rocking, rocking back and forth, her fingers metronomic, pressure and pressure and Grant, softly, careful to be careful: "So what happened?"

"Me," she said. "That's what happened. Shit, Grant, you're so dumb sometimes. I got it too, I'm as crazy as he ever was, the neighbors and Regina said it was what killed my mom," and Robin's flinch noticed by both of them, Grant's mouth open to say something kind but Saskia there before him, faster, sharper: "Fuck that. I know what you're thinking. If they die it's their own fucking fault, Robin, come on. If they want to blame us for that then we can blame them for making us crazy, I mean it's a circle, it just goes on and on," and then ostensibly to Grant but maybe more to that fourth figure, that sense of time: and with immense bitterness, "You don't realize what it's like for us, all the energy we put out just to live. Any one of us is better than ten of you. It's *hard* to live the way we do, you know it? And another thing," more quietly, the leprechaun released to lie on his distaff side, next to a pile of expired coupons and the roll of a grocery store flyer, "nobody understands this but it's *beautiful*, it's really beautiful. Like in your drawings," to Robin who did not smile, whose face in strained relief showed as a symbol shows some other room, some other father and mother and the illness like a tent to cover them all, sick kids, sick families, everyone in orbit about the gravitational pull of the illness. "Do you know when I was a little girl there were marks on the sidewalk that told me my name? Interference patterns," not dreamily but as if she spoke another language, words and meanings Grant on his own would never apprehend but that came somehow from her mouth already translated into simple words and phrases he could understand: not the way Robin understood her, through his fingers, through the aperture of gaze alone: but competent, enough, enough to get by.

And in one motion past Grant's quiet face she grabbed up both salt and pepper and hurled them to the floor, the coupons next to flutter like the wings of agitated birds and then she was throwing everything, reaching, grabbing, anything she could get her hands on was in the air or on the floor or in some windmilling combination of both states and she was screaming something, past coherence and Grant was still, still as Robin rose sorrowful and this time simply left the room: to stand in the living room where Grant followed him, uncertain of his own response both committed and not, stand shoulder to shoulder to see out the window the neighbor again, staring in at the house, motionless on the sidewalk and Grant with a moment's fugitive gladness (past the screaming and the crashing) realizing anew and with a sharper insight that there were levels and levels of touristry and that he was not as far on the outer rim as he might have imagined. No, he was here in the inner circle or at least the anteroom, where things break and people howl and pain is always there; time's sister in her hood and cloak, her hands worn fleshless and nude as a skull, busy hands in constant terrible motion in the use of tools the name and history of which each person knows intimately without ever wanting to know.

The smashing sounds stopped. Saskia came out

of the kitchen to sit before the silent television and count her fingers, thin and trembling fingers, over and over again. After a few moments Robin came to sit beside her and help her count.

"It's beautiful," she said, her voice trembling. "It's beautiful here," and Robin's nod each time she spoke, yes, that nod said, yes it is. It really is. As beautiful as his drawings, the art of pain; as beautiful as a flayed and pinned, still-beating human heart condemned to constant motion by the knowledge that the only thing more painful was to stop.

"It's beautiful here."

Yes it is.

Without expressed decision from any of them, the pattern established: three times a week, Grant's work hours permitting: at varying times, for varying reasons but every reason the same, Robin in the light, Saskia in the dark, Grant in between and the very alchemy of that triple presence was itself to Grant a new variant, a more rough and intoxicating kind of experimentation but one which to his silent relief he need not direct, or chaperon, or attempt to keep under control: he was the bystander here, they were the ones. The ones who talked to Angela, the ones who talked about Clearwater. The ones who talked back to the television or sat on the front porch naming the birds. The ones who went into silence as if it were a deep gray room, Robin more often than Saskia; the ones who screamed, Saskia all over: as if inside her were some endless tunnel from which the darkness expelled its benisons and threats, its own ominous insistence upon its continuing presence in her life: the lord of pain, the angel of darkness who slept sometimes curled like poison in her breast, who slept and dreamt and muttered; if the sleep of reason breeds monsters, what then breeds from the sleep of angels, the permutations of those dreams? Untranslatable, but present in her screams, in her angers: in her tears: and in her stories.

She told a lot of stories; she liked to talk. The wild card, queen of jokers, Scheherazade with her own fathomless agenda, who knew why she chose the stories she chose to tell? Of madness as the place of absolutes, of black and white and nothing between but the dead air of unconsciousness. Of lying naked and groaning in seclusion, tortured past the limit of speech, vision, tactile sensation and the end of the world and waking in three days (like Lazarus, like Christ) just in time to rise, wash, dress in weakness and stumbling exhaustion and go to dinner with her parents at a restaurant where her manners were that of a duchess and her father tried without success to discern with what exact poison his food had been laced.

"It used to bug the shit out of my mother," leaning back on the sofa, her head on Robin's shoulder, Robin who sat so still in the refracting light, Robin who needed the light more than ever now but not, it seemed, Grant thought, he hoped for the same reason. "Two crazies. Regina never got over it. He could see the thoughts everybody was having except himself. And me. He always said he couldn't see through my head and it really used to piss him off."

Together, two as one they made up histories for Angela: princess, captive, man in the moon; they slept like children on the floor, naptime in the heavy gold of afternoon, Grant awake and silent reading *Outdoors* magazine and wondering why things like whitewater rafting and rock climbing did not now seem in any way adventurous or imbued with true risk. On the floor, there, that was risk: her dirty hair, his thin face, their legs tangled in a kind of asexual innocence that was as transparent as it was brief: they would start fucking soon, Grant thought, watching them sleep, feeling the dull pressure of his own erection, they almost had to. It was obvious to anyone or at least to him that Robin was thoroughly and totally in love, crazy in love he said to himself and smiled, a little, ignored his hard-on, went back to his magazine. *Outdoors*, outside, why wasn't there a magazine called *Inside*, one to explore the treachery and huge vistas of the mind, that most dire of all terrains, least understood, last mended? He could be the foreign correspondent, dispatches from the back of the front. What It's Like to Be Normal. Why I Am the Way I Am. Saskia had tried to explain it to him more than once, with varying degrees of irritation and success: it's like glasses, she had said just that morning (her head not on his shoulder, perched like a bird on her own independent neck), the difference between wearing them and not wearing them when you need to. If I wore glasses your world would be the way I see without them. Do *you* see?

Eyes, all eyes and looking into his: not smiling but not yet exasperated, giving him the benefit not of doubt but of silence: and his nod, I see. I do see. It's a difference in perspective, it's a—

"No!" loud but not shouting, not screaming; not yet. "No no no, that's not it *at all*." And off to the kitchen, his kitchen this time to watch Robin give Angela a bath with a paper towel and a drop of spit, to ignore Grant when he entered, later, to begin to fix the dinner she would overload with salt and ketchup before eating.

Despite the misunderstandings, the feeling she evoked in Grant of being a tourist in his own home, a looker-in, a mere watcher, despite the other feelings she evoked, it was for Grant a time approaching not epiphany but the golden state before, a time when all three of them could sit together—his kitchen, her kitchen, his living room, her front porch—and talk, and listen: and laugh: and sometimes achieve in their triune togetherness something that Grant felt (and hoped to be true; he was not sure; he was not sure of anything these days) they could not have achieved separately: a kind of

collaboration between sorrow and madness and
happiness and the dark, fear as well as quietude,
her laughter as well as her screams. As well as
Robin's silences. As well as his drawings.

Which had begun again, effortlessly, as if they
had never stopped: a flow so immense that Grant
could not even feel envy for Saskia's role in
prompting them, could only stand in silent grati-
tude to watch the flow. No less dark for the light in
which they were produced, no less harrowing for
the smile Robin wore as he displayed them, no less
excruciating to view—infants in torment, enucle-
ated eyes borne in hands blessed by the stigmata,
shadows and dead rooms from which it was certain
nothing good could ever come—and apprehend:
more and more, tumbling from him to spin and
glitter like fluid past gravity's embrace, like happy
blood, like sperm, ropes and ropes threading
through the air, and Saskia clapped her hands
when she saw them, or hooted in pleasure, or—
sometimes; rarely—wept in slow hitching growls
into her hands: "You see everything," she told
Robin, those eyes wide and wet with fury and her
own remembrance. "You see every fucking thing in
this world and you know what to do about it, don't
you? Don't you," without question, it was no question, between them it seemed there were no
questions at all. And Robin did not smile, or shrug,
or even seem to hear her at all: but he was listening, oh he was listening, Grant could feel it from

across the room, see it in the muscles of Robin's back, the angled bend of his neck: strung on her pleasure like a mouse on wire, like a pinned and crucified insect in some harsh laboratory light; he heard everything she said and, Grant thought, the things she did not say he heard most and best of all. Love will do that, he thought, watching them both, love will open doors, love will find a way. A way in. All the way in; *ignore it*, sternly; sternly. Since that day in the kitchen, his ugly jealous flare and its insidious aftermath, that fierce internal pettiness like a dog with a sore he had tried in shame and self-disgust to ignore the beauty of her, Robin's obvious love, infatuation, call it whatever you wanted but it was as there as a fire, as a flare, as a bursting vein or a spurting cock and when she gave it back —inevitable, she would have to give it back, she was giving so much already with that leaning head and touching hand and eyes, eyes, eyes—then, well.

Then what? he asked himself, watching her fingers busy on a fashion magazine, tearing to pieces each ad that featured a woman's face, busy little fingers, busy little scraps of hair and lips and eyes around her like some dry flesh confetti and looking up, suddenly, into his own regard, giving him all those eyes like looking down the barrel of some infinite weapon, *here it is: take it.*

Take it.

And Robin asleep, there, close enough to be

touched by her busy hands, sleeping in the sun, another one of his naps: he slept a lot lately: tired maybe from his exultation, the wondrous drain of work (and what work: oh Robin the things you do now), tired from being in love. Sleeping in the sun with his two totems, rag Angela wrapped around his wrist, silent Saskia ripping up faces and eyes, his fingers moving, moving in his sleep as if he grasped, reached, found and held in the endless sun of the country of dreams the things he had not fully understood he needed until he saw them drenched and gilded with that slow eternal light: and a smile, exquisite, across that pale face, eyes moving as if in roving pleasure beneath the shivering lids, socketed with pain but now a pain escaped through the combined influences of Saskia, art and sleep: Robin *in excelsis*, Robin renewed and restored to a place where Grant in all his scramblings, his plannings, his reading and his experimenting had never begun to even glimpse, let alone make manifest the way: it was in a different sense a miracle that he, Grant, had not in his clumsiness and greed done more damage, damage unguessed and ineffable, more damage than the hospitals and the doctors, the aides and the group homes, Johnna and Alison, more damage than the executioner disease itself; be thankful for Saskia in more ways than one; it was a miracle things were turning out the way they were.

How were they turning out?

Saskia set down the magazine, let the scraps scatter; Robin stirred a little in his sleep. The light Vermeer moved across the floor. "Come on out on the porch with me," Saskia said. "I want to have a cigarette."

Grant quietly behind her, that dirty hair in a perky twist, strange childish braids and a T-shirt too small across her small breasts. He did not like it when she smoked, sometimes she burned herself: through carelessness, smoking too close to the filter or letting the cigarette smolder in her unfeeling fingers, insisting she did not feel the pain. Ugly purple burn on her index finger; it doesn't hurt. Irritably. It doesn't *hurt* I said. Robin's mild remembrance, a woman in the group home who had suffered from a terrible infection, something in her breast that the physical doctor to whom she was brought (against her will, which to Robin had seemed almost past mentioning: of course, his manner seemed to imply, it was against her will, everything they do to us is against our will, why should that have been any different? If she wanted to die from that infection, let the slow suppuration spread and spread and spread through her body like the crawling fingers of schizophrenia itself, why then they would have stopped her: it was as simple as that) had as she told Robin later snarled and swore at the aide who had accompanied her into the examining room, gave her an injection (the effects of which she did not at all enjoy) while still snarling that this woman must be in incredible pain and what the fuck was the matter with them anyway to delay treatment for so long. And the woman of course told them all she had felt nothing, no pain at all; no one had listened; Robin had not in the retelling of this story been surprised. That was the way things were; you were crazy, for God's sake, who was going to waste their time listening to you? Especially about anything important, pain or medication, come on.

Now: the pluming smoke from Saskia's nose, she liked to blow smoke, she liked to play with the lighter but mostly, Grant thought, to tease him (or maybe that was sheer ego, maybe she never noticed at all how nervous her games made him: fire and smoke, smoke and mirrors, mirrors and the silver stare of empty eyes). Her head tilted back, mouth pursed into half a smile: "Regina asked me yesterday if you were crazy."

Think before you speak; he did. "So what did you say?"

That pleased her; seeing this his own pleasure was absurdly immense; he had made her smile: all by himself, no Robin involved. "I said you were a guy I knew and if she didn't like it she could fuck off."

"Well, thank you." The arch of hand and cigarette, the dissipating blur of smoke. Her eyes. To say something: "She was over yesterday?"

"In my dreams. With her fucking dogs and I

told her I was going to blow them up in the microwave if she didn't keep them out of the house, I'm sick of slopping piss. Piss everywhere. Piss hiss miss kiss. Kiss me, Grant."

His deliberate nonreaction: like an echo of word salad, it was just that, just words until: her face before his and her mouth against his mouth, cigarette breath and the soft pallor of her lips, pressed against his and: blood flurry through his body, fingertips and cock, running everywhere and: herself drawing back in silence, a bare step away, one hand still on his arm. "You like me," she said.

"I—yeah, of course I like you, I—"

"I see you looking at me. At my tits," a sudden foxlike stare, accusation? Invitation? In his body the swirl of desire and confusion, betrayal and lust, his hands were on her hips now, lightly, lightly. Behind them through the window Robin in the yellow square of light, sleeping still, sleeping in innocence and trust and *(he can see through everybody's head but mine)* her voice, dry: "Don't worry." A pause. "I love Robin."

"I, I care about Robin too, I'm his friend," stumbling, the nubs of her hipbones beneath his circling thumbs, connections made and reinforced with each moment, flesh to flesh and she kissed him again, sun and dirty hair, the smell of her body beneath the fresher odor of grime and then she was back in the house, slow-closing screen and when he peered like a felon abashed through the window she was there on the floor, lying beside Robin, eyes open and blind to the rush like water of the incoming light.

Now he slept to dream of her, waking aching and hard and jacking off in the shower to the memory of that kiss, the feel of her hipbones, the imagined taste of her nipples, hair forced clean and long through his fingers, the canted bone of her pelvis ground against him in an ecstasy of need; her face in his mind, her stare: and other memories, other images as well. Robin asleep beside her, herself asleep across his legs like some loving pet, some half-wide creature pretending to be tamed. Fixing him a sandwich, sloppy meat mixture, something she made herself and Robin eating it like a child, one-handed and smiling, smiling up at her. Dirty T-shirt stretched tight, arms reaching high to pin up his drawings with pushpins, tack them to the refrigerator behind magnets that said ONE DAY AT A TIME and GOD DOESN'T MAKE JUNK! Mouth slack in unselfconscious pleasure as Robin scratched her back, his fingers gentle claws, up and down, up and down; Robin whose thin hands seemed always in motion, Robin who never slept the night, did he wake now from his own dreams, his own hard-ons, his own lusts and tremors, what? What if he did? And Grant looking at him, special pallor, hair longer and paler now, scar on his forehead seemingly without blood, without the tissue brand, not dark anymore: no barometer at all. One of the changes, another one of the changes wrought: by what? Time? Imperception? Saskia? Saskia.

If he took the time, Grant, time off from his job say or from his new job that apparently involved watching Saskia (and Robin: together: never forget that, never for a moment forget that togetherness, that unique bond that you, now, you can never share, Mr. Normal, Mr. Mental Health; she is in tune with him, more receptive than you can ever be to the nuances and stoppages and starts, the silences and screams, urging him on in her own way with those special goads made from the material of their shared illness in a secret way that you can never fathom, irrevocably excluded by your most conventional brain, your emotions, your perceptions from the bond of madness shared, the wild country of the black sun and mercury sky): if he were to take the time to enumerate those changes in Robin, what would he see, how long the list? Saskia an accelerant, always that and her influence maybe on them both which was warping his perceptions further, both their perceptions, all of them together one complicated puzzle, one inedible stew: the hammer finds the nail, who had said that? His mother? father? The hammer finds the nail. Aphorisms, portents, signs and signals: this morning the rush and glitter of the clouds above him, through his bird-shit windshield like some special scrying-glass: rain tonight, rain before mid-

night like an old wives' tale; and on the way home,
groceries for three hurried in the car and beside
the curb as he pulled from the supermarket parking lot the small roadkill body curled like punctua-
tion, as if death had posed a question life could not
answer. See your future in the dried patterns of its
fur, in the leaves overhead and the wind that drove
them: see it in Robin's eyes, clear eyes but remote,
afar in some new peculiar way, even when he
looked at Saskia, even with the eyes of love. See it
in the way he handled Angela, totem, talisman,
confidante, crutch; see the pure sustained disrup-
tion of all sleep patterns, up for hours, sleep for
days. See that craving for light never diminished
and only sharper now, growing, pores open to the
light, sleeping in its color; on rainy days, at night he
lay in the circle artificial, lamplight as oxygen; and
see his work, the darkness there infused, burned
through, shot like arrows full of light: white light.

White heat: Saskia's smile: Robin's hand with
the pencil, moving, stroking its way across the
smaller whiteness of the page. The motion of
clouds across the moon; the sound of circling birds;
the smell of dried coffee in the bottom of a cup.
Saskia's breasts, loose beneath a T-shirt; her sullen
unfocused stare; the butting tube of his own erection, pressed warm as a gun against his fly.

He had not touched her since the day on the
porch, had not said one word, made a gesture,
risked a glance or not at least when she was look-

ing: he thought anyway: who knew what she really
saw? Together all the time, the three of them, he
only absent at work (and they had cut his hours
again, fewer contracts, bad times, too bad but he
did not really care, in fact was glad: who wanted to
sit there, listen to John and his cruel and asinine
jokes, look at photographs so poorly done as to
cause him actual pain if he had been disposed to
care? Less money, yes, that was not good, he was
going to have to do some thinking about that but
then again they were spending so much time at
Saskia's, at the Holiday House, the lights on there,
the food from the cupboard, home away from
home and all of it free: there was that. And anyway
less work meant less time spent at work, it was a
simple and worthwhile equation) and when he was
present, well. Separate but equal. Baby makes
three and he behaved himself, didn't he? Looked at
the drawings, not at the way she bent over Robin,
the way she squeezed his hand, ruffled his hair
(or the way Robin looked, ruffled and squeezed;
oh there were all sorts of ways to be good here,
weren't there?). Looked at the newspaper and not
the obvious spill of her hair, that foxface stare, that
grimace as Robin scratched her back, his hands under the T-shirt, her nipples peaking as nails met
skin: looked at none of that, he was a good boy,
Grant, he was a good friend. Wasn't he? Wasn't he?
Wasn't this something only a good friend would do?
    But you kissed her on the porch, didn't you?—

the memory assaultive, speaking to him in his own voice but with an authority he could not know— you would have fucked her in a minute too, right there in front of God and daylight if she had yanked down her pants you would have been in her in half a minute, in the time it takes to point and shoot. Admit it, to yourself if no one else: admit too that you would do it now, you want to do it now, you want her as she smiles to Robin, as she admires his art (that you admire too, that you admired first; don't mention that, no, a good friend would not mention that I Was Here First), as she lets him light her infrequent cigarettes, as she storms to him about the hospital, the doctors, the fucking aides and the asshole therapists, grumbles about Regina and her dogs, weeps about her parents: her mother mostly, her dead father sometimes too.

Weeping now, a little, her hand against her mouth; Grant unsure if she recognized the sounds, the feel of the tears, sometimes she said she did not feel them rolling down her face, once she had wept in the grocery store, pushing the cart past the cookies and crackers and screamed at him for pointing it out, screamed at him then pushed her face into Robin's chest and would not speak again for hours. And Robin patting her, petting her, running one hand down her hair as he did now, not asking as Grant would have *What's wrong? What's the matter?* Was it because he knew already? or only knew that there was no answer she could have given, nothing really to say?

Light down her face, that artificial touch; Robin's hand in her hair. In his other hand the pencil and before him on the page another face, some suffering god, half its skin flayed to strips and curls, in its eyes a patience like the patience sorrowful of death itself. In half a page of pencil strokes, in a handful of lines. Staring at Grant as Grant stared at Robin, and Saskia, tableau and her tears, her voice roughened and strange and dry: "—red shoelaces, red hair, red hands, redhead. Deadhead. Shithead bastard fucking son of a bitch you made me this way, you *made* me this way! I didn't ask to be this way! I want to be this way, I am this way, I *am*!"

The suffering god. The open mouth as she wept, the hair, the dirt, the eyes.

"My mother's dead, *oh*," as if it had just happened, as if it happened anew each moment in the contracted eye of the god on the page. "My mother is dead, she died of an aneurysm, she died of a stroke and they wouldn't let me see her, they wouldn't let me go to see her. She loved me. She loved me. She gave me aspirin, she hit Koslowski, she hit him with a chart, a dart, she hit him in the park," mumbling now, weeping into her hands, Angela between them like their child, mute and lonely baby in the shared squared circling light, "hit him bit him, hit him and bit him, oh Robin she's *dead*. She's dead."

"She's dead," Robin said. "Yeah she is." Petting her in slow and formal motion, as if his hand described the spokes that drove the wheel of the world. He was crying, too. Did he know that?

I know it, Grant thought, when I cry.

They stayed up all night, crying and mumbling; he fell asleep sometime after two, woke in the rainy dawn to hear her voice, still in gear but failing, dragging like the feet of penitents, like the chains of prisoners rustling against the stones; woke again after nine thirty to rise and, heading for the bathroom, his aching bladder, his aching heart: see them lying on the living-room floor, half in the nest and half out, new drawings prodigal before them in careless, heedless sprawl: his hands on her hair, her head in his lap, mouth open and Angela lying in the shared clasp of their bodies; asleep. They were both asleep, Hansel and Gretel, children in the forest, lovers in their bed.

And for Grant a lunge, a stab immense of pity, hot self-pity as consuming as orgasm, bitter and final and dry: That stupid toy means more to them than I do, don't they understand anything at all? Don't they care? Who do they think is doing all the work here, huh? Who cooks, who works, who pays the bills, passes out the meds, who cares? Not them. Not them, they're the free ones, free to be

crazy crazy crazy as a shithouse rat and who does all
the work and has none of the fun? Me. Me. I'm the
one, the good friend, the forgotten man, and nobody cares at all, do they? Nobody cares at all.

In the bathroom he pissed and pissed, it
seemed it took forever and after he was done he
stood, hand on his penis, mouth down like a stroke
patient's, like Saskia's dead mother and unwilling to
pass them again, go back to his empty bed; felt
himself harden as if against his will, felt himself
thinking of Saskia, of going in there now, right now,
Robin disappeared as if in a dream and Saskia
there before him, breasts and hair and eyes and
spread legs and open mouth and his head back,
now, his breath in his mouth harsh and rare as poison gas

and the door opened, opened right on him with
his cock in his hand and Saskia was there, wide
awake, unsurprised, staring at him with the narrowed ferocity of dream

and put out her hand

to touch him.

"Come on," not smiling, staring at him with
those eyes like a sleepwalker, like a catatonic and
he was so hard it hurt, there in her hand, the heft
of his cock and her pale palm around it, shifting up
and down and in a minute he would come in her
hand, all over her skin like ointment, like the un-
guent that anoints but she let go, turned, walked
out of the bathroom and into the living room—

"Come on," not to hurry him, as if in a condition, a state past the reach of pure chronology and he went, he followed as if through a tunnel made from her flesh into the living room, shuffling with his underwear half on and tented out, ridiculous the angle and Robin awake now but only peripherally, gazing at them both as if he could not understand their presence in this room, together, beside him, literally beside him and Saskia crawling up on the couch, pulling off the T-shirt—small breasts, surprising large nipples that were not hard, soft like a girl's, soft soft and she pulled down her panties, spread herself on the cushions: to Grant: for Grant: "Come on," she said again and then turned to Robin who was staring, now, as blinkless as she and she put her hand to the side of his face, a gesture of almost mystic tenderness as Grant in the agony and confusion of heat and dream pulled off his own underwear, knelt between her canted legs and "So you'll never have to wonder," Saskia said, "so you won't be jealous anymore," her voice like medication for a sickness, an illness, her hand on Grant's cock tugging him, guiding him, sliding him in. All the way in; as Robin held her hand, that hand to his face as if the skin beneath would transform, would bubble or burn or turn to metal but it did none of these things, Grant staring at nothing and it was over very quickly, two or three pulls and gone, done, one canine little groan and out, breathing as if he had just run forever, up and down hills, in and out of valleys whose alignment he would never guess or grasp. Into a shame and a terror he had never dreamed he could feel, for which inside him existed no accommodating apparatus; crouched loose and miserable on the violated couch, one Judas drop at the end of his empty cock: but: Saskia and Robin now as if in some other place entirely, some room he could never hope to glimpse or enter, her arms about Robin's neck, pressing his silent face to her breasts: "Anything," she was saying, over and over again, "anything for you. For you, anything for you," as if past and through the tunnel of some difficult and hazardous operation, a night endured, a danger cheated; as if she had done something hard and frightening to emerge victorious with his name on her mouth, her hero's mouth open for his wreathing kiss.

And Grant clumsy, climbing away and into the hall, the bathroom, swabbing himself without thinking, without the climate for thought at all. He went back to bed and slept for three hours, the way a drunk sleeps, the way a man who has just been released from prison goes home to his own bed to sleep there for the first time in years. And woke to silence in the outer room, and the realization as calm and emotionless as an X ray, the picture of a tumor crouched warm beneath the heart, that she had done all of it for Robin, for Robin's wonder and jealousy, undertook it like a mission to bring to Robin peace, and security, and freedom from envy:

and none of it in any way was for Grant, or for herself at all.

As if this had made acceptable a long-open door Robin and Saskia became lovers, noisy and vociferous lovers but with a curious almost sweet modesty, Grant never caught them fucking, never saw them naked but he heard plenty, oh boy. Robin's wonder, "Oh, *oh*," and Saskia's growls, her cries, her exultations: "When we fuck I can hear angels, I can *hear* them," not hyperbolic figure of speech but burning fact, if she said she heard them she heard them; and she, having mimicked the thought angelic, herself an angel of a kind unencountered outside of very private and particular heavens, the heaven of the back wards, blue walls, seclusion rooms, cold packs, falling into a blunt voracious silence audible to Grant from his own silent perch upon his bed: paying bills, writing checks. Checks and balances. Night and day. It cost money to keep the lights on all the time: reminded of this not only by his own indebtedness to ConEd but the redoubtable Regina as well, he and she had finally met there in the driveway, he alone with a trunkful of junk, newspapers he was trucking to the recycling bins, Regina returning from some pissmission with her dogs, smelly little dogs with rheumy brown eyes and matted hair around their mouths and assholes as if neither were regularly scrubbed. Tangled on leashes, snuffling and growl-

ing past yellow teeth and "You're her friend," Regina said, her voice pleasantly low and completely
at odds with her wicked-witch appearance, the appearance of her scruffy dogs. "You and that other
guy."

"Yeah," Grant said, pleasant himself; no point
in causing friction with the neighbors, especially
this Regina who had been some kind of friend of
the family for a long time, Saskia's childhood, her
difficult adolescence, her father's madness and
then her own played out before these considering
eyes now considering Grant, there in the driveway
with the papers and the Greek chorus of the dogs
about his feet. "His name's Robin, and I'm Grant."
A pause; still smiling, what to say next? Something
nice, if possible, if necessary make something up.
"Uh, you're Regina, right? Saskia says you—"

"She's crazy," said Regina simply, as if this was
something Grant had not guessed but needed to
know. "Her father was too. She told you that, I
guess; well, he was. Look at this house." Rags,
artifacts, ribbons and bows, deflated reindeer,
cornstalks long and brittle like the casings of giant
insects, huge empty chrysalis here and here and a
wind brisk enough to make them rustle, like the
second coming of the creatures they housed. "She
won't take any of it down, either. None of it. I
tried, one time. The other neighbors were complaining, they called the cops." One of the dogs at
leash limit pissed on Regina's tree, sapling staked

and tied but curved, still, like a stubborn spine, a bone resisting treatment; without malice she yanked the dog stumbling back. "Health hazard, all this stuff, a fire hazard. What if it burned down, all this plastic?" Staring at him as if he might have a differing opinion on the dangerous flammability of plastic; Grant said nothing, hand on the trunk, newspapers damp and square within. "They said they were going to write her up, a citation, but I talked to them. I said you go on ahead but she'll never make it to court and you'll never make it stick either. I said I knew her mother, God bless her, she was a saint. Two of them, crazy in that house, father and daughter, they finally took him away, you know. And she was living through all of it and Sassy in the hospital, fourteen years old and she tried to cut her arms with a soda bottle, broken soda bottle right there on the back porch and I drove them to the hospital and they admitted her, and I drove her mother home and we sat in my kitchen and I cried with her. I cried with her," with grave emphasis, as if this was a point he might not fully grasp but if they were to continue at all would need to, "and I cried with her again when they took Sassy in at Clearwater, I been to Clearwater so many times with her I can't tell you. And when she died in the hospital, with that stroke and her mouth all pulled down like she was crying all the time, do you know what she said? You know what she said? Watch Sassy, she said. Watch her, she might hurt

herself, I love her so much. That's what she said. I
love her so much and then she died. Right there.
From the stroke."

Grant was still looking at her, that gravity, that
mouth but for this had to look away; at the sidewalk, the house itself, the newspapers in the trunk.
Looking back in time to see the wise nod, yanking
at the twined leashes again. "The house has been
paid for for years; I pay the taxes, there's a, what do
you call it, an escrow account. She had money," in
a suddenly smiling aside, if together they had finally found the one bright spot in the whole sad
situation. "That was one thing she had. So Sassy at
least doesn't have to live on the street. Is that what
you do?"

"What? —No," in a dry confusion, as if con-
fronted at the end of a tunnel with a door marked
inexplicably with his name. "No," he said, "I'm a
photographer."

"And he's her boyfriend? Her other friend, I
mean, that kid. He's crazy too, isn't he? Did she
meet him in the hospital or what?"

"No," again, conscious of the wind and the
dogs, the smell of the dogs, her stare on him: whatever else she might have been, whomever else she
had cried with, there was a wicked witch in there
too, a great dry engine of curiosity and no little
malice, the eyes on him like lights from a room he
did not want to enter and finally he shrugged,
closed the trunk lid; smiled a final distancing smile.

"See you," he said, and walked diagonal past the whipping plastic, flat reindeers, cornstalks and rotten stub of pumpkin stuck by that rot to the porch and then he was inside, closing the door, smelling the old-rag smell with a nostalgia he had not imagined he could feel, here, in Saskia's absence. The Holiday House; his second home.

They fucked there too, Robin and Saskia, fucked their quiet heads off in the living room and both bedrooms and down the basement and when Grant, in a hot quandary of embarrassment, had brought up to Robin the concept of safe sex, of contraception Robin had looked at him as if at a child and said softly, "We use rubbers, Grant, for God's sake. Do you think we're crazy or what?"

"Well, you know," his shrug abashed in the light of Robin's high-planed stare, pale stare as Grant shrugged again, "you need to be safe." And Grant thinking as Robin turned away of that dream-night, Saskia's hand on his cock, he had fucked her like a dog there without thinking twice, without any kind of safety at all, do you think we're crazy or what? One of us was that night and it wasn't her. Remembering as if on the deck of a ship sailing from the land of fevers, the sea of sirens: come on, she had said, come on and he would have walked through fire, through panes of slivered glass, he would have done anything at that moment to do exactly what he had done. It had seemed so important, it had seemed like life or death, get it into her, get it done. Fuck her. And now it was as if dispossessed of a notion that had led him into that fire, through that glass, now he could look at her, simply look without staring, without wanting her naked: and get impatient with her, angry and dodge her anger, watch her sleep and eat and kiss Robin and watch TV and feel not even the ghost of that terrible heat that had possessed him, feel only kindness and a concern that might be a kind of love; the things he felt for Robin, but without the intensity, without the pillar of fire burning in the center of his heart.

They never discussed it, that dream-night, the three of them on the couch; none of them brought it up although it did not bear, to Grant at least, the ceremonial stink of taboo, it was not a subject to be avoided, it was not something about which they agreed to disagree: it was not as if it had never happened. It was not even something accepted in a subterranean way, the way a family might accept alcoholism, say, or abuse from one of its members; it was simply not discussed, as if it were a dream in which they had all participated, a kind of silent movie in which each had had a part to execute: and had: and now it was over.

Far more important were things like the bills, money going out and not enough coming in; things like leaving the lights on, lighthouse burning day and night; things like Robin's art. Things like Robin's face, the scar almost white now, Angela hung like a rag around his neck, serene and sketch-

ing and his moving hands as pale and quick as the
legs of some dark-bred insect, something nurtured
far below the light now moving in cautious pleasure
in the tricksy shine of day. Artificial light; and Saskia beside him, dozing, her ratty head against his
knee; or reading the newspaper, cutting out all the
pictures of models, women in fashion ads; or
watching TV, foreign language TV and hours of it,
flipping channels to find it and the more obscure
the language the better; Grant irritated and in-
trigued by this habit and Saskia watching him, too,
watching him watch her, inscrutable, maliciously
amused: head cocked at a listening angle, the
woman on the program droning on and on in some
brisk Arab dialect and "Why do you *watch* that
stuff?" trying not to sound annoyed; very annoyed.
"You can't understand English half the time," and
her smile, not even pouncing: "I understand
plenty," and: well: maybe she did. Who knew? Not
him. Another road to the land of light closed to him
by virtue of his mental health, maybe she did understand, maybe she understood everything, maybe
in her head she could speak any language at all, all
the languages, every word ever conjured by human
beings and beings inhuman; when we fuck I can
hear angels, angels. Smiling at him like an angel
herself, a special and particular kind of angel; and
rubbing her head against Robin's knee again like a
pet, a half-tame wolverine, something bright and

toothed as a file, as the serrated edge of a knife
made to cut meat.

And Robin, half attending, half listening, not
quite all the way there: but not absent or if absent
then in a new way, not the way of sickness, not the
terrible red way of decompensation but a new ave-
nue, a new lane to the land where light is the order
of the day; Saskia talked about this place, had she
invented it? Had Robin? Grant did not know,
would not intrude by asking: he accepted it as a
given, Robin asleep in the light of three mismatched lamps, all of them shedding light like
grace on his face; and Saskia saying to Grant in a
brisk half whisper, "He has his own compass, he
knows where he wants to go. In his drawings," petting that sleeping face that beneath her touch did
not move or stir, strange as water sealing to the
touch that disturbs. "He's the bridge, you know?
The bridge home, he can show me, he can *take*
me," take her where, where? Where she needed to
be, to go, to exist finally and without anger: "Where
my kind of thinking makes sense," she said, "where
my way of thinking *is* thinking, where everyone is
like me." Isn't that Clearwater? but he didn't say it
and anyway didn't mean it, it was not what he had
meant to say at all because in a way, his way, the
way of the outsider he knew what she meant:
Clearwater was no more her home than the outside
world, even the Holiday House was no real home
for her: her home was in Robin's drawings, maybe,

if Robin could draw a place of knowledge without pain but she was saying something else, now, talking somehow to sleeping Robin and his face creased silent and wise as if he heard every word: and understood: and Grant catching only phrases, half heard like the whisper of fluid through cavities, through the pressured nooks of the brain itself: "—like it happens *to* me *without* me, do you understand?" her bent head, her whispering mouth to that pietà face, sleeping Robin with a pen in his hand, sleeping Robin sleeping in the light and he slept there through the hours of outer darkness, Saskia presumably beside him, Grant in the back bedroom falling asleep to the hum and drone of the small TV, three of Robin's newest pictures beside him: a dwarf in a box, a dead man smiling up through the dirt translucent, a woman fucking a dinosaur: all rendered in an exquisite emptiness, a lucidity of line and form that was not only transcendent but frightening: if he can do this with so few lines, so little, what can he do with nothing? And when might he decide to do it?

"Azrael," Saskia said. "That's the Angel of Death."

"I thought you were the angel of death," Grant said, mouth down to show he was kidding; but she wasn't. Unpacking the grocery bags, cheap soda and no-brand napkins, it was another bad money week, another week of very few paid hours and if things kept up like this there were going to be problems: changes: Grant did not want to tell them about it, any of it, all the hours at work now spent under the hammer unseen of suppressed anxiety and resentment, he knew what was happening: John's memos meaner and meaner, unpaid invoices, unpaid suppliers, payless paydays like a rodeo chute, like the metal ramp that leads from the livestock truck to the killing floor: but: what to do? Nothing. Stop thinking. Keep unpacking groceries, helping Saskia put them away according to her own system; keep listening to her talk about the angel of death, angels her new topic, she had been going through a period of enchantment, she said, angels had so much to teach. So much. If Robin shared this enthusiasm he did not mention it, spent his time as he was spending it now: sketching or dozing in the corner where the sun came in full and hard. Saskia's dirty hands on the slippery milk carton; dirty hands shaking lightly, slightly, her voice unusually flat.

"It's the Muslim aspect of the Judeo-Christian angel Raphael," she said, as if she were reciting out of a book; maybe she was. What book? "His body is all covered with eyes," and now she smiled a little, now it was like something she had seen herself and maybe that was true, too, who knew? Best to believe everything, everything; your own eyes and everything else. Grant pausing, hand around a jar of cheap peanut butter, sleeping Robin and rapt Saskia: "And every time one blinks, a creature dies."

"What kind of creature?" Grant said. "A person, or what? An animal?"

Shrugging, as if it were not her problem. "I don't know. A creature, is all. Somewhere in the world a creature dies when Azrael blinks. Every time he blinks—"

and Robin suddenly sitting up, bolt up, straight up as if his back had been in the instant broken in place: paper and pencil tumbling, eyes wide and voice loud and dry, prayer, curse, incantation: "All his eyes are blinking, all his eyes are blinking *now*"

and Saskia frozen, an animal in the light of his voice

and the plastic jar fallen like a brick from Grant's hand

"Blinking," Robin said, "on and off," and fully conscious, looking at them, a mild smile and from that smiling mouth a sudden gush of fluid, colorless and huge, arterial and enormous tumbling profligate to the floor

and Saskia's shriek consuming like fire the air in the kitchen and she lunged for Robin, threw herself at him as if saving him from a speeding car, save him save him and she crashed sideways into the chair, knocked them both down, the plasmalike fluid all over his chest, not blood, not vomit, something different and worse and still smiling with his leaking mouth he said, "Don't you see them? The eyes?" and then only to Saskia, "They're all over *you*" and the reiteration of her scream, her scream, her hands in wild flurry across his unhurt chest as if trying to close a wound, a hole, the exit from which the liquid leapt renewed, hideous and pale and he coughed a little, delicately, one hand at his mouth and more plasma, less plasma, thick as snot in her dirty hair, on her dirty hands that swept still across his chest and Grant as if literally paralyzed, unaware that he must breathe, finally the strangled gush of air and he was beside Robin, kneeling, his hands shaking so terribly he could barely turn Robin's chin in his hand, turn it toward the light: "Let me see," he said. "Robin, let me—I have to—"

Robin coughed again. "I made a mess," he said, still very mildly. Pale face, white scar, spatters and drip all over; all over the drawings, the lines obliterated by wet dominance, ruined beyond saving. "But that's okay," as if he were another person speaking to himself, to Robin who had made the mess. "We'll clean it up."

And Saskia still on her haunches, staring, her hands moving back and forth across his chest as if they must never do anything else; the jar of peanut butter in the puddle on the floor; Grant rising to stumble for paper towels, scrolling half a roll with shaking hands, towels for the mess and Robin's smile, full and beautiful, wet and bright as a gorging lion's, as the hot nourished smile of Azrael, smiling and staring and blinking his thousand eyes.

PART FOUR
GODS OF EARTH AND HEAVEN

A path not of illumination but thrall. To become at last what one beholds—and dare not know the difference.

BARRY N. MALZBERG

Men would be angels, angels would be gods.

POPE

"Do you love him?" Saskia's red eyes hard as marbles, one hand flat on the wall like a cop's, like a judge at a last-chance hearing, hair on end and witch-snarled through a cloud of smoke from one cigarette after another after another. "Do you love him?"

"What does—"

"Do you *love* him!"

"*Yes*," Grant angry, whispering, eyes aching; he had not slept for hours, hours, had sat up shaken and terrified, Robin cleansed, whole, hurt in no place Grant could see. Each twitch and sleeping underskin shudder bringing for watching Grant that leap again: gout and spatter, all over everything and his mild smile, fluid like blood on the drawings, all his eyes are blinking now. "Yes I love him," viciously to Saskia, weak in his sleeplessness and fear. "What does that have to do with anything?"

"If you love him," cold, cold and Grant saw her own fear, here was something beyond even her, beyond her own wild and expected terrors—she knew what to fear but this, oh this was something different, "don't make him go. Don't send him to—"

"For Christ's *sake*, Saskia, he needs to see a doctor!" What was that stuff, oh God; even blood would have been better, blood was something Grant could understand. "He needs to get checked out, he needs to be—"

"Be what? Put in the hospital? Taken *care* of?" Another cigarette; lighting the wrong end, upending it, lighting it anew. Snap and click and fire. "You know where they'll send him. Pandora's box, that's where they'll send him."

Leaning against the door, eyes closed, hands in his pockets like suicide stones; it had been almost seven hours, nothing had happened but sleep, Robin waking once to piss—reassuring the pale urine, just regular pee, no strange fluids there: Grant bent over the toilet like a priest reading entrails, I see fortuitous times for you, I see a long journey—and then Robin in mild somnambulism back to bed, to sleep again. He had not asked for Saskia; he had not noticed Grant.

Who stood now in the stink of smoke, head back, eyes grainy and dry and feeling the terror of true responsibility, a lonely terror and a selfish one: responsibility is where love lies down before power, chained heart and open hands, the place that says I will serve, I will consider, and in the end I will decide. What to do: make a choice: decide, because

Saskia is not free to do it or rather is too free, so many things masked in reversal—doctors and hospitals, pain and sorrow—that in walking her course there would be no purchase, no safe place: everything like the house of mirrors, which way? Which way do we go now? You choose: hospital? Or not? Doctors or not, medication or not? Which helps the most, hurts the least?

Saskia staring at him from the threshold, light and smoke, and Grant standing like a father over Robin's bed, statuary-pale and the only hint of explosion sodden Angela around his neck, he would not suffer her to be removed. Wanting to touch that face; wanting more than his next breath someone to tell him what he must do.

Nothing happened for another hour. Saskia fell asleep, finally; he hid her lighter and slept next to her, there on the hallway floor, so he would know if she moved: to go to Robin, to take him away. Would she do that? What else might she do?

What are you going to do?

I don't know, like rain clouds, like the silent sound a tumor makes as it grows beneath the unsuspecting, the innocent and untroubled skin. I don't know, I don't know, I don't know.

Robin woke, ate nothing, pissed again and again; refused to speak about the fluid, to answer questions; smiled; said little. "I'm fine," he said to Grant, over and over, to Saskia who sat glowering at them both, her still-hidden lighter unfound: she lit her cigarettes off the stove, she almost burned her hair, her fingers. Grant called in sick, made vegetable soup for lunch, ate half a cup out of a mug that said SEXY SENIOR CITIZEN. Robin would not eat anything. Saskia poured the rest of the soup down the toilet, flushed it to watch the chunks of vegetable spin around; to Grant it looked like vomit, he felt like vomiting, he felt sick all over. At quarter to five, through a rain so heavy it had flooded past the sidewalks, Grant put on Robin's coat and took him home.

Sleeping, sleeping. Whoever thought anyone could sleep so much? Is he going to vomit like that again (but it wasn't vomit, you know it wasn't, nobody in the world ever puked anything that looked anything like that)? Should I have taken him to the hospital? What should I do now?

8 PM, the note said, the first note on the notebook paper, written with one of Robin's drawing pencils. GINGER ALE. 9 PM SLEEP. MIDNIGHT SLEEP. 10 AM WATER. 10:30 AM SLEEP. With each entry his handwriting deteriorated. Saskia called nine times, wilder and meaner each time; Regina called once to say Saskia had asked for a ride to their apartment, and been refused; Grant could see that negating face, Regina shaking her head; could see the answer of Saskia's eyes, her powerlessness, her rage; but still was glad she was not there, he

needed to be alone with Robin, to watch him, to think. Think think think.

Robin had not spoken since he returned; into the nest, drawing one picture over and over: the slightest lines, so pale they were almost past viewing: a face, suffering. A suffering face. It hurt to look at it, hurt as if looking caused the pain. Over and over again. 2 PM GINGER ALE. 4 PM SLEEP. 5 PM SLEEP. 6 PM SLEEP. He would not eat, Robin; he would swallow only liquids, clear liquids. He did not move beyond the motions of drawings. He did not speak.

Grant called in sick the next day, too, speaking slowly and precisely as if the language of the everyday world had become a currency with which he could not properly navigate, a path whose markings were too plain to see (and that, his mind told him, *that's* because you spend all your time with crazy people, you might be crazy yourself now and not even know it, you might be mad as a fucking hatter but *how could you tell*?). And John came on the phone, too loud and too fast, as if he had been berating Grant for hours already: "I could fire your ass right now. You know that?"

"Yeah," Grant said; laborious his printing, he had been awake for more hours than he remembered; he was unsure what time it was now. His watch was hard to see. "You could."

"What the fuck's wrong with you anyway? You sick?"

"Yes," Grant said. "I'm sick. I'm really, really sick. I just threw up a whole can of vegetable soup."

"Shit, I'm not a doctor, don't tell me about it." He said something else Grant did not hear, then hung up. It took Grant a moment to put the phone back; instantly it rang again: Saskia.

Robin, drawing again. Over and over again.

"Let me talk to him, Grunt. Grunt grunt grunt, you fucking pig let me *talk* to him!"

"Saskia," and then could think of nothing else to say, through the ache and dry buzz of his exhaustion he could not even summon the energy for anger although he felt he had a right to be angry with her, screaming at him was out of line, especially now that she had found her lighter. Right where he had left it. "Saskia, he doesn't want to talk. He won't talk to me. He won't talk at all."

"He'll talk to me, you fuck, put him on put him on put him on—" and on and on and he dragged the phone to Robin who put it to his ear and kept on drawing; Angela around his neck had begun to stink, a dry iron smell like old blood; and said nothing at all. Nothing at all. When Grant replaced the phone it instantly began again to ring.

7 PM WATER. 8 PM SLEEP.

Robin's hand on the pencil as if it were a key; the same face everywhere, all over the room: the hurt face, the face in pain: who hurt you? Who did this to you? Robin's face white, white; from what?

Internal injuries? The stuff he had vomited had smelled bad; what did that mean? What did any of it mean? Should it be the hospital, or not? The lady or the tiger?

Help me, oh God, God I don't know what to do. It's all up to me and I don't know what to do. Did Johnna ever feel this way?—Johnna, the name so strange, as if from a past so attenuated that evoking it now was as formal and distant as prayer: Johnna, help me, I don't know what to do.

The next time the phone rang he let the machine pick it up: not Johnna but John, telling him that he was fired.

"I want to talk to Alison," Robin said.

No words for days into hours, hours into days, Angela around his neck giving off the odor of garbage, the stink of old blood; water and soda, clear liquids, no food at all; while Grant had slept unto numbness, slept six hours straight with legs drawn up and head in his hands, Robin had been busy, busy: putting up the drawings, taping them everywhere, all over the walls, all over the doors, the cabinets, taped onto the floor where no one now must walk: that face, over and over, it was as if an obsession had come to life to manifest itself on every surface visible to the stunned avoiding eye: look here. And here. And here, too, it's here, it's like pain: it can't be missed, it won't go away. No matter how much you want it to, no matter how hard you try.

"I want to talk to Alison."

Voice a little dry but very serviceable, Grant was surprised, dull surprise of a dying animal that wakes from sleep to life: hands numb to the elbows, without feeling, his legs as if paralyzed when he tried to stand. Robin's scar as pale as a searchlight, pristine against the yellowish surface of his skin, a jaundiced look, what was jaundice? Some liver thing? Bile, wasn't that a liver thing, wasn't that something he should know? Blood and bile. Blood and water. Someone had taken the phone off the hook. The answering machine reported through the medium of light that there were nineteen messages and a full tape; guess who.

"I want," again, gently, very gently, "to talk to Alison."

"All right," and Grant found his own voice less than useful, less than robust: a thin harsh little voice, like an adolescent's, like a boy's. "She might —Robin, she might not want, you know, to talk right now. She might be too—"

"I know she doesn't want to talk to me," Robin said. "She never did. But I want to talk to *her*."

So. What now? and for once that gave no difficulty: he had the number: he dialed it for Robin, gave him the phone. Stepped aside (and gingerly, gingerly, watch out for that face) and walked on legs that bent as if for the first time ever, walked into the kitchen to get a drink of water, to eat something, to fix something for Robin to eat; if he would eat it. Would he eat it? Make it and find out. Keep it simple, stupid.

Stirring some chicken soup in a pot, canned soup, thin the gleam of grease across its surface, little square pieces of chicken as small as erasers; the soup did not get hot; he had forgotten to turn on the gas. Gas stove, gas oven. Was Robin talking to Alison now? Was she talking to him? Listening to him? The hurting face, everywhere. Soup on the spoon. Peering for a moment at Robin in the living room, Angela in his hand, squeezing, squeezing but not to injure, not to crush: as one holds a talisman, as one holds the end of the lifeline, the way back, the way home. Where was home, for Robin? Not with Alison and their parents, not the hospital, the group home; here, with him? Or with Saskia at the Holiday House? Saskia had called him the bridge. Saskia had called him nineteen times. Would she be coming here next, was she on her way? Had she been here already, and he, Grant, asleep enough not to hear her? —No. Saskia in the apartment would have been something he could not have missed; she had not come. Yet. What was Robin saying? The spatter and boil of the soup, white bubble of scum. Grant burned himself on the pot's lip, pouring it into cups, he could not trust himself to carry bowls. In the living room Robin lay with his eyes closed, the phone cord wrapped around his neck, around and around until the ends pointed out straight and jaunty, clear plastic jack-ends like little nubs of bone, prosthetic bone for a body unimaginable, a new body, a body made of plastic and light. Grant stood staring, one cup in each hand, staring like a doctor at a patient who has just died and by doing so refused all possible medical help.

"Robin?"

Squeezing Angela. Squeezing Angela.

"Robin," holding the cups, the hot soup. His fingers felt thick. "Robin," are you okay? Why of course he is, just look at him. "Robin," closer now, bending over and

Robin's eyes very wide

looking at him

staring at him as if from a space too far to be measured, far and far and farther away and he opened his mouth, mild lips in sudden rictus, wide, wide, and Grant in terror dropped the soup, boiled splatter: expecting the plasma again, the leaping fluid: but instead it was his voice, just his voice, just Robin saying:

"She didn't want to talk to me. She said I was dead."

Silence. Heat through his pant leg, scalding, a pain as sharp as a bright color. The soup had burned him in its tumbling splash, there were noodles on the floor, little split worms and commas of white: and the white squares of chicken: Robin picked one up and attempted to feed it to Angela.

Cords around his neck like chains, like rosaries: devotions in silence. His eyes did not seem to blink.

"Alison said I was dead."

"You're not dead," Grant said.

"How do you know?" and then immediately, "Angela doesn't think so, too. Either. She doesn't think so either. Angela doesn't think so."

"Are you—" Hurt? Angry? "Are you hungry?"

Pushing the softness of a noodle onto Angela's dried-blood face. "No thank you," politely; most politely. "Not now."

The noodle limp and white between his fingers. The smell of soup, and grease, and fear as a great wind, a barren shunt of air and possibility: and tragedy: and rage. Grant standing there with the spoon in his hand and then as if prearranged the knocking at the door: Saskia.

"Let me in."

Not loud, not yet.

"Grant, let me in. Robin, let me *in*."

She did not look as if she had slept at all in their time apart; she looked grimy and witchy and wild, not like death but the terror that attends it. She was smoking a cigarette without removing it from her mouth; the ash grew long; she smelled terrible. She had, she said, walked all the way.

"Regina wouldn't drive me," past the cigarette, clenching teeth. "Regina said I was *too upset* to go anywhere. Regina said *Think of your mother*, my

mother, what the fuck does my mother have to do
with anything now, what the fucking hell does my
fucking dead mother have to—"

"Robin called his sister," Grant said, to say
something, to break into the rant before like a fire
it fed upon itself to grow larger, and larger; the
pain face on the walls, on the floors seemed to
agree, seemed to swim and swirl in the graceful
fact of its approval; perhaps he was crazy now too,
perhaps his perceptions had been altered past the
breaking point, perhaps he was in an altered state
to stay, now. You cross the border once too often
and you never get back. Never. No matter how
much you might want to, no matter how often or
how plaintively you insist *I've had enough, please, I
want to go home now.* No more home; everything
is here, now, and this is the place you must stay; as
if a person with a fresh new handicap might tell
himself to get on with life, get up and walk, only to
be forced down by the brute fact of the new: You
cannot live that way anymore, your apparatus is
gone, is changed forever. No more of the old life,
no more of anything but the look in Saskia's eyes,
her cigarette and her smell, and Robin there with
the phone cord around his neck, Robin and Angela
and the pencil in easy reach.

"His sister?" Saskia said, with suspicious pleasure. "What, Alison? The ice queen? The snow
princess? I know all about Alison, I saw her all the
time at Clearwater. Didn't I? Robin, didn't I?" No

answer. Robin was looking only at Angela, head bent, the scar rising past pallor to a color as sweet and fresh as a blushing peach, a color Grant could not remember having seen before; but surely this world was full of new things, new experiences, was it not, this world across the border, this permanently altered state? Sure it was. "I saw her in the dayroom, sitting so she wouldn't touch her brother the patient, her sister that she hated, her dad and her kid, I saw her all the fucking time. All clean and knees together. Runs away when you ask for a cigarette. Doesn't want to look at the crazy people, the looney tunes, oh yeah I know all about Alison, me and my mother used to laugh at her, me and my mother used to sit there and just fucking *laugh* at—"

"Stop it," Grant said. "Just stop it, Saskia. If Robin—"

"You stop it. *You* shut up, you're the one, you're the one who doesn't make sense. What do you know about it, anyway?"

There was no answer to that, not even here in the brave new terrible world so he did not attempt one; instead went into the kitchen, mugs in hand, for a towel, something, to wipe up the soup, do something constructive, perform some understandable action and while he was trying to remember where he kept the towels he felt her entering passage, felt her standing behind him as she might stand with an ax, say, or some bright hideous tool:

turn around. Turn around and he did, to see her eyes full of tears, mucus rimmed around her nostrils; the cigarette was burned down to the filter now.

"He won't talk to me," she said. "He'll talk to fucking Alison but he won't talk to me."

"Just, just slow down. All right? Please?" Her tears called answering tears from him, it was amazing, he had not cried in so long, so long, so long. "Just slow down a minute and let me think. Something's going wrong here," and they looked at each other through tears and the appalling light of the truth spoken: something *was* going wrong here, somewhere a turn had been taken, back there maybe with the springing fluid or the long sleep attendant like a handmaiden, hovering like a ghost and now there were circumstances, there were forces with which to be reckoned but his reckoning power was gone, he could not meet anything new, he was reduced himself by the strange new novelty to something less elemental than Saskia, far less so than Robin but nothing familiar or solid left on which to balance, no purchase place, no ledge. Nothing. But Saskia, crying with rage, with jealousy, crying and pounding her fist on the counter, the fallen cigarette filter jittering with every blow.

"All right," he said. "All right. Let's just stop a minute."

"*Fuck*," weeping. "Regina wouldn't drive me either, the cunt, the fucking bitch. Wouldn't make me any coffee. She said it would *make me nervous*, can you understand that? Who's the crazy one here, for Christ's sake, she has got to be flippo-nutso, she has got to be the craziest woman in the world to say coffee makes me nervous," pounding and pounding and no sound from Robin in the living room, no sound, nothing at all and he, Grant, still standing there in the midst of his memoryless-ness, his absence of rational thought or calm or any of the tools made so dreadfully necessary by this new and tentative situation, this deterioration over a period of several days, had it been several days, what day was it anyway? No sense asking her and anyway she was asking him something, wasn't she, the words had sounded like a question but with her you never got a second chance and already she was slamming around the kitchen, cupboards and drawers, pulling out a coffee can, cold water from the faucet and clicking at the coffee maker, pouring and slipping, "Fucking *shit*!" in her frustration, her tears and her terrible anger and Grant trying to help her, trying to take her hands, take the coffee-pot away and turning on him, now, her teeth bared, her rage incendiary as if years of bitterness leaking poison through the cracks had reached finally the point of ignition, as if she would literally explode before his eyes: "Don't tell me how to do it, don't you tell me how to do it!"

and Robin there, neither had seen him, perhaps he had just appeared like the sun over water, an angel in a Bible story: fear not. No words, his scar as pink and gentle as a bouquet rose and: smoothing her face with his fingertips, stroking the coils of her hair dreadlocked with dirt, a sound like wind—*sshhh sshhh sshhh* from his mouth, slow susurration, *sshhh sshhh sshhh* and though like feathers to iron it did not touch her anger it seemed to Grant, past the border but still no closer to the heart, the great beating engine, the confraternity of the mad, it seemed to his open and watching eyes that the flashpoint had been averted, that it might be safe now for him to move, to quietly resume the task, the making of coffee, the pouring of water. To move in safety and in the realization that, even through this curtain, this inherent scrim of powerlessness, he still might be able to achieve for her, for himself and most importantly for Robin a different kind of safety, a kind of drawing-in and a surcease from the

"fucking *bitch*!"

"No," and Robin's voice almost conversational

"Fucking stone-cold fucking bitch, I called you a hundred times, a hundred times Robin and you wouldn't talk to me, it wasn't just Grunt, it wasn't Grunt it was *you* and you wouldn't *talk* to me and she wouldn't make me *coffee* and then you talked to *her*, to *her*, to—"

"no," again; deeper, and the scar darkening to a pure and aching shade, the color of a broken heart

"—rather have *Alison* than me and she *hates*

you, Robin, she hates you and she's always hated you because she's scared of you, *scared of you*, you're her CRAZY BROTHER and she's SCARED OF YOU"

"*No*"

and Grant staring at them, fingers tight on the wet handle of the coffeepot, staring as if they had moved miles in an instant, their faces and figures wavering in the trickery of his exhausted sight, trying to speak enough to be heard: "You guys, stop it, listen, stop it" the way one might address a falling building, an edifice in a state of such terrific dissolution that the bricks, the mortar and the stones would begin like deadly rain to fall in instants; and he beneath with his prissy parasol, his umbrella of words saying stop it, stop it, stop it you guys

oh please stop

because I just can't bear it anymore, I've had enough, we've all had just about

"not like *my* mother, my mother *loves* me, she came every day and she wasn't afraid and she gave them cigarettes, anybody who wanted one, she used to give away whole *packs* of Kools and nobody scared her and *I* didn't scare her and she didn't—"

"Shut up Saskia, shut up shut up shut—"

"loved me loved me, Robin she loved me but Alison *doesn't love you*"

"*No*," not a scream, not a cry

and with one arm he shoved her, long piston motion not to hurt but to remove, the way he might push her from the path of a car and then turning, in the sweeping discus motion, to smash his hands against the cabinets, the counters, smash them again and again as if they were a fire he must extinguish, smash them so Grant, frozen, heard the sounds of breakage, of tissue and of flesh in collision, of bone through the gasp and cry of Saskia's shriek, fire-engine shriek and the phone began ringing, ringing, ringing and Robin smashed his hands again, his face locked into an expression so terrible and remote, that of a man who does a duty he loathes but will not pause nor be dissuaded from the doing, who will see it through until the end

and the ringing phone

and Saskia screaming "Robin stop it Robin DON'T ROBIN DON'T!"

and his hands again, *whack* like a board against the cabinets

and Grant reaching him at last, grabbing him, his own arms wrapped around Robin's in a trembling and ineffectual grasp although his muscles cried out in the motion, cried out from the force and Robin was away from him, arms hanging down at his sides in hideous loose inaction but with his body, his torso and his legs and his feet he began to destroy the kitchen, yanking and battering, heaving and thrusting and the smashing of glass, the ringing phone, Saskia's screams like an instrument played with all the passion of a god

and knocking, banging, pounding at the door

pounding at the door

and Grant's own voice in the melee, how long had he been shouting, what was he saying? Oh God, oh Jesus *God* and grabbing Saskia he flung her toward the living room, toward the pounding door and then with a violence he did not in the acting moment believe he locked an arm around Robin's neck, a chokehold to drag him away from the refrigerator, out of the kitchen

toward the pounding door

where Saskia was already turning the handle on police, was it police or only building security, somebody official and only two for all that pounding but Grant could not stop for them either, bullied past them with the frenzy of the panicked and into the elevator, Saskia slamming at the buttons, Robin trying to struggle free and then they were out, into the street, toward the parking lot and "My keys, get my fucking keys" as like some terrible triune beast they struggled, panted, gasped and staggered through the sunlight, weak and warm and beautiful, to his car: Saskia starting the engine with the discovered keys, a huge flooding roar and Grant threw Robin into the back seat, threw him down and sat half-atop him, saying "Go just go just drive this fucking car, Saskia Saskia *drive*"

and the sound of her weeping, the car bucking into reverse, then drive, then gone, very slowly, thirty miles an hour as Robin lifted his face on a long intensifying angle, tears and blind eyes and

turning his gaze up and up and up as he began to
scream

and scream

and scream.

"Saskia?"

It was hard to talk, Grant's throat aching, all the
muscles of his arms and back in pain. Robin lay
asleep in the corner, in the shiver and spill of sun,
Angela miraculous around his neck, necklaced as
well by bruises where Grant had choked him. His
shirt was torn. His hands were so grotesquely swollen that they had lost all definition, turned into hideous cartoon blobs; now he slept with them cradled
to his chest as if they were wounded children who
might somehow be calmed by the contact. Saskia
beside him raised her gaze with a stare so truly
empty that for one long moment Grant thought,
with simple and exquisite pleasure, of standing up,
of walking out; of leaving the house, leaving them
both forever and ever, of never never never coming
back.

"What," she said. There was no inflection in her
voice, no human feeling; maybe she was contem-
plating her own escape. "What," again when he did
not answer at once.

"I think," Grant said, "his hands are broken."

"I think you're right."

They stared at each other, out of words. Light
through the windows, light on Robin's face, his

arms, the suffering and pity of his hands. Light on
everything in the path of the sun; the soft spangle
of dust, the angles and declensions, the feeling of
stasis and waiting in the air, waiting for what but
not for long.

He knew he had to go back. He had no money,
nothing but his keys; he had to get his wallet,
his checkbook, clothing, the Medicaid number,
Robin's things; he would have to face the apartment manager, security, maybe cops. Malicious destruction. Reckless disregard. Creating a nuisance.
Would they try to detain him? No. No. "Will you be
okay?" for the fifth, tenth time, Saskia hunched as a
gargoyle beside sleeping Robin, blood on her
cheek, a bruise as if fragmented from some priest-
less ceremony. "Are you sure you'll be okay, like
this?"

"No."

"I won't be very long."

"Just go."

He had washed his face, brushed his hair,
changed into a clean wrinkled shirt scavenged from
one of the used-clothing bags: anonymous denim,
too tight across the shoulders. Fake pearl buttons
hard for his jittering hands to manage, hard to find
his keys, exquisitely hard to leave them there, Saskia staring and Robin, oh God his hands, please
God let him stay out so he won't feel the pain. Pain;
this time they would have to take him to a hospital,

they would have to do something. Something. And no medication for, what? Forty-eight hours? More? Cracks in the ice; the slow march of decompensation. The medication was sitting in an orange plastic bottle in the bathroom at the apartment. He could stop at the pharmacy and get a refill; he could stop and get some aspirin, extra-strength; no aspirin in the house, nothing so much as a cough drop, Regina was a firm believer in clean living and the only pills available were Saskia's neuroleptics, which, she told Grant without anger, without even being asked, she was faithfully swallowing. Still.

"I can't leave now," she said. "Not now."

She had wept then, eyes running, the muscles of her face knotting like gears unmeshed and grinding the engine of pain and Grant had wanted to comfort her, hold her, say something to her but instead stood in his own stupid agonies, hands empty: dirty beaten Saskia, sobbing till her skinny body bent like an arrow in a bow, sobbing till she retched; and Robin in the next room, sleeping, maybe unconscious, his shattered hands against his body, raveling Angela around his neck. And Grant in charge of everything, in charge of them all.

You wanted to feel, his memory reminded. Some real sensation, isn't it? Who would ever have thought a straw man like you could ever hurt so hard? cross the border the way you do? Isn't it something? isn't it something *else*?

"I won't be long," he said again and looked

once, last, at Robin. "Keep the door locked," he said.

"No, I thought I'd have a party," with a hint of venom but she was really too dispirited, there was too little left now to waste on sarcasm, to waste on him; hunkered down beside Robin she was an emblem of displacement, she was every refugee, every pained lost victim in the world, in the history of history's thrust and impersonal grind: she was dispossessed; she was alone, and empty; she did not look up as he gently closed the door.

At the apartment it was both more difficult and easier than he had feared: the manager was out but the assistant manager, a lean sleepy man who by Grant's appearance—was it a look, a certain smell, what? the way he held his body, his posture, the way he tried to smile at the man that unnerved the other so?—was made hasty and less thorough perhaps than he might have been. Keeping too far for courtesy in the elevator, talking all the way up: "—and damages, there was a lot of breakage, you know, the refrigerator's all dented up and one of the cabinet doors is—"

"I'll write you a check," Grant said. "Will that be all right?"

"I guess," the man said. "Sure."

The apartment had not been entered since that headlong moment of departure: things were as they had been, smashed, dented, that suffering face all over; God. As the man waited Grant moved through the rooms in silent haste, gathering the necessities, taking what he needed as if in evacuation: hurry, hurry, for the god of war is here, the plague is coming, the tanks are over the hills. Pills, toothbrush, some clothes he grabbed at random. His photographic equipment, oh God; when was the last time he had even thought about it, even considered the act of photography? It had in toto less true meaning than an adolescent artifact but in the end he could not bear to leave it behind; down to the car with the portable stuff, the rest—what would he do with the rest? He could not now stop to consider. What else? A coat for Robin. Drawing supplies (and how with those hands will Robin draw, did you think of that, you think of everything don't you so why didn't you think of that?). Wallet and checkbook; the assistant manager named a number; Grant wrote the check, almost certain it would bounce.

"What do you want to do about the furniture?" the man said.

On the deck of the *Titanic*: where shall we send your suitcase? "I'll be in touch," he lied, feeling less guilty about the rubber check, they could keep the kitchen table, they could ransom the bed (in which he had lain awake worrying over Robin, reading the hidden books; in which, more anciently, he and Johnna had performed the juiceless acrobatics that at the time had passed for lovemaking), they could sell his suits and his empty portfolios and the framed and matted pictures on the walls, his oeuvre, his testament. No. His testament lay broken-handed, brokenhearted on the floor of the Holiday House, Saskia beside him in sleeplessness and emptiness and pain; these were only pictures, stupid photographs he could barely remember shooting. He had thought of his work as potentially important; he had wanted to use his—what? "talent" was too strong—his facility, then, he had wanted to make proper use of it and what had all that gotten him? Nothing; less than nothing. He remembered an argument here in this kitchen, here in this denuded and shattered room, an argument with Johnna about the responsibility of the artist, her own long-winded diatribe: the idea of seeing the artist through the wrong-side funnel, the little hole at the bottom is the art, she said, and you're seeing through that, while the artist sees the other way, the large end of the funnel is personality, the small exit hole is the art and after all of that he had laughed, naturally and without artifice, without even the intent to hurt; and she had thrown her cup in the sink so it cracked, hairline split down its bottle-green side and shrilled at him: "You think you're so fucking smart!" and the truth was he had, he had; but he didn't now, oh no, now he knew what he didn't know and so paradoxically probably *was* smarter than before. You think you're so smart; no I don't; then you must be; perhaps she too had been as well.

He had argued with Saskia here too, two women, two shrieking voices but how different, oh, what a difference there was: Johnna's tight-assed shrink voice dissolved into Saskia staring, the bright angel of God's own madness staring him down, staring him into a spot where there was nothing but light: "There isn't anything wrong with us," cold, cold and bright, *"you're* the ones who're cut off. You can't see what we see. You can't know what we know," and she was right about that one, she was absolutely and incontrovertibly right and now the assistant manager was saying something, perhaps had been, was speaking to him in the tone one uses with intractable teenagers or wavering drunks and Grant surprised them both by saying crisply, "I don't have time for this now," an exit line and the man did not stop him, did not try to make him stay, he had never in his life been able to do anything like this; perhaps the confrontation with and surrender to the inevitable, the process, had given him this new and temporary power, perhaps it would desert him utterly when he arrived where he must be, back in Saskia's house: back before Robin, Robin's gaze in the constant unending light.

And thinking, as he drove, car full, one camera bag nudging him somewhat painfully in the hipbone, pressing like a lover importunate, pressing and gouging like a nag, a shrew, a harpy: his own thoughts like harpies, singing and shouting: and thinking with true black clarity They're crazy, Saskia and Robin, they are medically defined to be mentally ill, they're the only friends I have; what does that say about me? and remembering Saskia's ice-cold kitchen stare, you could catch it you know, it's possible you could have it right now and not even know it; was she right? Not about catching it, that was absurd and they both knew it, there were predilections and precursors but none applied to him; but there were other methods, not contagion but collusion: what had become normal to him was strange, strange to the rest of the world, strange as Robin's liquid and light, strange as the slow smacking roll of Saskia's lips as she placed with staggered staples another Christmas card over the fat leaf pile of the rest. You can't see what we see, you can't know what we know. Altered states and altered states, a difference of commitment; of degrees. Maybe you had to want it so badly it became part of your genes; maybe you had to lose your fear. Or maybe the fear was necessary, an evolutionary thing, safe passage through the land of the living, the land of the healthy and the sane.

Pulling into the driveway he saw Regina, leashed dogs and mouth pulled to such a tight lipless line that his whole body warmed with fear, instant the roil, the nauseous bubble in his throat. She walked directly to the car, stood as he rolled down his window; motor running; the dogs smelled like bundled hair and urine, and dirt.

"That boy's hands are broken," she said, as if he

were responsible. "Every finger. And I offered, I said I would drive him to the hospital, I told him I would bring him straight back here but *she* said oh no, not the hospital, the hospital's just the first step back to the funny farm and he wasn't going anywhere. And he started throwing up, then, just all over, all this loose white stuff and she—"

A sound, half a groan and he slammed the car into park, pushed open the door into Regina's legs, her stance beside and left her there, into the house to find them in the living room, in the last of the sun: Robin awake, lying still on the floor between old-clothes bags and a rolled blanket as Saskia taped his hands: thick mummy bandages, two white clubs at the end of his arms. The tape was snarled, sticking to Saskia's hanging hair, filthy and loose and the look she gave him through its curtain was hideous in its rage.

"Took your fucking time, didn't you?"

"Saskia—" but he gave that up without a struggle, there was no sense to it now. Robin's gaze was that of one who does not speak the language, one who must fashion by implication and need his own understandings; you're trying to help, his eyes said, as Saskia swore, ripped at the tape, as she pressed and handled his hands that must be nothing now but pain, all pain in those fingers, those pulped knuckles and bones. I know, his eyes said. I know.

"Robin," and Grant found he was weeping without volition, crying as simply as a child cries:

because he was sad. Because it hurt. Tears dripping from his chin; mucus heavy as blood in his throat and "Oh *Robin*. I'm sorry. I'm *sorry*," wanting to touch him, to put his hands upon him but afraid to cause pain, more pain, further pain, oh Robin oh my Christ I am so *sorry* and Robin shook his head, raised one arm a little, a little as if he would touch Grant, comfort him: "It's okay," he said. "It's not that bad, it's not really bad at all."

"Regina was here," Saskia said through her teeth. "She had her car all revved up for the hospital. She—"

"You, you threw up again," Grant said. Robin nodded. The bruises on his throat looked uglier, more severe. "Like before?"

"No." Saskia's answer. She hurled the tape against the wall, muffled bounce as it struck to land behind the television. "All white. White white white. All over. I left it for you to clean up."

Snot beneath his nose, a hinging pain in his back as he rose to stand, to walk into the kitchen, to see like blood upon the floor, the chair, the edge of the table: vomit, whiteness, nothing that looked as if it could come from a human body, nothing he could imagine coming from him. The roll of paper towels was almost empty; from beneath the sink he took another from its package, white paper imprinted with blue flowers, acres of flowers, patterns turning wet and gray as with leaden hands he swabbed, he sopped, he wept until the floor was clean, the chair was clean, the table was clean; and from the living room the accompaniment of Saskia's croon, the wordless clucking of the battlefield, of the hospital, of the morgue; and from Robin, its recipient, no sound audible at all.

"No hospital," Robin said gently, like a parent breaking bad news to a child, breaking a promise. "I already told Regina that. Saskia fixed my hands, I don't need a hospital."

Grant in exhaustion feeling as if he might never sleep again, sitting with folded legs beside Robin who lay, now, on the sofa, heaped with moldy-smelling afghans poisonously crocheted, between them on the floor the water glass ignored, Robin was not, he said, thirsty, he was not hungry, he did not want to eat. Clear liquids, only liquids and now only enough to swallow his pills, swallow some aspirin for what must be hideous pain in his hands. Around them the room all light, every lamp and overhead constellation-bright though blades of sunlight reached as well through the windows; it was nearly noon. Saskia was in her bedroom, working. On a project, something for Robin she said and said nothing else, disappeared with a staple gun and a bag of folded curtains, emerging only to pee, once, and to tell Grant what to say to Regina if she came.

"Tell her," outrageously dirty now, dry sweat and vomit-stained shirt, she had not washed, slept, changed her clothes for days, brushed her hair (although she had brushed her teeth, using half a tube of toothpaste to do so; Grant had watched some of it as he shook out Robin's pills), "tell her to fuck off and die, fucking hag. Tell her I said so."

"No," Grant said, but with such wooden pleasantry that Saskia laughed: a real laugh, her face in that aching second translated past dirt and terror and pain into the first wild beauty he had seen, Botticelli and Bosch, a construction of exquisite subtlety and brute force. Dancing in the church basement, calling out, calling to him; to Robin. Robin her darling, Robin lying in state in the next room; Robin for whom she now worked, constructing something, making, she said, a new nest to replace the one left behind, a place of safety and of peace. "It'll be okay," she had said, not to Grant beside her in the bathroom, not to herself in the mirror. "It'll be okay."

Grant's hand in motion, to touch very gently her hair, matted as fur; to kiss her cheek. They had fought terribly in the night, dead midnight and Robin groaning in his sleep, tossing in the path of the lights he had insisted they aim directly upon him, searchlight in his face and as they sat past its conjunctive beam, in the far dimness without, Grant's thoughts ox-slow as he considered many things, the angles and shapes of this new situation, where everything had changed past changing in such a short time: for Robin there would likely be no more drawing, not for a long while and maybe not ever, he had in some permanent way almost certainly destroyed his hands; and past that destruction something else, a growing, the whole process accelerated terribly, tremendously, like the widening arc of disease, disaster; and past those thoughts like broken rocks, like concrete the new revelation, Saskia confessing in one long monotone how she had convinced Robin that all the internal changes, his love for light, his love for and affinity with Angela, the subjects which he chose (or, she said, which chose him) to draw: all of these worked synergistically, all of them together were turning him into an angel. I knew he was an angel, she had said to Grant, helplessly aghast beside her, I could smell it on him, on his breath, I knew it I knew it I knew it; hands on his cheeks, breathing in his exhalations as if his face were a candle flame.

And Grant in silence, and then in rage quieted by necessity saying, If you knew why didn't you tell me, huh? Why didn't either one of you break down and tell me, huh? but he knew why: the normal one, the outsider, the one with his face to the window, the gates, always outside looking in: you tell him, no *you* tell him. No. Let him wait, let him guess, let him find out on his own; well he was certainly finding out, wasn't he, he was certainly on the right track now but then again how could he fail to be, even he could see things were breaking down, falling in, falling on them all like ordnance from a clear deadly sky, they were all falling to-

gether: like Lucifer, the morning star, the angel,
the prince of birds, like a star's trajectory, like the
lines on a medical chart

and even more quietly now, as if in utter pros-
tration before the fact of this knowledge displayed
(but too late, too late, too late): "Why didn't you
tell me, Saskia? For Christ's sake why didn't—"

"I wanted him to go," she had said, looking at
nothing, her own twisting hands, twisting like gal-
lows rope. "I wanted to let him find out—but
Grant I'm losing him, I'm *losing him*," as if pro-
testing the fact of death itself, stubborn terrified
rage at her failure, at her inabilities, her impending
and inescapable loss and even in his anger he could
no longer sustain that sense of betrayal, she was
losing far more than he, for her there had always
been more to lose in a life so surfeit of loss. She
had not cried, he had not held her, touched her,
tried to bring comfort as if to the hall of the dead:
but in the dark they had stared at one another as
Robin turned, head back and forth and hands wob-
bling against the cradling chest, bobbing in their
cocoons like clumsy insects giving birth to life; they
stared and Saskia spoke, to them both, with an ora-
cle's independence of evil or good: "It won't take
long," she said. "It's not going to take long at all."

Now: the sound of her motion, a hectic vivacity,
back and forth in the unseen room and Robin smiling at Grant, a little, as Grant with hopeless tenderness offered again the water glass: to Robin's head-

shake: to the sound of Saskia's motion, back and forth, back and forth, back and forth.

It was all white, everywhere: curtains made of some heavy cotton staple-gunned to the walls, white paper taped to the windows, to the floor; the overhead now stripped of sheltering fixture to give all the light possible from its hundred-watt bulb; one drawing—the suffering face; how had she come up with that?—tacked to the door so with closure it became the only image in a broken sea of white. When Robin saw it he smiled, a sweet smile at Saskia who stood like a piece of dirt on a clean cloth, who smiled back at him; whose eyes were full of tears.

"Do you like it?" she said.

"Oh yeah," entering with a curious kind of hobble, as if without the gift of hands he could not properly find his balance; his shoulder touched the wall, rubbed against the fabric there. "It's all white," he said. "It's all white everywhere."

"I know," she said, as if this were something previously discussed; again the outsider but Grant did not take offense, no time to waste on that; something was happening here beyond a new room for Robin; and his words remembered, like a line in a book now returned with clarity ferocious, the line, the phrase, the words that tell you in the vacuum of your understanding what your life from now on will be like: I need it to be light in here; I need it to be *light* in here. Light, the province of day, light the home of angels, had it really begun so far back as that? Wearing Angela around his neck, guardian, confidante; his refusal to eat; his insistence on clarity, clear liquid, the gush and fanning splatter of the liquid from his mouth: and now nothing, no intake, burning clear as light itself on nothing, nothing, only the energy stored—where? In his broken hands? In his broken heart? There against the backdrop of white he was nothing but a little scarecrow, how had Grant failed to see this, how through familiarity had he allowed his perceptions to be so blunted? A little scarecrow with dirty hair and hands bandaged into clubs, skinny and smiling and curling, now, into a satisfied ball in the center of the room, directly under the light; as he once had curled into his sleeping-bag nest, rest, resting place, jumping-off point for the larger journey—where? Journey *where*?

"It's *all* light," Robin said.

Saskia was crying.

The white room; the one laborious drawing; his shattered hands. Light upon light upon light, twenty-four hours a day; everything turned to white, like a bone, a star, a scar, the scar on the inside of your heart where you cannot see but feel it with every move, every slow breath in and out until the final exhalation in which it breathes out from you like the spirit of God moving over the face of the waters, the suffering warm and ancient face of your own human and perishing skull; what *process* is this, what method brings this about? The engine of illness? The weight of desire? Some inner strength beaten and tortured to depths without limit, as if Robin's illness was only preparation, a kind of silent tempering, a crucible for this larger becoming, as if the caterpillar might at last come to understand the nature of the chrysalis, its confines found to be not cruel at all, oh God not cruel at all but only necessary, as even the known body must give way before the inexorable drive of transformation; of becoming; of turning into something else.

It's all light.

Call the doctor, Grant thought, in that holy silence, in the air of that room like a cathedral, a chancel for the altar of fire, of purity and death. Call the fucking doctor and call him *right now.*

Nothing good can come of this.

Sitting in the one pocket of dark in the house, Robin in his new room, his sanctuary, Saskia exactly like a guard dog stretched asleep before the door and he in this darkness, the talk with the doctor hurting like a migraine; he had been open about it, he had not lied, it would be wrong now to lie in this terrible atmosphere, this fierce new clarity and so he told them both, Robin especially, looking straight into his eyes: I am calling the doctor, he said, I have to tell someone. This is dangerous, something's happening here and I can't handle it alone. (There, his mind said, trembling hands and vision as if narrowed by a fatigue so severe it might never be overcome, always like cancer some lingering trace in the pockets and narrows of his flesh, his aching eyes forever doomed to vision: there, now. You admitted it and it wasn't so bad, was it? Was it? And wouldn't it all have been easier if you had done this months ago, instead of letting things slide, letting things drift and build and build and build and see what it gets you? You see what you get? Johnna was right, you know, Johnna and Maryann at the group home, they knew better than you did, saw more clearly, feared more accurately. They were right, and you, well, you know what you were; you know now what you are.) I just can't handle it, he had said and they looked back at him, Saskia with the narrowed stare of contempt one reserves for the traitor, Robin with a pale smile; his hands, he said, were hurting very much today but there was no need to call the doctor for *that*.

"That's not what I mean," Grant had said and Saskia then as if spitting: "No, he means the *head* doctor, the *shrink*. The head clown at the funny farm. The biggest nut in the basket. The oddest fucking ball on the—"

"I know what he means," Robin had said, and no one else said anything after that, no one talked at all but the doctor, talking in Grant's ear, talking on the phone and saying all the things Saskia would have predicted, giving no help, no aid, not at the story of the clear liquids and the vomiting, not even when Grant in his desperation said, "But there's some kind of process going on here, I'm telling you it's not normal, I'm telling you that he is turning into something that I—"

"Schizophrenia," not unkindly, "*is* a process. What you have to understand is that there can be so many manifestations of the inner illness, there can be so many changes in personality in the course of the disease that he can seem like a different person," and segue into the litany of relapse, changes in sleep patterns, in activity level. Changes in social activity, in bodily perceptions, in hygiene, in levels of concentration. "You say he's still taking his medication?"

"Yes." Swallowing it like viaticum, Grant himself placing it upon his tongue. "I'm making sure that he does."

"Then it's more than likely not decompensation, unless of course he's becoming resistant to the medication but that's not usually—"

"Doctor for fuck's sake," from the depths of his panic and frustration, the phone like the barrel of a gun against his head and trying not to yell, or swear, trying not to scream, "I've been living with him for a *long time*, I would *know* if this was decompensating and it *isn't* decompensating, I *know* he's been taking his meds and I *know* that he's not—"

"The only thing I can suggest," overriding now,

still kindly but in a different mode: Dealing with the Hysterical Family Member, Part One: The Consultation, "the only thing I can suggest is for you to bring him—"

"He won't go," flat.

"Have there been any overt—"

"There are *no grounds*," are there? and would he invoke them if there truly were? If there were more to tell the doctor, the police, a judge? Your Honor, he's sitting in a white room; Your Honor, he's turning into an angel. Your Honor, he won't eat, he could tell them that: Robin in court, Robin in a hospital. The look in Robin's eyes, the tube in his arm; his own voice saying to Robin—in the driveway at the group home, the promises; were they now lies? I'll take care of you. I'll never let them do that to you. I'll never let them take you away. The idling engine; his lying mouth. Angel Robin in a room full of light.

"This is too much for any one person to handle alone," said the doctor who was still talking, providing Grant for a moment with such black mirth that from his stretching mouth came a laugh, a little laugh like a cough, like the sound of strangling and the doctor said something else and Grant said "Thank you," as calmly as possible, "thank you," and once more for good measure; and then hung up and wept into his hands, right by the phone, head to the wall, crying as Saskia slept, as Robin lay open in his new cocoon, wept because he was stupid and he was helpless, wept because there was no one who could help; a hospital would not stop this, a doctor would bring no cure. They could fix his hands, they could change his medication, they would do everything they knew how to do and then what? Then what? Would they make him better, would they heal him? Would they stop him from metamorphosis and turn him instead into, what? A patient? An outpatient? One of the people in the dayroom, in no room and part of no day at all; what? What?

Crying more quietly now, seeing with an inward sight himself: unkempt, unwashed, snot on his hands and stains on his clothes, red-eyed from sorrow and lost sleep and how sane was he, now, how rational his thoughts? Maybe this will end, he thought, maybe this is something he has to go through and maybe he'll get *better*. He won't get well but maybe he'll get better and we can go back, go back, go back to the way things were, go back to the beginning, go back without any more experiments at all because

you wanted, his mind reminded, *an altered state; you wanted to know what it would be like to change perceptions, to feel at the highest limits and beyond; you're the one who wanted to know*

because things were completely out of control now but if they could be mitigated by time, if enough time were to pass then maybe, maybe then they would be

*looks like you got what you wanted, didn't you?
too bad it's at Robin's expense, you didn't think of
that though did you, you didn't think this thing
through, did you*

maybe then they would be safe
too late

together, both of them, all of them; safe together in the quiet and the dark. The friendly dark,
that hides the scythes and blades and angles of the
light; the loving dark to cloak mistakes, and an-
guishes, and blame as real as any grinning skull. He
cried there until he could not cry anymore and
then rose up, to wash his gritty face, to make something to eat: food Robin would ignore, Saskia too
unless he forced her and he would force her: he
would say Your fasting won't feed him, it won't help
him, you have to be strong. You have to be strong.

I'm losing him, she had said. Grant I'm losing
him.

Saskia, he did not say but could have, Saskia
I'm losing him too. Just like I'm losing you, like
we're losing everything, every day now, all the
time.

Stiff on the plate, sticky macaroni and she ate like a
prisoner, she must have done the same thing in
Clearwater: fork in one hand, salt in the other, machinery motions and from where they sat they
could see, like a comet's tail, the light from his
room in which he lay, open-mouthed, scar-pale

with a new and pasty look, the air not so much of starvation—could a person starve, in a few days? how long did it take?—as purification, an emptying not for its own sake but to make way for what would follow to fill. Grant had tried again, and again, and unsuccessfully to make him eat something, soup, graham crackers; he had managed to get some juice down him, apple juice as clear and pretty, Robin said around the slim plastic of the straw, as angel's tears. There was an ambulance in his future, that was certain, Grant staring at a macaroni noodle stuck to the table, picking at it with the tines of his fork; I won't let him die. I will not let him die. I will not let—

"—fuck's *sake*," her shrill voice, had she been talking to him?

"What?"

"I *said* watch what you're fucking *doing*," and behind the words the instant tears, weeping again and her mouth sagging open, the fork tumbling from her hand as she put her arms down on the table, down on her plate and cried; and Grant thought with a longing more pure than a lover's for not death but silence, silence, an empty room, a long and silent night. Light from Robin's room; no sound at all. Was he dying in there, dying and smiling? Finally Grant had forced him to eat some clear soup, canned chicken broth, spoon by spoon like a baby, fighting his own desire to weep, to scream: to say Robin don't do this to me, don't *do* this to me but why shouldn't he? Why shouldn't he do this to you, for himself; after all you've done plenty to him, haven't you? Haven't you just done—

"—*die*," through half-chewed food and snot, raising her gaze, tears and rage and terror and "I just want to die, Grant. I want to die and stop watching him, I don't want to see what's going to happen."

"I'll tell you what's going to happen," he said. He did not trouble to lower his voice. "When he gets skinny enough and sick enough I'm going to call the fucking ambulance and they're going to come and stick a tube in his arm and *feed* him, that's what's going to happen, and if he rips it out I'm going to make them put it back in, or put him in the hospital, and when he gets better he can come out and start all over again if he wants but I am *not* going to sit here and watch him starve, I am *not* going—"

"Oh Grant," from behind him and turning he saw Robin, trembling in the doorway: no tears but the emanation of vast betrayal, the eyes of a child staring up through the water that drowns him, "you *said* you wouldn't do that. You said you would never let them take me away."

And what to say to that? I lied? I love you? I can't stand this anymore? "I love you," Grant said. "Robin, I love you and I won't let you die."

"I'm not going to die," Robin said. "It's not dying, what I'm doing." Silence. "I wish you would believe me."

"I believe you," Saskia said, pushing away from the table to stand beside him, to prop his swaying stance; dizzy, dizzy from the lack of food, of nourishment, would his scar, now pale, shrink or dazzle, would his hair start falling out soon, would his patched and balding head glow like a halo, like the shining skin of a star? The morning star. Lucifer. Raphael. Michael. Gabriel, Azrael, Israfel; there was a poem like that, he remembered, he remembered. *None sing so wildly well/As the angel Israfel.* And the stars all mute. Mute and silent in the silence of death, Robin I won't let you die, Robin I *won't* let you die.

"I'm not dying," Robin said. He was pale as a skull; Grant imagined he could see light through his wrapped hands. "Come and see."

The room is white. The air smells like dust. Robin lies in the center of the floor, wrapped in an off-white blanket, shaking and serene. Saskia the door guard, guard dog, lying outside with her eyes shut tight; she does not, she says, want to see; sweet Saskia who can change her mind without torment: Be an angel. No, stop! and see no division, no conflict there; if only I could be that way, Grant thinks, if only I could be the way she is because if not I

     and Robin puts out one hand to Grant and says, "Hold my hand"

and Grant does, feels the heartbeat too strong,
wild cadence; the skin of the wrist trembles, trembles beneath its force. Dust and white; silence and
then a noise, a thrum, a hum, a sound like an appliance left on too long, a burning hum, a sound like
wires singing, like the sound at the edge of your
sense of hearing, the sound only animals can hear
   coming from Robin's open mouth
   a sound without noise, higher, stretching the
edge of possibility; his eyes are open but it is plain
he sees nothing; his whole body now shudders to
the beat of his heart. His hand in Grant's is sweating. Grant is sweating, in terror, in thrall: staring
and staring: it seems as if the room is growing
lighter, whiter; the sound from his mouth enormous and barely there and in that mouth, past
those parted lips Grant stares: and sees
   light: it is all light
   inside. Light inside.
   There is light behind his eyes, glass balls swimming in sockets of white, light inside and
   the noise curls into the invisible as suddenly
Robin is drenched, perspiration all over his body,
his hair is wet as rain and he closes his mouth,
snaps it shut like a turtle, like the lid on a box; lies
in shivering silence, in the dark again as Grant beside him tries to understand: eyes playing tricks,
perception in flux, did he see what he wanted to
see or what was really there? and what did he really
see? Light inside Robin's mouth, behind his eyes,

light where none should be. What is happening, here? What is happening here?

And Robin smiles and says something, speaks: Grant cannot hear but miraculous at the doorway Saskia does, hears and understands: and says to Grant with a strange, nearly monstrous mixture of agony and pride unwilling, "He says he's almost there now; he says pretty soon. Pretty soon."

All of it in this room like air and dust; all of it as if it has taken less than a moment. All of it as insubstantial and terrifying as a dream, the dream from which you wake in the grip of emotion you cannot name, an emotion you wish you may never feel again; the dream, Grant knows in the sudden grip of memory, the burning flux: the dream he had had, of the door, and the light beyond it.

Past midnight, nearing the cruelty of dawn and Grant in his bundled darkness, not so much asleep as hammered by exhaustion into the trench of unconsciousness and: Saskia's voice: in his head? In his dreams? No. Her real voice. Her real voice: in a tone he did not know, a kind of keening sound, not loud but as plangent as real pain: and he was on his feet in an instant, bumping and stumbling down the hall to Robin's room: where she sat beside him, not cradling him, not embracing but touching, holding on as one would hold the relic of a saint, a saint's dead body.

"Behold."

That was the word, the sound she was making. "Behold," her groan ecstatic, over and over in the dusty air; "behold," and he pushed her gently to one side, pushed her to see Robin's eyes rolled back in his head, his lips stiff: his stiffening hands as hot and terrible as flesh in a fire and

"—behold—"

his mouth, pried by trembling fingers, full of nothing but dark air, his tongue so dry it was hideous. His heart had achieved a rhythm no muscle could bear. There was a phone in the hallway; Grant was talking to someone, he was unsure how this had happened but he was repeating the address, you can't miss it, he was saying. There's Santas and shit all over the house, you can't miss it. It's a holiday house. You can't miss it.

"—behold."

Robin's heart, beating; his hands like candle flames. Grant held him to his chest like a doll, a pet, a precious toy; a child; a lover. Saskia kept repeating her word, key to the kingdom of light, she the daughter of deeps and burnings he could never apprehend, who knew but she would join Robin, who knew if she were not already on her way? That body in his arms, that weight; he did not feel starved but he was noticeably thinner, they would see it, the ambulance people, the paramedics, they would know what to do. They would be here soon. Maybe they were here already.

In the end it was Saskia, groaning and mum-

bling, who let them in, Saskia who with her word
proclaimed, who ushered in more than men in uni-
forms, whose annunciation could no longer be
heard past the clashing sound of the gurney, their
movements, their bottles and their plastic bags; the
lights of the ambulance were bright, bright, but
their lights were not pure or holy, they were blue
and red, carnival colors to shine in revolution on
every surface, in all the watching neighbors' eyes.

"You can follow us," one of the paramedics said
to Grant as they muscled past him, out to the open
ambulance doors, Robin wrapped and strapped on
the moving altar, his eyes still open, his mouth
pushed decently closed. "We're going to First
Meth, it's the closest."

The sound of the engine; Saskia on the porch
and for once he did not consider her, did not reach
to take her hand, to take care of her, left her there
like one of the Santas, one of the rabbits or flags
tattered by the weather of circumstance, the blowing wind of time. Into the car, weaving and speeding in the light of false dawn; parking somewhere it
seemed he should not have, leaving the keys in the
car to enter the emergency room, sit in the inner
room of shock beside the drunks and the bleeders,
the screamers and the people on drugs, First Meth-
odist full to bursting seemingly in this artificial
morning, this false antiseptic light; waiting there in
the waiting room and it took nearly an hour for
someone to come and tell him that Robin's heart

had stopped beating on the way to the hospital, stopped, they said, and could not be started again.

Ammonia smell, cleaning; cleaning up the Holiday House, the white room made for Robin now stripped to its yellow print wallpaper, its ugly rug. Regina had given him half a morning in private, to clean up, to do whatever he felt was necessary but her eyes told him plainly she would be counting all the silverware; let her. How could that trouble him here, in this landscape as desolate as a planet in lost orbit, here on this morning after the funeral, and she had been there too, in attendance as Saskia's witness; Saskia now back in Clearwater; he would be going to visit her as soon as he was done here. Not much to do, not really, things to sort and gather, not much; Angela lost somewhere, in the hospital, in the morgue, the funeral home; gone. Dirty and small and gone, the suffering face on the wall gone too and who had taken that? He wished he had; he hoped it had been Saskia. Something to hold on to; to look at, to behold.

I'm not dying; come and see.

Alison had not even bothered to accuse him of killing her brother; maybe she did not believe he had. He had managed, there in the emergency room, to talk to a doctor who had been profession- ally kind: Heart failure, he said, we're going to pull his records of course but that's what it was. There were some indications—we wanted to do an autopsy, but the family refused permission. Maybe it's just as well. I understand he was receiving treatment for schizophrenia? Grant had not responded to this; the doctor did not push. Are you family, too?

No, Grant had said; his voice was stretched somehow, elongated, it seemed to take forever to say the word. No, I'm a friend.

Only a friend, not family, not next of kin; he had given them Alison's number, there still in his wallet like a miracle, the end of a magic trick. Don't give my name as next of kin, she had said; had she said that? Alone at the funeral home, strangely pretty in dark blue, her eyes so red they looked bloody; she had not wept during the service or the moments before but to Grant her sorrow was mute but obvious; perhaps now it was safe to feel for her brother, to cry for him and say his name. The parents had not attended; he heard Alison telling some friend, some avid relative in a gray suit that they were on tranquilizers, the doctor did not believe they ought to come. Was it true? How did he know? He was on tranquilizers himself, unprescribed tranquilizers, he had bought a double handful from a guy in the emergency room, a skinny guy with a dripping nose who had accosted him in the parking lot to ask for spare change, not seeming to remember their transaction only moments before; the pills were small but powerful and he was taking one every four or five hours. They did not exactly help but they seemed to keep him alive, enable him to look at Robin in the coffin, Robin in a hideous blue suit, Robin with his hair combed back to reveal the powdered landscape of his scar. His hands were below the line of vision, hidden beneath polished wood; nobody, Grant supposed, wanted to see them, they were evidence of a kind no one wanted to consider but what did it matter now? Hands into wings, light into brighter light, was he an angel now or was he just dead? Flowers as bright and false as the lights in the hospital, it was not easy to dry-swallow another pill but Grant managed. They nauseated him but he managed that too; he did not imagine he was going to care much for his body anymore.

After the funeral home, the nondenominational service during which the nondenominational minister did not once mention Robin by name—*he* this and *he* that and not a whisper about Clearwater, not a word about Robin's angelic nature, nobody here was going to mention any of that at all: then cremation, a denouement from which Grant was excluded; Robin gone into light and fire, fire and light. Burning. The morning star. When these tranquilizers wore off he was going to do some burning of his own, some experimenting, he was going to find subsumation in a state so altered it was beyond any possible recognition; a place not so much to hide from the pain but where pain was as much a stranger as he. He could get there, too, he was

almost sure of it, as sure as the bitter smell of the
ammonia, the way the newspapers lay in their paper sacks, piled like pyramid bricks; as sure as the
little cache of Robin's drawing supplies, his drawings taken from the apartment, his clothing, the last
of his medication. He had asked Alison if she
wanted these things—except the drawings, he had
never intended to give her those—and she had
stared at him as if he were crazy.

Maybe he was.

It was almost noon; he had a twenty-five-
minute drive to Clearwater. Paper and stink and a
lemony brightness, calm and limitless, the harbin-
ger it seemed of fair weather, of safe journeys to
places far away. He carried the small bags that held
the clothes, the drawings, Robin's leave-behinds
out to the car, separated the house key from his
own keys, left it lying like a note on the strange
clean kitchen table. In his mouth the pill was
smooth as plastic, sweet as honey from the comb;
he had three more left, and after they were gone he
would begin.